Second Edition

CLEO WHITE

Cover Art by Acacia, Ever After Cover Design

Edited by Stacey, Stacey's Bookcorner Editing Services

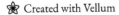 Created with Vellum

*For my Bookstagram girls, who taught me I don't have to do it
all on my own.*

Author's Note

This story contains graphic adult content not intended for readers under eighteen, as well as themes and mentions of topics which some may find triggering. These include; miscarriage, death of a parent, depression, suicide, infidelity and child abandonment.

Please read with caution.

One

∞

JOSEPHINE

THE CLAWING, undying need to make every single person in your life happy isn't an easy habit to break.

Even when you realize you're a people pleaser and recognize it's likely a big part of why you're so miserable, it would be easier to perform your own root canal than do something about it.

I'm an only child, for god's sake. We're practically programmed to be amiable. When other kids were wrestling with their siblings, I was playing chess with my mother or solving quadratic equations with my father. Family vacations usually involved a "short stop" at some sort of conference or think tank (though I still couldn't explain what a think tank is) and catered birthday parties to ensure the many adults in attendance wouldn't be forced to eat pizza and cheese puffs.

It sounds really ungrateful to complain about all that. A lot of people have *actual* problems with their families, and that I was beyond lucky to grow up with parents who loved each other and me. Not so occasional loneliness aside, my childhood was good. Which is probably what's made it so hard to be honest with them. Or myself.

At twenty-two years old, I've become exactly what they always hoped I would be. I'm the kind of college senior that my parents' friends *wish* they had, and while it should make me happy that I've missed my early-twenties hot mess era, all I am is embarrassed.

I've known something was coming, sensed the desperation building up inside me like steam in a kettle. This has happened before, and a good old-fashioned fit of sobbing into my pillow for half an hour usually clears it right up. Not this time. A full-on breakdown seemed imminent, and all I could do was brace for impact.

That being said, I might be depressed, but I'm not an idiot. Even without my therapist's prompting, I knew I had to step out of my comfort zone, and *I really tried to*.

I went to a party—and spent most of the time pretending to text a non-existent friend.

I got a haircut—and now I have to manage curly haired bangs on top of everything else.

I joined a tennis club—spoiler alert: tennis sucks.

None of it was enough. The pressure has kept on building, becoming more unbearable by the day, and somewhere in there, a dangerous reality has made itself known: *I hate my life.*

Not in an *"I want to die"* kind of way, thankfully. I'm not suicidal, I'm just tired of working so hard to succeed at something that has done nothing but make me miserable. Even with all that self-awareness, I didn't know what I was going to do about it, but sucking it up and continuing on as I did before wasn't an option.

A meeting with my advisor last week confirmed I'm only a few credits short of graduating early, which means that if I play my cards right, I will finish my undergraduate degree by the end of the year. Then, I'll have my pick of grad schools, and after that, a soulless, mind numbing job that will probably take me right from *"I hate my life"* to *"I want to die"* in no time.

No wonder I've felt ready to explode.

I just didn't expect it to be triggered by a little black dress laid out on my bed.

In Mom's defense, she probably thought she was being helpful. I've been crazy busy the last few weeks, studying and taking finals to wrap up my anticlimactic junior year. The party tonight is her thing, and I'm sure she wants to make it easy for me to attend. It's hardly the first we've hosted this year, or even this month. As President of Weston University—the same school I attend—most of Mom's job seems to be schmoozing donors and keeping the legions of overworked, underpaid academics happy.

Everyone wants to have face time with their boss, my brilliant mother. My brilliant mother who took the time out of her busy schedule to purchase a beautiful, expensive dress for me to wear tonight. A dress that is perfect on paper and will probably fit me flawlessly, but is all wrong in all the ways that matter.

Staring down at it, blood rushing in my ears and my heart beating far too hard for a girl who just spent the better part of an hour plucking her eyebrows, the terrible, undeniable truth seemed to wash over me.

This *stupid* dress was a *stupid* symbol for my *stupid* life. I didn't like it, and yet there wasn't a question in my mind that I was going to put it on, anyway.

With a hand pressed over my lips, I take a few steps away, my back hitting the wall. I barely feel it. This is it, the moment I knew was coming, only I don't cry my eyes out or scream into my pillow.

My phone is in my pocket, and I rip it out, struggling to get my hands to stop shaking long enough to type out the

3

email that has already been mentally composed, recomposed and checked for grammatical errors about a dozen times.

Doctor Novak,

I'm reaching out to inform you that I will not be returning to Weston University for the fall semester. I'll be taking some time off to focus on my mental health and reevaluate my plans for the future. Could you please advise me on what steps I can take to ensure re-enrollment is not an issue if/when I should choose to return.

Thank you in advance for your advice and time.

J. Sutton

I press send as quickly as I can, and the moment I do, I drop to the floor beside my bed, breathing heavily and searching myself for signs of regret. There's still time to undo this. I could email Doctor Novak right back and tell him I had some kind of mental break and to please disregard my previous email. The man has worked in academia for decades. I'm sure he's heard it before.

Instead, I set my phone on the mattress behind me, staring blindly at the opposite wall. *Did I really just do that?*

There's a quick knock on the door and my panic notches higher.

"Jo!" Mom calls, cheerful and utterly unaware that I've destroyed my perfect-daughter status. "Are you dressed? The caterers are still getting set up and people will be here any minute. Would you mind showing them where everything is?"

It's a struggle to swallow. "I'll be right there!"

Footsteps retreat toward the stairs, but I still don't move. Did I seriously just withdraw from school? My mother is the

4

president. The president of an ivy league university's daughter doesn't *drop out*. Do they?

I open my phone again and check the "sent" folder.

Yup. Apparently, the daughter of university presidents do sometimes drop out of school. Or, at least, this one does.

If this had been even slightly planned, I would have prepared Mom for this. She is so proud of me, she cares about my education so much, and now I'm throwing it all to the wind for... what?

I have no idea.

Oh god.

Am I having a mental breakdown? It doesn't feel like a mental breakdown, but I've never had one before, so what do I know?

Getting to my feet is a struggle, but I manage it. Bypassing the ugly black dress at the end of my bed, I head to the closet and flick on the light, staring around hopelessly. *It's all the same.* Every garment in here is black, dark blue, brown or gray. They're all made of some fussy "dry-clean only" material, and usually come with a matching cardigan. There isn't a single fun, colorful summer dress or pair of cute but impractical shoes.

Even my underwear is beige. Not panties—*underwear*. There is most definitely a difference, and nobody could look at these things and tell me otherwise. I'm twenty-two years old. If this isn't my panties era, will I ever have one?

How did I never see it before?

How is it possible I didn't notice that I hate my clothes?

My stomach churns as I snatch my least tragic dress from its hanger. There are a pair of almost fashionable heels that always give me blisters, but I put them on anyway.

My panic flairs as I check the time and realize another potential complication of my hastily made life-choice.

In only a few minutes, Weston faculty and staff will begin

descending on the president's house for free drinks and finger food. How did it not occur to me that my advisor, Dr. Novak, the man I just emailed to inform him I was dropping out, could very well be among them?

Crap.

The kitten heels turn out to be a blessing in disguise. While I have no practical experience in the matter, I would guess that vaulting down a set of two-hundred-year-old polished wooden stairs while wearing pumps would end in bloodshed.

God, why did I have to blow up my life tonight of all nights?

If I'd just... *sucked it in*, I could have told my parents I had a headache, and spent the night hiding in my room while the indistinct murmur of voices and obligatory laughter drifted up through the floors. They wouldn't have questioned it, and nobody would have missed me, or wondered why the president of Weston University's twenty-two-year-old daughter wasn't in attendance.

I'm panting by the time I arrive in the foyer, looking wildly around for signs of my mother. The front door is still, thankfully, closed and the only people in sight are a set of frantic looking caterers lighting the candles beneath the chafing dishes in the dining room.

"Mom!" I call, endeavoring to sound casual, and not like I'm having a full-blown crisis and did something stupid for the first time in my boring, vanilla, *underwear* wearing life.

Heels click on wood floors, and seconds later, my mother comes into view wearing a dress very similar to the one she laid out for me and a pair of pearl earrings she brings out for all these things. "Hi, sweetheart." She looks me up and down, frowning slightly. "Did the dress not fit?"

"Um. Maybe?" I wade through my disjointed, panicky thoughts. "Is Dr. Novak coming tonight?"

"I'm not sure. I'd have to ask my assistant." She turns toward the study. "George! George, are you ready?"

My father appears with his tie hanging loose around his neck, hands shoved deep in his pockets and wearing the usual faraway expression he gets when he's been working on a particularly challenging equation. In some circles, George Sutton is a legend, but I've never quite been able to work out how such a brilliant man can also routinely forget his way to the kitchen.

Mom moves over to knot Dad's tie, smiling at him fondly.

I'm almost dizzy with disbelief. This is happening. I'm actually doing this. *Right now.* I've painted myself into a corner, and the only way out is to make a really big mess.

"I have to tell you guys something," I squeak.

Two sets of eyes settle on me, and I take a deep breath, my chest aching with anxiety at the inevitable disappointment to come. "I'm withdrawing from the fall semester. I haven't been happy, and I have to take some time to figure out what I want."

Somewhere deep in the house, someone drops a plate, and all three of us wince.

Mom recovers first and blinks at me, utterly bemused. "You want to be a physicist, Jo. Like your father. That's what you've always wanted."

She's right. I have always wanted that. "I think I thought I wanted that, because I'm good at it, and it made both of you so happy. It's not enough for me, though. I'm not sure what I'm going to do, travel maybe, but I need to make a change."

I'm pretty proud of myself for the delivery. It sounds as if I'm actually sure about this, like I'm confident this isn't a big, fat, stress induced mistake. Even if I'm melting down internally, I keep my chin up, and my voice doesn't waver even once.

After a few seconds of stunned silence, Mom's, however, does. "This isn't the time, Jo. We'll discuss it later." She checks the elegant gold watch on her wrist and frowns. "Please go help the caterers find what they need."

My shoulders slump, but she doesn't need to tell me twice. I'm grateful for any chance to catch my breath. Thankfully, the caterers need a lot of help and I'm able to kill almost half an hour before I've officially started getting in the way, and I head back toward the entryway with a sphere of dread, approximately the mass and density of a cement bowling ball, sitting at the bottom of my stomach.

Arguments with my mother have been few and far between, but that's all over now. As she'll soon learn, the decision was made before consulting her, and even if it upsets her, I have no intention of backing down. The execution might have been a bit shaky, but if the sudden absence of unbearable pressure building inside me is any indication, I needed to do this.

Dad is nowhere to be seen as I slip back into the entryway, taking the place beside Mom just as a thin, white-haired man hobbles into view.

"Dean Michaels. Thank you so much for coming." Her expression is pinched into a polite smile. "You've met my daughter, Jo, I believe? She'll be entering her senior year in the fall."

Subtle, Mom.

I barely suppress a grimace as the man's watery eyes settle on me. In institutions as old as Weston University, change is slow. Dean Michaels, the head of the English department, who is about two decades past retirement age and can barely string together a coherent budget proposal, is proof of that.

"Oh yes." He nods, shuffling past us into the foyer. "She's a beauty. Looks just like my late wife's sister."

My mother's left eye twitches, and she opens her mouth, no doubt to let forth a long list of my achievements, none of which have anything to do with my face, but I squeeze her arm and give her a look as the man heads off without further comment. "Not worth it," I mutter under my breath. "He'll forget this conversation even happened by the time he gets to the sitting room."

On any other night, she would appreciate the joke. We'd share a conspiratorial smile or a quiet laugh. Now, all I get in response is a tight nod. The moment he's gone, Mom rounds on me. "You are one semester off from graduating, Jo," she mutters, careful to keep her voice low. "If you're burned out, you can take time off before grad school."

I don't meet her eyes, choosing instead to stare at the ugly portrait of one of Weston's former presidents hanging opposite us, a hollow ache growing inside me. "Mom. I don't want to pursue theoretical physics as a career," I croak, trying again. "It doesn't make me happy. I've been struggling for a long time."

The depression diagnosis we never talk about hangs heavy in the air between us.

She blows out a long breath, her eyes on a couple getting out of their parked car across the street. "There are a lot of things you can do with a physics degree that aren't being a physicist. Law is an option, or medical school—"

"I have no interest in either of those things."

She whips around to face me, her expression rigid. "So what are your plans, Jo?" Her voice has taken on a hysterical edge and, glancing around, she lowers it as she continues, "I can't stop you from dropping out of school, but your father and I won't be funding your *soul searching expedition*. What is your plan here? The only job you've ever had is babysitting. I doubt that will pay your way around the world."

I'm pretty sure there's just a gaping, empty hole where my heart used to be. I assumed she would be mad, but my mother had never spoken to me like that before.

Then again, I've never gone head to head with her before tonight.

Another couple arrives at the door, and I'm only vaguely aware of Mom greeting them smoothly, the image of dignity and professionalism.

As they head off to greet their colleagues, Dad shuffles back into view, frowning down at a packet of heavily annotated equations. More people are coming up the walk, and while I'm fairly confident that I'm being a coward right now, I seize my opportunity to book it.

If Mom notices, she doesn't try to stop me.

The house is full and busy. Parties like this happen all too often, with different groups or departments showing up in hopes of getting some time with the woman in charge of their budget requests. It's not just an obligation for me—*nobody* wants to be here.

Any other night, I would make small talk, mingle and stand in as Elizabeth Sutton 2.0. Tonight, I need to be alone.

Going back upstairs would mean getting past Mom, and I'm not willing to risk another soul withering lecture. I grit my teeth as I weave through the little clusters of Weston employees, breathing easier as the population dwindles the further I move from the main living areas. The library door is ajar, and I push through it, glancing around hurriedly.

Empty.

Groaning in relief, I push it closed behind me and sag back against the cool wood, pressing the heels of my palms into my eyes until white spots appear in my vision. I let out a frustrated little shriek. "Shit, fuck, crap, mother freaking crapping crapsicles—"

"*Ah*... Excuse me?"

A gasp rips free from my throat and I turn so quickly that I almost fall over, staring in horror at the man I completely missed in my rush. He's standing in an alcove before a table littered with puzzle pieces, and he looks almost as mortified as I feel.

He's handsome.

It's not the kind of thing I typically notice, or at least, I don't typically notice it so noticeably. This guy—*man*—makes it hard not to though. He's older than me, quite a bit older if his graying, light brown hair is anything to go by, but the sudden tightness in the muscles below my bellybutton suggest I don't have a problem with that.

"Hi," I squeak, heat rushing to my face.

He clears his throat, looking anywhere but at me. "I'm sorry. I didn't mean to startle you." His low, melodic voice is colored by an accent, French I think, and—*phew*. I didn't think guys like this existed outside of my Kindle. I'm woefully unprepared.

My answering laugh verges on hysterical. "I think I'm the one who should apologize here. I don't normally walk into libraries and start making up curse words."

The stranger's lips twitch. "It's quite alright. No harm done. I may borrow *crapping crapsicles,* actually."

Purely to give myself something to look at apart from his very handsome face, my eyes fall to the partially assembled puzzle laying before him. "That good of a party?" I edge closer, tilting my head to make out the picture on the box, a watercolor landscape.

"Is it a party?" He muses wryly, picking up a glass of whisky from the corner of the table and taking a sip. "I thought it was more of a campaign to get in the good graces of Madame President."

My heart flutters, because if he's talking this way, there's no way he knows who I am. We haven't met before, which means he thinks I'm a colleague, and I can't bring myself to correct him. "Are you in her bad graces?"

11

The stranger snorts, returning his attention to the puzzle. "I'm afraid so. Not that tonight will make any difference."

I want to ask why, or at least find out his name so I can be nosy and question Mom later, but I keep my mouth shut and edge closer to the table, watching as he selects an edge piece and slots it into place.

"If it helps, there's no way she's as angry with you as she is with me." Spotting another that fits, I reach out and take it, pressing the small bit of cardboard into the correct position. When I lift my gaze again, I meet a pair of pale blue eyes.

My stomach flips.

We both turn away, but the brief eye contact is enough to reduce me to goo. Gazing blankly at the jumble of tiny colored pieces before me, I scramble for something to say. I want to keep talking to him, but he's fallen silent, absent-mindedly turning a piece between the long fingers of his left hand.

Again, it's not the type of thing I take any notice of, but now I can't help it. *He's not wearing a wedding ring.*

"Sorry to crash your puzzle," I finally manage quietly, trying my best to pretend there aren't butterflies occupying the place where my abdominal organs are usually located. My heart is still tender from the fight with Mom, but removed from the weight of her disapproval, I can breathe again. "You can tell me to get lost if you want. I'm sure I can find my own hideout."

He huffs a laugh, and as I sneak another peek over at him I see he's smiling. "I'd rather you didn't. It's far less pathetic to be found doing a puzzle with a beautiful woman than on my own."

Beautiful?

I'm positive I'm blushing like a madwoman and no amount of telling myself to *calm the hell down* helps. I've had crushes in the past, and sexually frustrated way-too-old-virgin or not, I have done *some* stuff. It's been a while, but I'm not so innocent that a man calling me beautiful would prompt this kind of reaction.

Except I kind of like him. Not just his face—which is more than like-worthy on its own—but the way he talks. The accent is part of it, but the casual formality of it reminds me of the heroes in an Austin or Brontë novel. He reads, I'm sure of it, and it says a lot about my level of nerdiness that the image of this man sitting in bed with a book in his hands is downright erotic.

Though not as erotic as how I would persuade him to put it down.

Dear god, who am I right now?

I realize I've been silent for too long when he speaks again, his tone unsure. "That was inappropriate. I apologize if I've made you uncomfortable."

Oof. If I wasn't sold before, the respect would seal the deal.

"You didn't make me uncomfortable," I blurt out, and look at him again. "I'm sorry. I've had a bad night, and I'm not very good at... this."

Whatever *this* is. Flirting, maybe?

He slots another piece of the puzzle into place before looking back up at me, and his crooked smile makes the muscles below my bellybutton tighten. "If it helps, I don't make a habit of complimenting the appearance of strangers at parties. Or *attending* parties for that matter. So the fault here might be my poor execution of the compliment."

"I thought we established this isn't a party."

The corners of his eyes crease as his smile widens, and *god*, I can't stop looking at him. What is happening? He has to be older than me—a *lot* older than me—and would definitely not be talking this way if he knew I was the daughter of his boss. Is that shitty of me? It's not like he asked. Or, maybe he does know, or at least guesses that I'm a student and he isn't bothered?

About thirty minutes ago, I was vaulting down the stairs to get to my mom and confess my impulsive bid for freedom. Now, my education situation isn't even in the top five priorities.

"Will you tell me your name?"

My heart performs a funny sort of flip flop. *Oh boy,* I'm in so much trouble. I swallow. "Josephine. Jo, I mean. Pretty much everyone calls me Jo."

A round of muted laugher sounds from elsewhere in the house, and I glance over my shoulder toward the door, pulse racing.

"Josephine," he echoes, as though testing the way it sounds on his tongue—which is definitely better than mine. I've never particularly liked my name. It seemed stuffy and ordinary, with too many letters to fit comfortably on DMV forms. When he says it though...

"Do I get to know yours?" I ask, trying desperately to play it cool while every single cell in my body seems to be vibrating with excitement. I might not be very experienced, but *I know he's interested.*

"Ellis." He chuckles, and a hook low in my belly pulls in his direction. *Ellis.* Formal and a little old fashioned. Quiet, unassuming and eloquent. It suits him. I lower my gaze, giving myself a few seconds to *chill the craping crapsicles out.* It doesn't work, because his next question knocks the wind right out of me. "Do you have plans after this?"

Two

ELLIS

WESTON UNIVERSITY BOASTS a total of twelve libraries and mine, Montgomery, is the largest. It's a beautiful place, full of sweeping, finely carved mahogany and endless rows of leather-bound tomes. During my very first visit here, I'd drifted from the tour group of incoming freshmen, wandering deeper into the seemingly endless building, filled with a sense of rightness I'd never experienced before.

The hushed voices of study groups, the smell of dust and ink, the glow of computer screens and rustle of turning pages might have seemed mundane to some, but to me, it felt as though ancient magic lived within the very walls of Montgomery.

Through wars, political upheaval, technological advancements, and countless generations of Weston students, this place has been a sanctuary, standing steadfast against the sands of time and shifting memory. It thrilled and comforted me in equal measure. So much so, that I built my entire career around it.

Now, as a grown man with more than my fair share of cynicism, I see past the romantic facade. That's what happens when you truly know a place. Not passing through, or using it to facilitate another purpose, but living and breathing it every single day.

I know the places where the ancient slate roof leaks during heavy storms, the stairs that creek and the shelves that slant. All those things are my responsibility now, but they're not my *only* responsibility. There are other things in my life that come first. Things that mean more to me than an old building stuffed with books.

It was never supposed to be like this. That's the line I've told myself whenever I had to take days off, or leave work early, or bring a cranky six-year-old to an academic library in a feeble attempt to do my job.

Unfortunately, what my life was *supposed* to look like doesn't matter much to Weston University. This morning, when I opened my email, I had yet another email from campus administration reminding me that while they're very understanding of my *"circumstances"*, my allotment of personal time has run out.

I'm not sure what I hoped to achieve by coming here tonight, perhaps to show my boss that I care about my job? Whatever the case, it didn't make a difference. Any hope I had that attending this party would put me in favor with the formidable university president was proven woefully incorrect nearly the moment I walked through the door.

"Mr. Delvaux. Thank you so much for coming. Will you call my office Monday morning? We should schedule a sit down."

Christ. My stomach dropped like a lead balloon. Losing my job... It's not an option. For one, positions for academic librarians with decent pay, good healthcare and a flexible schedule, aren't in high supply. Even if I did manage to find something, changing jobs would almost certainly mean moving out of the state, uprooting my daughter, and trying to sell the overpriced house my ex-wife fell in love with.

I was fortunate to get *this* job, and the only reason I did was because my mentor was retiring. Not only that, but I like what I do and where I do it. In a life that's been rife with stress the last few years, I'd like to keep one damn thing for myself.

Now, that desire is standing on shaky ground.

Without bothering to make small talk with my colleagues, I snatched a drink from the bar and strode blindly through the house. It was amusing, but not all that surprising, to end up in the president's home library.

It's a stately room, lined in deep wood shelves and row after row of books that are all likely worth more than my mortgage payment. The house is owned by the university, and given as a perk to the current president, so the room looks the same as it did when Sutton's predecessor threw similarly stuffy "parties" in this house.

The plan was to lick my wounds, get a grip, and head back out to salvage the night as best I could. After all, what good would brooding do now? I'd already shelled out a small fortune for a babysitter and got my hair cut for the first time in about four months. I might as well make the best of the evening, do my best to ignore the ice cold dread seeping through my veins, and enjoy my first night off in god-knows how long.

None of the plan included meeting someone. I've been single for so long that celibacy has become something of a habit. Even if it had occurred to me to look out for a single, pretty coworker to flirt with, it never would have struck me as a possibility that I stood a chance with *her*.

If it weren't for the few seconds in which she vented her frustration in made-up curse words, I would have embarrassed myself.

The woman is breathtaking. *Literally, breathtaking*—I think I forgot to breathe when I first laid eyes on her.

Everything from the elegant curve of her neck to the bow of her lips, hits me like a truck. Hers is the kind of face that would look at home in one of my daughter's princess books, not gazing shyly up at me in my boss's library with desire in her eyes.

My life is no fairytale. These things don't happen to me, and it was downright disorienting when it became apparent I wasn't the only one experiencing this attraction, try as I might to deny it. No matter which way I thought about it, I simply couldn't wrap my head around *her* wanting *me*.

Josephine.

Even her name makes me throb.

I'm not the sort of man who pursues younger women, or any women at all. God knows I'm not in a place where I could even think of dating.

Her being attracted to me is more than I could possibly have hoped for and I barely recognize myself as we slip out the back door, my hand pressed firmly to the small of her back. This is the sort of thing that happens to other men. Not me. Not now, certainly, when I can hardly remember the last time I had sex.

Has it been three years? Four? *Merde**, I think it may be closer to five.

Is it wrong to hope she'll fuck me? Because I really, *really* hope she'll fuck me. Just the thought of it is almost too much, and I have to drag my attention onto something else so I don't do something ill advised—like pin her to the side of my boss's home and make her come on my fingers.

I don't take it for granted that her leaving with me like this

---

* Shit

is an act of trust, and I'm determined to ensure she doesn't regret it.

My mouth is dry as we round the far corner of the house, making sure to give the door a wide birth as we head toward the street. People are still arriving, and cars are parked up and down the street. Across the road, the University campus is sparsely lit, though I can still make out the roofline of Montgomery Library rising above nearly every building in it's vicinity.

"Will you let me buy you dinner?" I ask Josephine quietly, not removing my hand from her back. "One that isn't composed of finger sandwiches or puffs with unpronounce-able ingredients?"

"What do you have against charcuterie?" she teases, and there's a breathy quality to her voice that suggests I'm not the only one reeling from this turn of events.

The sound of her heels clicking on the sidewalk seems to be in time with my heartbeat as I turn us toward my car. Thankfully, I took the booster seat out for the babysitter and used the opportunity to clean out the mounds of calcified fish-shaped crackers I discovered beneath it.

For once in my goddamn life, the stars seem to be aligning in my favor.

"I'll admit, my ancestors would turn over in their graves if they saw what I consume on a daily basis. It's embarrassing. I have no taste at all."

Josephine giggles as we stop beside my car and I hurry to find the correct button to unlock it, as though the split second's pause will cause her to rethink leaving with me. Her lips curve in a pleased little smile as I open the door for her and step back, watching as she moves gracefully into the darkened interior.

The heavy thud of the car door closing makes my pulse leap, and as I walk around the front to the driver's side, conscious of her eyes on me, I still can't quite believe this is happening. The most beautiful woman I've ever seen is sitting in my car, waiting for me to take her... As my hand finds the door handle, I falter.

Where the hell am I going to take her?

It's 8 P.M. on Saturday in a college town. The only places open are bars and the twenty-four-hour diner which is notoriously lax with food safety, and mostly patronized by drunk students. Neither of those options are going to impress Josephine, and food poisoning is not how I want this night to end.

"So, I might not have thought this through entirely," I admit as I sit down behind the wheel, peering at Josephine through the dim light. "Any ideas on where one can get dinner this late?"

Her eyes widen in alarm. "Oh..."

I wince. "Yeah."

She lifts a shoulder sheepishly, and my eyes are drawn instantly to the slope of her collar bone. I clear my throat, struggling to keep a clear head when we're suddenly alone in a small, confined space. "Would you think me terribly cheap if I suggested the grocery store? They have pre-made dinners I believe."

I believe. Hah. As if I don't eat meals from the prepared food section at the local market almost every night. Try as I might, my daughter's food preferences don't extend far beyond chicken nuggets, white bread and the occasional butter noodles if she's feeling generous. I'm a decent cook, but a dinner for one is too grim, even for me.

"Not at all!" Josephine says hurriedly, offering a bright smile to show she means it. "That's totally fine."

Okay, then.

This is happening.

The cards are so stacked against me here, it's fairly preposterous. If it were one of my friends describing this situation to me, I'd advise them to turn tail and run with some self-respect intact. I can't do it, though, and not just because fucking her would be the highlight of my decade.

I like her. Already, I can tell she's sweet and funny and clever. If my life weren't... well, my life, Josephine is exactly the sort of woman I would pursue.

The unpleasant truth is that I have nothing to offer her beyond tonight. I cannot imagine a universe where a beautiful young woman would sign up for *more* with a single father librarian who hasn't gone to the gym in a year and a half, has enough emotional baggage to fill the luggage claim at JFK and whose career is hanging by a thread.

For god's sake, if I don't like my life, I have no business dragging anyone else into it.

"So what department are you in?" Josephine asks, breaking through my self-pitying internal monologue as I pull out onto the street, leaving President Sutton's party behind us.

I clear my throat. "I'm staff, actually. I run Montgomery."

"You run the library?" Her voice drops in disbelief. "Seriously? That's the coolest job ever."

Fiddling with the thermostat for something to do other than preen at her approval, I keep my gaze on the dark street before us. "And you? What's your department?"

"Physics, concentrating on theoretical if you want to get specific." There isn't enthusiasm in her tone, and when I hazard a glance over at her, Josephine looks a little embarrassed. "I'm probably going to be taking some time off."

Theoretical physics? Shit. I should have guessed it would be something like that. There's something quietly intelligent about her, as if she's spent a good amount of time figuring out how to cover it up so as not to make people uncomfortable.

I wish she wouldn't. There's nothing I'd like more than to be wildly intimidated by this woman.

Turning into the brightly lit parking lot of the grocery store, I park as close as I can to the building out of concern for her feet in those shoes. Turning the keys in the ignition, the car falls silent, and we look at each other from our respective seats.

My heart flips. "If it makes you feel better. I have my dream job, and I still have to talk myself into the building most days."

Her lips twitch. "Want to trade places?"

"The physics department would *not* be pleased to have me," I inform her with a wry smile. "My last math class was a requirement for my undergraduate degree and I squeaked by with a C."

"*Oof.*" She giggles, her eyes sparkling in the light of the neon supermarket sign.

I know it's not the moment but still, the urge to kiss her is almost overpowering.

What would she taste like?

Would she moan?

Are her lips as soft as they look?

"So. Grocery store," I say to distract myself and gesture to the brick fronted building before us. "Would you like me to go in? Those shoes don't look comfortable."

Josephine waves me off, already unbuckling her seatbelt. "I'm fine."

She's *not* fine—that much is clear by the time we get through the sliding doors. I can hardly stop her, but I stay close as we move through the familiar produce section toward the *more* familiar prepared food stations.

It's strange being here this late. Normally, I come midafternoon and try to get in and out as quickly as I can before Zoe gets overstimulated. I certainly don't wear a vest, crisp white shirt and slacks, or have a beautiful woman at my side.

"So, what are we having?" Josephine asks mildly when we stop before a display of soggy fried chicken.

"Not this." I poke at the cover on a rotisserie which appears to have melted into the bottom of its container. This might be a pretty feeble attempt at a date, but surely I can do better than that.

Beside me, Josephine bends to adjust the back strap of her heel, and I wince at the sight of the angry red line left there.

Without pausing to consider how bizarre a thing this is for me to do, I step in front of her and crouch down, looking back over my shoulder at her, I frown expectantly. "Get on."

Josephine lets out a startled laugh. "Seriously? I'm heavy!"

I scoff. "If you're actually heavy, I'll dump you on the floor in the freezer section. Get on."

She has the cutest *trying not to smile* face. Warm hands find my shoulders and I wrap my hands around the back of her knees. My pulse leaps at the feeling of soft, delicate skin, and the warm weight of Josephine's body pressed against my back as I straighten up.

Merde[*].

I didn't think this through, but then again, none of tonight has been thought through so why start now? Maybe I'm reacting to the stress of my work situation, or maybe her effect on me is really this great, but the result is the same, regardless. I've never felt so outside my own head in the company of a new person, so unworried I'm being a bore, or that something, somewhere is going wrong.

Tonight, I'm doing what I want. It's thrilling, and as I begin to move again, Josephine's *not heavy* weight on my back, I feel damn near invincible.

An elderly woman pushes her cart past us, scowling straight ahead, and Josephine has to stifle her giggles against

---

[*] Shit

23

my shoulder. Adjusting my grip on her legs, I move toward the nearest cooler. "Do you like sushi?" At this time of night, there's a lackluster selection, and even I wouldn't consume what remains. Without waiting for her decision, I move on.

"Maybe I *like* graying supermarket mystery-fish sushi." Her breath tickles my ear, and I hear it hitch when I give the back of her knees a little squeeze.

I feel myself grin as I stop dead in the middle of the aisle. "I can get it for you, if you'd like. It's not too late."

Her arms tighten around me. "Oh no, we've already come this far. We should leave it."

"Are you sure?" I begin to turn back, but the arms around me squeeze tighter.

"I don't know what I was thinking with that one." Josephine giggles. "Such an easy way to lose a game of chicken."

As we move forward again, I frown, wracking my mind for an American game called *chicken* and coming up blank. I've lived in the United States since college, nearly twenty years now. The occasions where I've felt out of my depth or unsure about some cultural or linguistic subtlety have grown less frequent as time passed. Still, it happens, and I find myself a bit embarrassed as we near a display of pre-made salads and sandwiches. "What is that game? Chicken?" I ask the woman clinging to my back.

"Oh!" She sounds surprised. "It's not an actual game. Or, I guess it is. Anyway, it's basically like calling someone's bluff, seeing how far you can push a situation before they admit defeat."

I lean down to get a better look at the selection of goods in the cooler, my heart stalls as lips brush against my neck. My hands slip an inch higher on her thighs.

Chicken, indeed.

"That?" I point to a sandwich sampler at random, too

busy reeling at the feeling of her soft, bare skin in my hands to think about anything else.

Josephine nods, her warm cheek brushing my jaw. "Looks probably edible."

"Unfortunately, home-cooked meals aren't something I come by often, so I'm quite familiar with the selection. *Probably edible* is the best we're going to manage." I sigh, keeping my voice low so the kid behind the counter doesn't hear us.

I lean forward and Josephine reaches over my shoulder to grab it. The few other customers stare at us as we pass them on our way to the front, and we make a scene trying to coordinate use of the self-checkout. By the time we make it outside, mediocre dinner secure, Josephine is stifling her laughter in my neck and I can't stop smiling.

Her body is pressed snugly against mine, and we seem to be far more comfortable touching each other than two near-strangers ought to be. As we cross the dark parking lot, something sharp and panicky lodges in my chest.

I don't want to take my hands off her. What if this is it? What if we eat, I drop her at home, and then we never see each other again? A reckless daring is expanding inside me with each step closer to the car.

What would happen if I kissed her? Should I wait for her to make the first move? It's been years since I had to think about these things, and now the most beautiful woman I've ever encountered is within reach and I have no idea how to reach out and take her.

Though, admittedly, I have no shortage of ideas on what I would do to her if I managed it.

Experimentally, I drag my thumb over the skin just above her knee. The quiet gasp she makes in response goes right to my cock.

My heart is pounding when we stop beside the car and I

crouch down, allowing her safely back onto the ground. Immediately, I miss having my hands on her.

"Thank you for saving me from blisters," Josephine tells me shyly, tucking her curls behind her ears when I turn to face her.

My mouth is dry. We're standing less than three feet apart. Why is this so difficult? Her signals suggest that my advances wouldn't be poorly received, yet still, I don't move. "Promise me you'll throw those shoes away when you get home," I joke weakly.

She nods. "Probably a good idea."

Silence falls between us. This is the part where we should be getting back in our respective seats to eat the dinner I promised her, and yet we aren't moving.

Is she wondering whether I want her? Is she hoping I'll touch her?

The possibility of her feeling unwanted is what does it. If one night is all we'll have, I know I would never forgive myself if I allowed nerves and feelings of inadequacy to stand in our way

To hell with it.

Three

JOSEPHINE

UNTIL THE DAY I DIE, I'll never be able to explain how I got here.

The library, I remember.

The walk to the car is perfectly clear.

The supermarket is a bit of a blur. Even so, very memorable.

It's not until we're back in the car that the details get fuzzy. Actually, it might have been Ellis letting me down on the asphalt beside the passenger door.

Our entire time in the store couldn't have been longer than ten minutes, and yet when it was over... It's like we got used to touching each other, and we didn't want to stop.

I remember my back hitting the car, the sound of a paper shopping bag hitting the ground and the way he kept his eyes on my face to gauge my reaction as he lowered his lips to mine. Whatever he'd seen there must have been confirmation enough.

It's after that when the details blur together.

"*Christ*, Josephine." My lower belly twists at the rough, hungry way he groans my name. We're in the backseat of his car, cloaked in darkness, and come to think of it, I really don't care how we got here.

My clit has a pulse, my dress is bunched up over my hips and my thighs are spread wide over his lap. Beneath me, Ellis is palming my ass, muttering words of praise in between kisses so desperate they make my toes curl.

I'm not in control of myself, and I get the sense he isn't either. This is instinctual, my body responding to his in a way that I've never experienced before.

"You feel so good," I pant, enjoying the sight of his neat hair mussed up from my hands and the look of naked desire on his face. His hands drag up my sides to my breasts.

Ellis *groans*.

The obvious effect I'm having on him only makes me more eager, more willing. Liquid heat is pooling between my thighs, soaking through my panties and probably his pants too. My inhibitions are nowhere to be found, and all I can think about now is getting closer to him.

Like he knows, Ellis reclaims my lips in a bruising kiss, and one hand dips between us, brushing tentatively over my cloth covered sex.

My gasp is drowned out by the rough, animalistic noise he makes. "You're so wet." He presses a little harder and swallows my moan as he begins to stroke me. The light from the street is muted by the tinted windows and a new layer of fog on the windows that definitely wasn't there earlier. We're in our own world.

"I never do this," I admit, my breathy voice breaking as he finds my clit, rubbing in firm circles through the slick cotton.

Ellis grunts, his breathing heavy as he pauses in his ministrations. Through the hazy light, his eyes meet mine. "We don't have to."

Sex. He means we don't have to have sex. I know we don't have to, even having only met this man a few hours ago, I'm positive he wouldn't lay a finger on me if I didn't want it. He definitely wouldn't do this if he knew I hadn't before.

I want to, though. Maybe it's reckless, and a little stupid, but everything inside me is screaming *"yes!"* and for once, I'm going to listen.

Holy shit, I'm doing this. Finally.

Holding his gaze, I reach between us, palming his thick erection through his slacks. It twitches under my touch, and Ellis's lips part, his fingers moving more firmly over my clit. For a moment, the only noise in the car is our ragged breathing and the rustling of fabric.

"I want to," I whisper, realizing he was waiting for my consent.

Wow, that's so hot.

I suck in a startled breath when my panties are hooked to the side and cool air hits the arousal coated lips of my pussy. "You want me to touch you here?" Ellis murmurs, his voice a dangerous purr. He strokes the skin along my seam without pushing further, his touch featherlight and agonizing.

Helpless to do anything else, I nod.

He doesn't move his eyes from my face as he presses forward, finding my clit with his bare fingers. I squeak. Ellis groans. "Is all this for me, *mon amour?* Have I made this pretty little pussy wet?"

"Yes," I whimper, and another gasp rips from my lungs when he lowers his fingers and pushes them smoothly past my entrance, filling me.

My hand is still between us, pressed to his cock, and I feel it twitch. "You're so goddamn tight. *Merde*, we'll have to go slow. I need to get you ready." There's no mistaking the hunger in his expression at the prospect. "I'll make you feel so good, Josephine. You'll come on my cock like a good girl, won't you?"

His praise does something to me. Wetness floods over his

fingers and the muscles below my bellybutton tighten while my thighs go loose.

Interest flickers behind his darkened gaze. With maddening control, almost gently, he begins to finger me. I lean back until I hit the driver's seat, offering more space for him to work. *God, it feels so good.*

"Ellis," I whisper, forced to stop stroking his cock so I can hold on to the head rest behind me.

His fingers move faster, curving them to brush a spot that makes me tighten up all over. He's found a rhythm that seems to be dragging the orgasm from my body so much faster than I was prepared for, and through the darkness, I see his lips curl. "You liked me telling you what a good girl you are, didn't you?"

I'm starting to shake. "Yes!"

He groans. "You like knowing how hard you make me? How much I'm going to enjoy this?"

His words are hitting me so hard. Without realizing it, I've started squirming and bucking into his touch, pushing myself down on his hand in my eagerness to come. "Yes!" I cry again, too loud. If anyone happened to be walking by the car, they'd know exactly what we were doing in here, fogged up windows or not.

Ellis groans. "Come on, *mon amour*. Come for me. My cock aches. I need you to make it better. You'll do that for me, won't you? You'll take the ache away?"

Another yes, this one high and keening, my arousal soaking his hand as he works me closer, two fingers inside me and his thumb on my clit. I was already close, but his words have sent me spinning off toward something much more powerful.

I'm in a trance, completely at the mercy of my need for him. Ellis's tongue darts out to wet his lips, and fisting the back of my hair with his free hand, he drags me back to kiss him.

Almost without warning, I come. It's nothing like any orgasm I've had by myself. This is intense and overwhelming, forcing me to buck and grind against the hand between my legs, my choked moans swallowed by the man it belongs to.

Nearly the moment I come down, trembling, Ellis lifts his shining fingers to my lips. "Clean me up, *mon amour*. Then we'll get that sweet pussy filled, yes?"

Yes. Absolutely, one-hundred percent yes. Any qualms I had about abandoning my too-old-virgin status are long gone. I want this.

He watches as I suck my own release away, dragging my tongue over his fingers to ensure I get every drop.

I want to do it perfectly for him.

Ellis hums in approval, but as he lowers both hands his belt, his expression transforms from hungry to horrified. He curses. "*Damn*—I... I don't have protection."

Almost in unison, we look to the store, just in time to see the front lights flicker off, a sign they've closed for the night. *This isn't happening.* This isn't seriously happening, is it? But then I gasp and lean sideways through the space in the seats, fumbling with my purse on the passenger side.

"Yes!" I pull my hand out of the side pocket, lifting the tiny silver packet I found there victoriously. "From the people always handing them out on campus." I giggle as Ellis fumbles with his belt eagerly, looking extremely relieved.

"I would have gone door to door begging," he grunts, and I stare between us, watching as he frees his cock. He's tall and well built. I should have known he wouldn't be a small man, but still, the thick length jutting into the space between us is intimidating.

That's going inside me?

I watch, heat spreading through my core as he rolls the

latex over his length, the sound of our heavy breathing filling the car.

"We'll go slow," he promises, and—still half expecting to wake up and find myself alone—I lift onto my knees, allowing him to guide our bodies into alignment.

Will he be able to tell I've never done this before?

"This is what you wanted, yes?" he murmurs, nipping at my bottom lip. "Take it, *mon amour*. Sit on my cock. Let me have it."

We kiss slowly and my hands grip his shoulders as I begin to lower myself onto his cock. It's... a lot. Too much. Everything.

"Ellis." My voice breaks and I cling to him, every muscle in my body tensed around the intrusion.

He kisses me as we pause, making out with his cock barely inside me. My body seems to be relaxing though, and I need to make him feel good. Without giving myself time to tense up, I let my pelvis drop, impaling myself.

He swallows my noise of shock.

It hurts, my walls are stretched too far, I'm burning and I don't know if I can hide it. Ellis seems to know, though, because his fingers find my clit, rubbing in gentle circles. "I'm sorry," I whisper, squeezing my eyes shut. "You're just... you're really big."

"Don't apologize. I've never—*Jesus Christ*—you're tight." His voice is strained, and his free hand is pushed up beneath my dress, clutching my waist. "You're doing so well, Josephine. Take your time."

His praise helps. I melt against him, relieved. I'm not sure why it's so important to me that he doesn't realize it's my first time. Maybe because I want him to see me as a real possibility, a woman he might fall for, not an immature college student.

I like him so much.

The pain is starting to fade, and his touch on my clit is

spreading pleasure through my abdomen. "Okay," I whisper, wiggling in his lap. Ellis groans.

My fingers bite into his shoulders as I find a tentative rhythm, rising and falling over him, my eyes all but rolling back every time my butt lands on his thighs.

"Is this okay?" I whisper, my forehead pressed against his, our lips brushing.

His strained laugh passes through him and into me. "*Mon amour*, nothing has ever felt this good. I'm losing my mind. Tell me how to make you come. I need—*god, that's so good*—I need to make you come. This won't last as long as I'd like it to."

For some reason, this turns me on even more. I'm surrendering to this, to him, and my noises of pleasure grow louder as I start to move faster. Ellis's fingers are flying over my clit, as I give in to what I need.

It *is* so good. I want to do this again and again, to learn exactly what he likes, exactly how to turn him on and drive him insane.

"Such a good girl, riding me so well. Come for me," Ellis orders through clenched teeth. "Squeeze my cock."

No more encouragement is needed. I do exactly as he says, coming so hard that my entire body shakes and my eyes squeeze shut, too overwhelmed by the pleasure surging through me to think of keeping them open. Ellis is in control, his hips lifting off the seat, drilling into me from below. It's rough and fast, filling the car with the sound of our skin slapping together, and then it's over before I've fully recovered from my orgasm.

With a low curse, he pulls me down, sealing us together as his length twitches inside me, filling the condom with his release. I watch, panting, hypnotized by the way his jaw locks and his breath stutters.

"Jesus." He lets out a choked laugh. "That was, *ah*, unexpected?"

I giggle, warm all over as Ellis pulls me close, kissing my neck, my collar bone, my lips. His cock is still inside me, softening, and with a reluctant sigh, I lift off him, pulling my clothes back into their rightful places as he removes the condom, shoving it into an empty water bottle from the floor of the car.

There's an ache between my legs from what we just did, and I have to fight a smile as he pulls me sideways back into his lap, kissing me deeply. "Should we actually eat now?" I ask, beaming up at him when we finally break for air, our foreheads still pressed together.

Ellis lets out an amused huff, then, as if he's remembering something, stiffens. Shoving a hand into his pocket, he pulls out his phone and we both stare at the screen. It's 10:05.

"Damn it," he hisses, turning his apologetic gaze to mine. "I have to go. I'm late." He must see the look on my face, the horror—because who has plans at ten o'clock at night?—as I realize we never discussed whether either of us was seeing someone. His throat bobs, and he shakes his head, dispelling my unspoken assumption. "I, ah, have a daughter. The babysitter is waiting."

Oh. Okay. I definitely wasn't expecting that. This isn't something I would discuss with a guy my age. Having kids definitely isn't on most Weston student's radar, but Ellis is older. It was probably silly of me not to think it was a possibility. Should it bother me? Or at least put me off? Probing my own feelings, I find that it isn't. I love kids. Definitely not a deal breaker.

"I understand," I assure him, because I do. Of course, if he has a babysitter, he can't stay out all night.

"I'll take you back to the party," he promises, and we stumble out of the back seat into the quiet parking lot. There's no one in sight except a couple standing at the bus stop down the street, and Ellis stoops to retrieve the bag of sandwiches we left abandoned on the ground with a sheepish smile.

As we pull out onto the street, I smile over at him, suddenly shy. "Thank you for tonight. I... well, I really needed it."

"I did as well." He reaches across the center console to take my hand, squeezing it. "For the record, this isn't something I do either."

Yeah, I got that impression. Especially now that I know he's a father. Tentatively, I smile. "What's your daughter's name?"

I can tell he wasn't expecting that question. He glances at me as we roll to a stop at an intersection, eyebrows lifted in surprise. "Zoe," he finally replies with a hint of pride that makes my heart squeeze. "She's six."

Dr. and Dr. Tran's twins are a little older than that. I babysit for them a lot during the school year, and it's pretty much the highlight of my week. "What is she into lately? Princesses? Or is she out there defying gender stereotypes?"

Ellis chuckles. "Not Zoe. Anything pink or sparkly is good with her. I found a recipe for sparkle paint on the internet and we did her room a few weeks ago. I let her pick the color at the store and it's... *bright*."

I laugh at the pained fondness in his voice. "If you sell your house, the new owners are going to hate you. That's awesome, though. Where was pink sparkle paint when I was six?"

My heart falls when we turn, and I realize we're back on my street. A few cars are still parked along the sidewalk, and lights are on inside the house. Likely, my parents haven't even realized I left. It's only been an hour or two, and I feel like a new person. The kind of person who's bold and strong, who goes after what she wants and takes it without apology. I love it.

Ellis pulls over and puts the car in park, looking over at me with his lips turned down. "I suppose this is goodnight."

Be bold, Jo.

I hold out my hand. "Let me see your phone." He obeys, unlocking it and handing it over. Neither of us speaks as I open his phone app and create a new contact for myself, adding a little sandwich beside my name as an afterthought. "Goodnight," I tell him when I've handed it back.

A large hand curls around the back of my neck, pulling me in to meet his lips. It's slow and sweet, the kind of kiss I would have expected to be our first if we hadn't gone so feral for each other.

No regrets.

Feral is awesome.

His hands linger on me even after we break apart, and my smile is huge as I get out of the car, starting down the sidewalk. Ellis pulls away a moment later, and I watch his car until it vanishes around the corner. I've never felt like this before. It's illogical and romantic and probably stupid, but I can't shake these big, unfamiliar feelings that have come out of nowhere.

This is the start of something.

Four

ELLIS

IT'S strange how you can pass a building every day and hardly give it any thought.

Weston University's administration building is a towering, brick structure located at the edge of campus, right beside the staff lot where I park my car every day. I must have walked past it on my way to and from Montgomery Library thousands of times by now, without ever doing more than offering it a passing glance.

In the ten years I've been employed here, I've only stepped foot inside three times. The first was to meet with human resources when I was first hired as an associate librarian, fresh out of graduate school. The second was when my mentor, Marian, retired and I was appointed head librarian. I was invited by the former president to discuss my vision for Montgomery's future. The third was just after President Sutton was appointed. She took it upon herself to sit down with all the school's senior leadership, looking for institutional problems dismissed by the previous administration.

All three occasions were brief and forgettable. Apparently,

having no significant experiences to associate with the place led me to all but ignore it. At least until I received my summons for a meeting with President Sutton—set Friday morning, nearly two weeks after the party at her home—which may or may not spell the end of my career at Weston.

Suddenly, after years of ignoring it, the building was all I could see. Walking to my car or to Montgomery, it loomed in my periphery, an elegant, ivy covered reminder of how fragile my place here has become. Sitting in my office—*trying* to work—my eyes seemed magnetized to the corner of the window where a small part of the roof was visible.

It's saying quite a lot that the impending meeting wasn't the only thing distracting me this week.

Even now, as the last minutes before the meeting tick down and I walk over the groaning, ancient wood floors in the building that's followed me like a spectre all week, my mind returns to *her*.

Grimacing, I force my attention back to the problem at hand. As I turn down the hall leading to President Sutton's office, now more than ever, *I need to focus*. Unfortunately, I have no idea how I'll convince this woman that I'm worthy of a little more patience when nothing about my situation has changed.

My wife is still gone. I still can't find a nanny. Even if I could find a daycare with an available place for Zoe, I haven't come into a miraculous inheritance which would allow me to afford it.

How has my life boiled down so low?

I've made it a habit to avoiding thinking about my ex-wife whenever possible. It's the past. Miranda made the choices she did, and even if I'm still cleaning up after them, there's no point dwelling on it. I have my daughter to consider, and I don't want to be the angry, bitter man who is too stuck in the past to appreciate what he has now.

At moments like this, though... I *am* bitter and angry.

I did everything right—*everything* I was supposed to—and where did it get me? Instead of staying in the small village where I grew up, I ventured out into the world and got an education. I married my college girlfriend, got a good job, bought a house, and dedicated myself to being a good father and husband.

If life came with a correct order of operations, I've followed every step, and everything is *still* a goddamn mess.

All the assurances that Montgomery Library is my priority will count for nothing unless I can offer some assurance that this coming semester won't be like the last—with me missing appointments, deadlines, and leaving the building halfway through the day, never to return.

I feel as though I'm walking to the gallows as I make the final turn into the president's wing of the building, and find myself standing before two assistants stationed at desks before a set of polished oak doors.

Swallowing past the heart lodged in my throat, I attempt a perfunctory smile. "Ellis Delvaux. I have an eleven o'clock meeting with President Sutton."

The man closest to me nods, clicking around on his computer for a moment, before gesturing to a small waiting area on the far wall, which is equipped with a couch, two chairs, and a potted plant. "Take a seat. She's just finishing up a call."

I sit, my knee bouncing as the quiet tapping of keys and hum of the air conditioner press in on me. This is unbearable —the *waiting*—and in desperation, I allow my mind to turn to the woman who I shouldn't be thinking of at all. The beautiful distraction, who has proven herself to be far harder to forget than I anticipated.

It was supposed to just be sex, and while my carefree bachelor days are long behind me, I can't say I remember dwelling so much about a one-night stand after that one night passed. Granted, I never broke a half decade long dry spell by having casual sex with a woman who looks like my most sordid fantasies come to life.

The events of that night... sometimes I can barely breathe thinking about them. Not just the way her body moved with mine, or the soft, erotic noises that escaped her lips when she impaled herself on my cock, or even how good it felt. No, like the old fool I am, I can't stop recalling the way she smiled over her shoulder at me when I dropped her off.

It won't happen again.

More time has passed than could be considered acceptable for not calling. She asked me to. She gave me her number, and I didn't use it. That's the end of it. If I tried to reverse course now, it would undoubtedly be seen as disingenuous. Besides, my situation hasn't changed since that night and it may even get worse before the day is over.

I've made my bed, now it's time to lie in it. It doesn't matter how many times I tell myself that I made no promises or led her on. In the back of my mind, I know the truth. There was something there, a connection, and even if we never discussed it, she expected me to call.

Sleeping with her was selfish. Not telling her I'm unable to offer more was downright cowardly, and it's almost a relief to be pulled from my spiral of self-loathing by one of the assistants addressing me.

"Mr. Delvaux? President Sutton is available now. You can go right in."

I stand and, with the distinct feeling I'm walking to my doom, cross to the oak door, knock once, and enter.

President Sutton is seated at her desk, making a note on a yellow legal pad, and nods at me in greeting. "Mr. Delvaux. Thank you for coming."

"Of course." I take one of the antique leather chairs in front of the desk, wondering as I do if everyone who sits before this woman is as intimidated as I am.

While my interactions with President Sutton have been fairly benign thus far, her reputation is something of a legend at Weston. Her husband—one of the most celebrated physicists in the world—is the less accomplished of the couple.

The president finishes her note and leans back, setting down her pen and offering me a polite smile. "Firstly, you should be aware that I've had at least four directors of smaller campus libraries in this office over the past month, insisting they can do a better job of running Montgomery than you can."

My hands tighten on the arms of the chair. This news doesn't surprise me. My appointment was controversial and while I've done well, the last year especially must have done quite a bit of damage to my professional reputation. "I acknowledge that my performance hasn't been as high as it's been previously. My personal life has been something of a mess, but I assure you I am taking every possible measure to get things sorted out."

President Sutton watches me ramble on, her shrewd gaze appraising. "While I'd like to believe myself above idle gossip, I do hear some things."

My stomach twists. "*Ah.*"

"Yes." She sighs, and there's something in her expression I hadn't predicted. Kindness. Folding her hands neatly on the desk before her, President Sutton offers a gentle smile. "I hope you don't mind me bringing it up, however, I do believe the extenuating circumstances merit consideration in this instance."

While I never wanted to be the man who relied on pity to keep his job, it appears I have no other option now.

41

"I appreciate that." My mouth dry and my voice strangely hollow. My pride wants me to tell her I have everything under control, that my attendance will never be an issue again, and my personal business is none of her concern. Unfortunately, neither of those things is true, and my pride won't pay the mortgage or ensure my daughter gets the care she deserves.

Pride has no place here.

"That being said," she continues, her expression becoming more grave as she does, "I cannot be as lenient as I would like. There are rules in place, and if I bend them for you, I'd be forced to bend them for everyone. Will your childcare situation still be an issue in the fall semester?"

Ice is spreading through my veins. "I'll make sure it won't be. I've been looking for a nanny," I assure her hurriedly. "It's been a struggle so far, but I'm hopeful with students beginning to look for housing for September, that the room and board will be sufficient draw. Unfortunately, after school daycare places for special needs children are very limited and, *ah*, expensive."

President Sutton must see some of the desperation written in my face, because she doesn't make any objection to my lackluster reassurances. She taps her pen against the mouse pad beside her, gazing at me thoughtfully. "Perhaps you should consider taking some time away from Weston."

If the floor opened up beneath my chair and swallowed me whole, it would be a relief. This can't be happening. Every time I turn, I seem to hit another brick wall, and *I'm fucking tired.* Losing the job I worked so hard for, being unable to provide for Zoe... "I can't do that," I choke out, and there's no keeping the panic from my voice now. "If I could just have a few more weeks to—"

My jumbled pleas are silenced when President Sutton lifts her hand to stop me. "This isn't a punishment, Mr. Delvaux. You would remain the director of Montgomery Library, and you'd receive a paycheck. However, something very recently came across my desk that might be a very good opportunity for you to take a *working* sabbatical."

Blood is rushing in my ears. "I'm... surprised."

President Sutton laughs lightly. "You're very good at what you do, Mr. Delvaux. Weston University is fortunate to have you, and I believe you're uniquely qualified for this assignment. The board agrees."

I know that I'll do it. Whatever she asks, even if it's mopping the cafeteria. This is so much more than I expected, or even could have hoped for. When I walked in here, I knew very well she could fire me, and now even the faintest possibility of an alternative allows me to breathe for the first time in weeks.

With the exception of a few hours spent in the company of a woman I'll never see again.

My boss takes a folder from the corner of her desk and passes it across to me. Opening it, I stare down at the contents, which seem to be a jumble of legal documents in French and English. There's a faded photograph of a clearly ancient, but beautiful, manor house. I know without seeing the address that it's in my home country.

"A rather affluent alumni of Weston passed away a few weeks ago and left his entire estate to the school. His family home, a chateau, located several hours south of Paris, is said to include an extensive collection of rare books. No one has catalogued these or taken an inventory, but it's thought that many are very valuable."

I look up sharply. "You're kidding."

President Sutton's eyes glint with amusement. "I'm not. Trust me, I was stunned as well. It seems insane not to have any sort of documentation. For insurance purposes, at the very least."

"Mad," I agree, staring back down at the photograph, which looks as though it came out of an old property record.

The chateau is stunning, composed of large, ivy covered stones and surrounded by open fields, with only a dirt drive leading to the structure.

She continues. "Obviously, we need someone on the ground to take an inventory, see what should be kept for the school, auctioned, etcetera. The school's trustee board has allotted a living and travel expense stipend, as well as a full salary and benefits for the length of the assignment. Naturally, with your experience in project management and expertise in rare books, your name was the first suggested. We recognize it will be a significant inconvenience to leave the country for an extended period, so they are willing to offer you a significant bonus upon completion of the project, dependent on the value of what you find."

Talk about emotional whiplash. Only a few minutes ago, I was convinced I was about to be fired, and now I'm struggling to keep a lid on my excitement. This is, quite literally, every librarian's dream. Or, at least, it's mine.

Zoe needs to be taken into account, though. Changes of routine are brutal for her, and my heart twists at the thought of how difficult it would be for her. While I always imagined I would raise my daughter bilingual, her difficulty with speech has held me back from using my mother-tongue more often at home. She would struggle terribly in a French-speaking school.

I swallow, scrambling to find the right thing to say. Finally, when I can't put off responding any longer, I smile tightly at my employer, endeavoring to appear more confident than I am. "I'd need to do some research into finding a nanny or tutor for my daughter. It may be a challenge conducting interviews from overseas, but I'm sure I could manage it with some time."

I'm actually not sure of that at all, considering how hard of a time I've had securing childcare in the city where we live, but I need to make this happen, for both of our sakes. If it means forgoing sleep and spending my days with Zoe and working at night, I'll do it. Whatever it takes.

President Sutton looks pleased with herself. "Actually, I have a solution to that, too." I lean forward, listening intently as she continues, "My daughter should be going into her senior year at Weston this year. She's very bright, responsible, and happens to have babysat for several professors here with children on the spectrum."

I sit up straighter. "Oh?"

There's something pained in her expression as she nods and continues, "She wants to take a year off. To travel and work. I know she would enjoy something like this, and it would provide you the freedom to leave immediately, which is important to the board. This estate is substantial, as are the costs of upkeep, and the house and land can't be sold until these books are appraised."

Hope is coming to life inside me. While I'm not entirely sold on allowing my employer's college-aged daughter to be Zoe's tutor and nanny, I can at least meet her. Besides, with nothing in my current situation here likely to change any time soon, what choice do I have? Every potential nanny I've interviewed has—miraculously—been worse than the last, and I wouldn't trust most of those people to babysit a cat, never mind my child. In this scenario, I would be in the same house as Zoe and this stranger, not across town hoping for the best.

And, perhaps selfishly, I *really* want to do it.

"I would like to meet her, certainly."

President Sutton nods, looking pleased I'm open to the idea. "I hope it wasn't too presumptive, but I invited her here today to make introductions. I'm not trying to pressure you, but for obvious reasons, the board is aiming for this to be put in motion as quickly as possible. We'd want you to leave for France as early as next week."

Next week? I'm so caught up in this that I barely register the first piece of information she shared. When I look up to find her gazing expectantly at me, I bob my head automatically. "Of course. I'm something of an expert in interviewing nannies these days." I chuckle dryly. "Or possibly a survivor."

She laughs obligingly and stands, crossing to the door and slips out, allowing me a few moments to catch my breath. My thoughts are moving at about a thousand miles per hour, jumping between relief at being able to keep my job, excitement at this assignment and worry about what will happen if I can't do it.

No. There is no can't, here. *I have to do it.*

Not only is this the opportunity of a lifetime, but it's my chance to keep my position at the university, visit my mother, and buy myself some time to find a better childcare solution for Zoe for when we return. Unless this young woman is wholly and completely incompetent, I'll be forced to say yes.

Two sets of footsteps sound behind me, and as I look around, it's as though—for the second time today—my world has been turned upside down.

President Sutton keeps moving past me, walking back around to her side of the desk, oblivious to the fact her daughter has stopped dead in the doorway, staring at me with just as much shock as I'm currently feeling. Her daughter, whom is not such a stranger to me after all.

No.

Tell me she isn't...

Tell me I didn't...

Josephine seems to shake herself, her expression going blank just seconds before the creak of an office chair indicates her mother has taken her seat.

Her mother, who is my boss.

Her mother, who just suggested her college senior aged daughter, travel with me and Zoe to France and act as her nanny and tutor.

"Come sit down, Jo," says President Sutton, lifting her hand to the chair beside mine and Josephine moves forward, not looking at me.

My ears are ringing, and my heart is beating so fast it seems impossible that neither of the women in the room with me can hear it. I'm trying to find a way around the truth that's staring me in the face, and there isn't one. The beautiful young woman I met at the faculty mixer, the one I felt such a connection with, isn't a faculty member after all. She lied? *No.* She *didn't* lie. I asked what her department was, not her job. Which means I fucked my boss's daughter in the back seat of my car.

And just when I thought my life couldn't be any more of a mess.

"Mr. Delvaux, this is my daughter Josephine, Jo, to most of us. I've already filled her in on the situation here, and she's fully on board." The woman across the desk smiles, oblivious to the underlying tension. "She's been wanting to travel, and spent the better part of her college career babysitting for Doctor and Doctor Tran's twins."

I'm barely listening to the words coming out of her mouth. Fraternization between faculty and students are strictly prohibited at Weston. Every year, my colleagues and I have to sit through a seminar on "workplace conduct" in which we're reminded of that (about thirty times in the space of a day). I'd always rolled my eyes at this, privately baffled by why anyone would endanger their career for sex.

Now, *I'm* that idiot, and if Josephine chooses to tell her mother what transpired between us... I might as well pack up my office. Maybe I deserve it, if my judgment is so flawed that I can't even enjoy a one-night-stand with a woman without it blowing up in my face. Bracing myself, I turn to look at her directly.

Experiencing guilt, horror and attraction all at once is a new one for me, but that's what happens when I meet her warm, hazel eyes. Josephine's hands are folded in her lap, her back is straight, and her smile is polite as she says, "It's nice to meet you, Mr. Delvaux."

Five

JOSEPHINE

> Unknown Number: Can we meet
> somewhere to speak?

> Unknown Number: Please return my call
> when you get the chance.

> Unknown Number: I'm available any time,
> just let me know. Your mother offered me
> the week off to prepare.

> Unknown Number: I've left you several
> messages. Are you getting them?

> Unknown Number: Josephine, we leave in
> two days. I'd really like to discuss the
> situation with you before we board an
> international flight.

AS I LAY flat on my bedroom floor, staring at the five texts I've ignored, it occurs to me that I might be being petty. Or a coward. Or both. Whatever the case, it's not a good look— but, *come on*. I went into what I thought was a meet and greet with a prospective employer for a job I *really* wanted to get, and instead found myself in the most awkward situations of my life.

Maybe there are some women out there who would have handled it with dignity and come up with some brilliant evasive maneuver to get out of the whole thing. Not me. I sat there, nodding mutely while my mother went on and on about what a good opportunity it is for both of us and how *the stars aligned*.

Yeah, they aligned alright. A little too well. Because now, I will be living with and working as a nanny for my one night stand.

The one night stand, who I haven't been able to bring myself to face yet. Partially because the shock hasn't quite worn off, and partially because the hurt hasn't either.

It was probably stupid of me, or naïve, but I really thought he would call. I haven't been on a ton of first dates, but there's been enough to know they're generally pretty awkward. Lots of silence and obligatory introductory questions, all while wondering if my hair is starting to get all frizzy in the back.

They're *hard*, but being with Ellis was *easy*. Sleeping with him didn't feel like a one night stand, or even sex after the first date. I went home feeling happier than I can remember being in a really long time, forgetting the reason I'd fled the party in the first place until my mother knocked on my bedroom door to apologize. We talked, and while she still isn't on board with me taking time off, she did admit she trusted my judgement and thought she had an idea of something for me to do.

It's pretty embarrassing that my heart sank a little at the possibility of spending half a year in another country when I'd met a guy I really liked. After all, I hadn't imagined the way he was looking at me, or the way he'd held on just a little longer when he dropped me off. Men don't want to steal a few more seconds of intimacy with one night stands, do they?

Then, one day passed. Then two. Then three... and I still stubbornly believed he was going to call, probably with a really good excuse about why he hadn't earlier.

He liked me, I was *so sure* of it, and I liked him back. Whenever I picked up my phone this past week, hoping to see a call or text from him and being disappointed each time, it hurt. Or I hurt myself by hoping this was the start of a love story. It isn't one. This is real life, and sometimes you lose your virginity to a guy in the backseat of a car, and he doesn't call.

Oof. When did I become a bad stereotype?

In Mom's office, as the horrible, awkward *star alignment* settled over us, I'm pretty sure Ellis and I both lost the ability to speak. Or, more likely, we were each trying to find a reason this arrangement wouldn't work, when my mother (who comes equipped with a genius level IQ and excellent deductive reasoning skills) listed off the reasons it *would*.

I told her I needed a change. Ellis needed a nanny comfortable caring for and teaching autistic children, and I'm qualified.

What could I say?

What could he say?

We were backed into a corner, and the only thing to do was agree.

My stomach twists every time I remember his set expression, or the way he stared at me with none of the warmth or familiarity we shared during our one and only night together. He couldn't do or say anything in front of my mom—*his boss*—but still, it stung, and it's yet another reason why I've been avoiding this meeting with him. What if he pretends nothing happened, or, worse, tells me it was a mistake? The jury's still out on whether *I* think it was, but I'm not sure my ego could stand the hit if *he* did.

Strangely, the whole thing hasn't turned me off dating as much as I expected. In an uncharacteristic show of defiance, it's only made me more determined to find someone who *will* call. Before I do that, though, I need to get through an eight-hour international flight and six months in a foreign country with the first guy who *didn't*.

While nobody seems quite sure of what the late, eccentric Weston alumni left behind, the consensus seems to be he was an avid collector of rare books, and his library is massive. Apparently, the school has allocated funds for Ellis to spend six months sorting the whole mess out. It could take less time, or more, depending on what he finds when he gets there. When *we* get there.

Six months in the French countryside.

It sounds like a dream come true. I should be excitedly looking up mini trips to take on the weekends and listening to *"learn French fast"* podcasts. Most people my age would fight me for this opportunity, but I haven't even started packing. My mother has been at a conference most of the week, and my father wouldn't notice if the house caught fire, so there wasn't anyone to ask questions about why I'm not over the moon. After all, I told them I wanted to take time off, to travel, and now I am.

Maybe.

Everything has happened so fast. The last few weeks have been an emotional rollercoaster, and everything seems to hinge on the talk with Ellis I've been avoiding.

Now it's Wednesday night and I'm lying on the floor of my not packed bedroom, knowing I've officially run out of time. Either I tell my parents I've changed my mind and want to stay the course with my degree, or I go to France. It's time to put on my big girl pants and do the thing. Reluctantly. Wearing waterproof mascara, just in case.

My heart is lodged in my throat as I pick up my phone and type out a text, pressing send before I can second guess the decision.

> Josephine: Hi. I can meet you tomorrow.

He responds within thirty seconds.

> Ellis: Hi! Great! I'm taking Zoe to Monkey Do at 1pm. We have a membership, so if you let them know at the desk they won't charge you. Do you want to meet us there, or come to the house later? I don't have a sitter, or I would meet you somewhere else.

His friendly tone disarms me. Was I expecting him to be rude? No. Frosty seemed likely, though, or at least cool and professional as he'd been in Mom's office. As I stare at the screen, considering my options, little bubbles to indicate he's typing appear then disappear twice.

> Josephine: 1pm at Monkey Do. Sounds good.

* * *

Monkey Do turns out to be one of those big, indoor play places.

As soon as I walk through the front doors, I'm almost bowled over by a harassed-looking mother who is carrying a sobbing toddler, and holding the hand of an older child who is whining loudly about having to go.

She shoots me an apologetic look as I double back to hold the door for her, and I offer an understanding smile in response. Her day is *clearly* way more stressful than mine. Almost being run into seems tame by comparison.

Once they've passed and I've stepped back inside, I pause, scanning the space. I'm standing in the small lobby area of a big, open room, all centered on a massive padded play structure. Brightly colored booths surround it, all occupied by parents or grandparents, watching their kids play while chatting with each other, scrolling on their phones or just staring off into the distance.

Fighting back the overwhelming instinct to run right back to my car, I blow out a long breath and stride forward, approaching the teenage desk attendant. "Hi," I begin, smiling tentatively. "I'm here to meet Ellis Delvaux? He said they have a membership and—" She buzzes me through the little gate without a word, and returns to staring at her phone.

I wipe my damp palms on the skirt of my summer dress and step through into the play area. Even while I'm practically vibrating with nerves, my heart lifts a little as I make my way past kids zooming in every direction. It's adorable in here. They've clearly gone to some lengths to make the space accessible to everyone, and it's kind of amazing to see differently abled children all happily playing together.

As I round the far corner of the play structure, dodging kids as I go, my throat tightens at the sight of a silver-haired man sitting alone at a booth twenty yards away. I stop dead. There he is. Ellis Delvaux. Librarian, single father, and the man responsible for my bruised heart.

Gone is the crisp white shirt, the vest and the neatly combed hair I saw the night of the party, and again in Mom's office. In their place is a faded *Weston Alumni* t-shirt bearing a red stain, disheveled hair, and dark bags beneath his eyes.

He's leaning back in the booth, looking off into the play area, both hands cradling a cardboard coffee cup. As I watch, his eyes close and he takes a long drink from it, allowing himself a brief moment of respite before returning to readiness. As if he senses he's being watched, Ellis turns, meeting my gaze from twenty feet away.

A shiver of awareness runs through me, and it takes some effort to drag my feet off the ground and move forward. When

I finally do, Ellis hurries to stand. "Josephine. Hi," he says, pale eyes searching my face. "Thank you for coming."

"Hi, Ellis." I manage a polite smile.

Clearing his throat, Ellis gestures to the booth in wordless invitation and we both sit. There's a Cheerio stuck to the shoulder of his t-shirt. "Ah, how are you?"

God, how did I forget how attractive his accent was? Every word flows like honey, smooth and sweet. He might have been reading poetry rather than making awkward small talk. Judging by the interested looks he's getting from the moms in the booth behind him, I'm not the only one affected by it.

"Fine." I set my bag on the bench beside me and lean back, trying my best to look confident and unruffled. "You wanted to talk?"

His throat bobs. "I thought we should clear the air." I'm not going to make this easy on him, so I wait, watching as he grapples with what to say. "I apologize if I led you on, if I've hurt you." His voice is strained, desperate even, but I refuse to read into it or wonder why. I already knew he wasn't inter- ested, so why does this final confirmation sting so badly?

"Okay. *Um.* That's fine," I tell him at last, letting my gaze fall to the scuffed tabletop. *Damn it.* That's fine? Why did I say that?

I was so determined to show up here and show him he hasn't hurt me, but I can't get it together. There's no way to pretend I didn't like him. *I really freaking liked him, and now he knows it.* As if this situation wasn't mortifying enough to begin with.

Steeling myself, I look up again and my eyes catch on a few of the moms sitting together at the table behind Ellis. They're eyeing me speculatively, but look away when they see I've noticed them, pretending to be engrossed in conversation.

My heart sinks. Maybe he's slept with them, too. Maybe he does this all the time, and I was naïve enough to fall for the sweet, bashful librarian act. Or—my stomach twists—maybe he just had a bad time.

Oh god, am I bad at sex?

"I handled it poorly," Ellis tries again, speaking in a low rush. "I hope, given the circumstances, we can set it aside. Start fresh? I'd very much like us to be friends."

My heart sinks. Right. The circumstances. "To be honest, I'm not sure this, me going to France, I mean, is such a good idea," I tell him tightly. "Wouldn't you be more comfortable with someone you don't have this kind of history with? Maybe there's another—"

"I looked at your resume," he interjects, eyes bright. "You're more than qualified. Zoe would be lucky to have you and..." His expression twists. "Frankly, I'm desperately in need of help, and not above begging. We wouldn't have to mention the way we met ever again if you'd rather forget it. You have my word. I'll be nothing but professional."

As we study each other, something hot and restless shifts beneath my skin. There's no earthly reason for me to believe him, but I do. Just like the night we met, there is something about this man that strips away all my second-guessing and reservations.

It's hard to accept that maybe Ellis isn't the villain in all this. He isn't the guy who didn't call, he's the guy who really *couldn't* call. Not because he got into a car accident or had a family member die, or any of the other excuses that ran through my head as the days passed without hearing from him. No, Ellis is just a tired, stressed single dad who is already so overwhelmed by life that he couldn't take *me* on too.

Maybe, just maybe, all my instincts about him were right. There might have been a genuine connection between us, but —no, I *know* there was. I feel it now, even as we sit stiffly on opposite benches of a bright yellow booth, a world away from our one and only night together.

It would be a lot easier if I wasn't attracted to him, or at least feel enough rejection and anger to lie to myself about it. It's no use, though. He's so handsome, even with a Cheerio on his shoulder and what looks like a smear of ketchup on his shirt. The sexy, surreal veil has been lifted, and now we can see each other in broad daylight. He knows who I am, I know who he is, and all the ugliness of our lives that we glossed over for one almost perfect night is laid out on the table between us.

I still want him.

God, that stings.

A horrible possibility occurs to me. "You're not just doing this because you're afraid of me being upset with you and telling my mother, are you?"

Ellis grimaces. "I would like to think my first impression of you was correct, and you're not the sort of person to be vengeful. Surely if you were so angry with me that you wanted to ruin my life, you'd have done so the day we met in your mother's office."

He's right, I'm not. Especially knowing he has a daughter to take care of.

Reluctantly, I nod. "So if I did come—" My sentence breaks off, though, because someone has appeared at the edge of the table.

The little girl is unquestionably Ellis's daughter. She has his eyes, his skin tone, and beneath a layer of baby fat, I can see a hint of the sharp cheekbones that got me into this mess to begin with. Her dark brown hair is pulled into two neat braids, and while Ellis looks more than a little worse for wear, his little girl is clean and obviously well cared for.

She bounces on the balls of her feet beside the table, hands flapping indignantly, and Ellis is instantly at attention. I watch as he reaches into the bag at his side to produce a pink, sparkly water bottle. Zoe snatches it and brings it to her lips. As she drinks, she looks over at me for the first time.

"Hello, Zoe." There's no need for me to pretend to smile at her. "My name is Jo. It's very nice to meet you."

Zoe pauses for all of half a second before thrusting the bottle back into her father's waiting hands and racing off to the row of silk sensory swings.

"She's adorable," I say as I turn back to Ellis, finding a composure in his expression that wasn't there previously.

"Thank you." He smiles gently. "She's made a lot of progress with her speech in the past year. I've arranged for her occupational and speech therapy to continue remotely, but getting her to cooperate might be an uphill battle."

Something about his tone, which sounds as though he's practiced being strong even when he's so clearly exhausted, makes my heart twist with sympathy. His hands are resting on the table before him, and for just a second, I wish I could reach out and take one. Does this guy have anyone in his corner? Who does he lean on when things get hard?

It doesn't matter. That's not what Ellis Delvaux needs from me. He needs a nanny, and I need to break out of my bland, lonely life now, before I get stuck in it forever.

Going to France with him might be a bad idea, but good ideas haven't gotten me anywhere. I've spent years doing the logical, responsible thing, and all I have to show for it is mild-to-moderate depression and a life about as interesting as drying paint. Agreeing to this is risky, probably stupid, and there are about fifty ways it could go wrong, but it *feels* right.

Something defiant and bold seems to rise inside me, and before I can second guess the decision, I nod. "We'll figure it out."

Ellis's entire demeanor changes. "*We?* You're coming?" he asks hopefully, eyebrows high.

"Yeah." I hadn't made up my mind, not fully anyway, until

coming here, but now... Well, now I just need to focus on keeping myself from catching feelings for the man before me. That is one bad idea I refuse to give into.

It seems to take a moment for this to sink in before Ellis sags with relief, smiling at me gratefully. "Thank you. Really, Josephine. It's very good of you to agree." He glances at Zoe again, then back to me, serious again. "Is there anything I can do to make you more comfortable around me?"

His question takes me off guard, and it takes me a moment to piece together why I'm so confused. I am comfortable around him. Which is weird. I shouldn't be, right? Even he seems to think so.

I shake my head and reach blindly beside me to grab my bag. "I'm okay. Really. I'll see you in a few days."

As I go to stand, however, Ellis's hand flashes out to catch my wrist. We both freeze and he drops it immediately, grimacing in apology. "I'm sorry. I know I said we could pretend it never happened, but before we do... I just—I wanted to explain properly. At least once."

He lowers his voice and, behind him, one of the moms who was eyeing him when I came in leans forward, trying to be subtle in her eavesdropping. "I should have made it clear before we... before anything happened, that I'm not in a place where I can even consider dating or a relationship. It wasn't a commentary on you, or the night we had together, or anything other than not having space in my life." His eyes search my face, as though the way to make this all go away is written there. "Zoe needs to be my first priority."

"I get it." It's not just me saying that, either. I really do understand, but that doesn't take away the sting of rejection, or the self-doubt I've carried around for the last few weeks. "I probably shouldn't have assumed you would. Nothing personal, right?" Embarrassment clogs my throat as I smile tightly at him, fighting the urge to look away. "Lesson learned."

God, he must think I'm so clingy for getting so bent out of shape over having sex one time. If he wasn't already, now he's probably pretty relieved he didn't call.

At my words, Ellis's shoulders drop slightly. "When I look back at that night... I likely would have assumed otherwise too, if our positions were reversed. I'm entirely in the wrong, Josephine. There's no excuse for my behavior, and I'm sorry."

I smile weakly. "You already said that."

He grimaces. "Once wasn't enough. Truly, I feel terrible."

"Don't. We're good." I scoot to the end of the bench, preparing to leave again, but something in his crestfallen expression makes me pause. "I'm not angry at you, Ellis. Really. You're a really good father for putting her first."

He lets out a hard laugh, and turns toward the play yard, rubbing absentmindedly at the stubble on his jaw. "I appreciate that. Some days I don't feel like one. Most days, actually, I think anyone could do this better than me."

I follow his gaze, spotting Zoe playing some sort of twirling game with another little girl, their giggles carrying back to us. Something deep inside me pulls taught. "I think you being so hard on yourself means you care very much. We don't hurt ourselves for things that don't matter."

It would be easier if I were still mad at him, but I'm not. Sometimes, there isn't a bad guy. There's just a stressed out single dad, who is doing his best. Ellis isn't a villain here.

When I tear my eyes away from Zoe, I find Ellis already looking at me. The corners of his lips lift in a halfhearted smile. "Would you like to meet her? Properly?"

I don't hesitate to agree.

It takes some persuading to get Zoe to leave *Monkey Do*, but Ellis manages it without tears. She eyes me skeptically as the three of us walk across the street to a small, quiet park and sit down in the grass at the foot of a big tree.

"*Mon coeur*, you remember I told you were are going on an airplane, don't you?" Ellis asks, and Zoe's head bobs up and down dutifully. "Josephine will be coming with us. She is going to teach you all the things Mrs. Burns does now, and spend time with you when I am busy working."

Zoe doesn't look at me, choosing instead to watch cars zooming by us on the street, but I smile at her, anyway. "Hi Zoe. My name *is* Josephine, but most people call me Jo. You're welcome to as well. I'm very excited to go on this trip with you and your dad."

"*Papa*." She corrects me with the tiniest hint of an accent.

Beside her, Ellis laughs softly. "*Oui, mon coeur. Papa*."

Holy cuteness. I'm doomed.

"I'm very sorry. I'll know better in the future." I glance up at Ellis, biting back a smile. "If it's okay with you, I saw an *i-c-e c-r-e-a-m* shop a few doors down from *Monkey Do*. I'd love to take her and shamelessly buy some cool nanny points while we get to know each other a little better."

He looks at me for so long, his expression flat, I start to think I've done something wrong. Before I can even begin to imagine what, though, Ellis nods. "Of course. I can answer some emails while I wait for you two. My car is over there, the blue one..." His words falter, and a dull flush rises on his high cheekbones, obviously remembering I have been in his car before.

I'm determined not to find it charming.

My attention turns to Zoe, who is watching me closely now, her lips pursed. "I was going to get some ice cream after meeting you guys, but I think it would be way more fun if you came with me, Zoe. If you'd like to. Do you like rainbow sprinkles?"

Unsurprisingly, Zoe is a big fan of rainbow sprinkles. She

has no qualms about abandoning Ellis, clutching my hand and humming merrily to herself as we head back toward the street. "I've seen pictures of this place online, actually," I tell her. "They have all sorts of really cool sundaes. There's one that even has an entire slice of birthday cake on top. Do you want to split that with me?" As I look to check Zoe's reaction, movement in the corner of my eye makes me glance back.

Ellis is watching us, the same carefully blank look on his face as he had when I proposed the ice cream, and I look back around hurriedly, my heart suddenly beating much harder than it was before.

Crap.

Six

ELLIS

THIS WEEK HAS BEEN nothing short of a nightmare.

I'm grateful for the opportunity, truly I am. But between wrapping up projects at work, making arrangements for the house, preparing Zoe as best I can, and worrying about the Josephine situation, the last days before we leave have taken their toll.

Once, I would have relished this kind of adventure. Now, an international flight (leaving at five in the morning) seems likely to end me. If it doesn't, Josephine will finish the job.

In the two days since we met at *Monkey Do*, I haven't been able to stop thinking about the hurt on her face. I felt like enough of a bastard in the days after our night together, even if I was certain a clean break was the best course of action. This is the opposite of that, and now, I have confirmation that I'm even more of an ass than previously thought.

Josephine... *merde*. She's lovely. More than lovely. The woman is an angel with fuck-me lips and an ass I would go to war for, and *I* made her feel unwanted. Me. The man who— only a few days ago—used air freshener as deodorant after forgetting to visit the store.

Lying in bed the night before our departure, try as I might, I couldn't think of anything other than Josephine. The way she looked at me in that library. Her arms wrapped around me as I carried her through the grocery store, and how my heart was lighter than it'd been in years. The sounds she made when I was inside her. And, worst of all, the rejection and hurt that flashed across her face when I apologized for *leading her on*.

While I wish I could deny it, that's precisely what I did. When she gave me her number, I didn't tell her I wouldn't use it. No, I just let her go off into the night, allowing her to believe something would happen that patently could not. Not then, and certainly not now.

It's all a mess, and I only manage to drift off for a few hours before my alarm sounds at three to get the luggage and Zoe out of the house in time to meet the airport shuttle. Predictably, my daughter doesn't respond well to being woken hours ahead of schedule, and there are a fair few tears as I struggle to get us ready.

When the van arrives, Josephine is already on board. I nearly swallow my tongue when I see the formfitting jumpsuit she chose to fly in, which is casual and comfortable enough, but clings to every curve of her body.

God help me.

Despite my assurances that we could keep things professional, there is no denying the effect she has on me. My cock is at attention from the moment she steps down onto the curb, offering me a tentative smile and kneeling down to speak quietly to a grumpy, teary-eyed Zoe.

It quickly becomes clear that I'm not the only member of this family who is taken with Josephine Sutton. By the time the driver and I finish loading everything up, I climb into the dark van to find the two girls already curled together in a pair of seats, examining a tiny travel game that Josephine brought with her.

They sit together the entire drive to the airport, and when we arrive, Josephine settles a pair of noise canceling headphones and sunglasses on Zoe's head without me even mentioning it.

Neither of us says much as we check in and make our way through security, with Zoe detaching from Josephine and clinging to me when it comes time to go through the metal detectors. It was only when we settle into stiff, uncomfortable chairs at the gate and my girl sees the plane that she starts to get excited.

"I'm going to grab a cup of coffee," Josephine tells me quietly, gathering her purse from the seat beside her as Zoe presses her nose to the gate window to see the luggage being loaded up beneath. "Can I get you anything?"

A voice echoes over our heads. *"Flight two-six-seven to Paris, Charles de Gaulle, will begin boarding in twenty minutes..."*

"Coffee would be great. Thank you." I reach for my wallet, but she's already waved me off and turned toward the coffee kiosk situated across the terminal.

A man about my age, sitting across from us, smirks. "Lucky man." He chuckles as he looks back down at his phone.

It registers, with a dull shock, that he thinks she's my wife. Why wouldn't he? We're traveling together. Zoe and Josephine both have dark hair. To an outsider, we must look like a family. I'm sure this won't be the only time someone makes this mistake over the coming months.

"Keep your eyes to yourself," I snarl before I can stop myself. Irrational, territorial anger rising inside me. Even if she isn't mine, it doesn't give some asshole the right to look at her.

Like I did.

Wisely, the man doesn't respond, and I alternate between keeping an eye on Zoe, hopping up and down beside the window, and checking on Josephine's progress in line. As if she'll pick up another admirer in the time she's gone, one who's observant enough to discern there is no ring on her finger.

She isn't meant to be mine, that much is obvious, but knowing it doesn't remove the vicious twist of jealousy whenever I think of her sharing something like we did with someone else. Hell, I can't even stand the idea of someone *looking* at her, a failing I certainly never experienced during my marriage.

My only hope is that living in such extreme proximity to her proves we aren't compatible, and any pitiful desire for *more* fades away. Jo is twenty-two. Surely she'll want to go out and party, travel on her weekends and date men in the village. Even if it makes my teeth gnash just to think of it, her moving on to more appropriate prospects would certainly serve a purpose.

I'm so preoccupied I fail to notice Josephine returning until a large coffee cup is pressed into my hand. Offering her a weak smile, I flip back the plastic tab on the top and take a long, greedy draw. "Thank you."

"Don't mention it." She doesn't look at me, busying herself with putting her phone in her bag.

A sour taste fills my mouth. Things will get easier, won't they? Less awkward? I really do want this to work out, and not just for my job. Better than anyone, I know that good childcare doesn't grow on trees, and all signs point toward Josephine being excellent with Zoe. If I couldn't find reliable help in a college town, what are my chances of finding a replacement in the French countryside should Josephine decide this situation is too much for her?

I am the reason my daughter is growing up with only a single father and no mother. The least I can do is keep my lust in check and allow her a positive female role model.

Unable to stand the silence, I glance at Jo's profile and speak the question that's been on my mind a lot over the last few days. "You never told me why you're taking time off school."

Her thumb nail drags up and down on the plastic rim of the coffee cup, creating a hollow clicking sound. "It's nothing dramatic." She lifts a shoulder, eyes following Zoe as she plops down on the ground to watch the luggage handlers with rapt attention.

"I'd still like to know." I can tell I'm pushing my luck, that asking too much of her right now might result in the walls between us going even higher, but I can't seem to stop myself.

Bright hazel eyes meet mine. "I did everything I was supposed to, and I still wasn't happy. This should be a really big, exciting time in my life, but there wasn't anything in my life to be excited about. I guess it occurred to me that if I didn't stop and make a change now, I never would."

Her words, so far from what I was expecting from her, hit me squarely in the chest. The feeling she's describing is familiar to me, the sense of bewilderment and injustice when you follow the rules to a T, and you find yourself unhappy anyway.

"Not necessarily." The corner of my lips lifts into a half-hearted smile. I lift my hand to the cavernous room where we're seated. "Change can take you by surprise sometimes."

Her gaze falls to her cup. "I—"

"Papa!" We both look around to see Zoe hopping up and down in excitement, pointing down to one of the luggage handlers who is waving up at her.

"Wave back, *mon coeur*." I feel my spirits lift as the first true excitement begins to set in. The circumstances might not be ideal, but this is a once in a lifetime opportunity, and the first chance I've had to spend any significant time in my home country since college.

My mother was over the moon when I called to tell her the news, and has already decided to come to the chateau for several weeks once we're settled.

There was a time when I would get homesick for France, but that faded away with every year I spent in the States. Now, I find myself itching with excitement to get home, to show Zoe all the things and places I loved as a boy... and Josephine. I would very much like to experience those things with the beautiful young woman beside me, too. Not that she'll be accompanying Zoe and me on outings, I'm sure by the end of her work days she'll avoid us like the plague, and—

"Zoe doesn't have any allergies, does she?" asks Josephine suddenly, interrupting my preoccupation.

I turn, blinking in surprise. "None. Why?"

Reaching into her bag, Josephine holds up a handful of multicolored lollipops, her lips curved in a sheepish smile. "I thought I'd better check with you first. They might help with her ears popping, but the sugar obviously brings its own problems."

"I'll take vibrating with energy over screaming in pain any day," I tell her wryly. Truthfully, there is a handful in my carry-on as well, but I resolve to leave them where they are. The idea of her taking the time to research how to make Zoe's journey easier makes me feel warm all over. To some, it might seem small, but for years now, I've been *everything* to my daughter. It's a nice feeling to know there's someone else who cares. Even if she's only doing it because she's paid to.

As soon as the conclusion crosses my mind, though, I dismiss it. Getting paid has nothing to do with it. There's a difference between taking care of someone and caring about them, and it couldn't be more clear that after only a few hours in her presence, Josephine already cares about my girl.

As passengers with children are called to board, Zoe gleefully takes her new nanny's hand, bouncing with excitement as we head toward the plane.

"Here we go," I say under my breath and Jo looks back, catching my eye.

"Here we go," she agrees.

Seven

JOSEPHINE

LE CHÂTEAU PERDU, our home for the next six months, is a three-hour drive north from Paris.

Zoe, who slept for more than half the flight, is cranky and fidgety when we finally get off the plane. Headphones still in place, she stares around the crowded luggage claim with wide eyes.

Other passengers from our flight are standing around us, looking rumpled and exhausted. I'm sure I haven't fared much better, but apart from a quick peek in the tiny airplane lavatory mirror hours ago, I haven't dared to check. Ellis, annoyingly, looks handsome even with his hair sticking up in the back and bags beneath his eyes.

Suspicion that I look like shit aside, the excitement is beginning to set in, because *I'm in France!* My international travel experience up until now was going to Toronto for Model UN in high school, and Bermuda on a cruise with my parents. Even with the complicated relationship with my employer, it feels as though weight I didn't realize I was carrying got left behind at home. I'm free, at least for six months, and right now that feels like all the time in the world.

"Can we stop somewhere for pastries?" I ask Ellis as the luggage carousel begins to move, murmurs of relief from everyone around us.

He eyes me curiously. "I would have thought you'd like a proper meal after... well, whatever it was we ate on the flight."

I laugh. "The menu said pork chops."

"That was *not* pork chops." Ellis makes a noise of derision and waves his hand dismissively. Then, catching sight of his daughter, winces. "Damn—Zoe, please don't touch the belt, you'll pinch your fingers."

Zoe ignores him.

Ellis's shoulders sag.

"Hey, honey girl." I bend down beside her, pointing to a fountain installed towards the street entrance. There are a few parents standing around it with their small children, throwing coins in. "Will you go make a wish with me? I'm sure Papa can handle the bags without us."

This is obviously deemed an acceptable alternative to getting her fingers jammed in a luggage carousel, because Zoe nods excitedly and allows me to take her hand. We walk side by side to the base of the fountain and stare down into the shallow water where thousands of coins from hundreds of countries are glinting up at us.

"So, you can't tell me what you wish for," I tell her, reaching into my bag to find a penny, "or it won't come true."

Zoe nods, taking this very seriously, and I find another for myself. She watches as I turn my back to the fountain and throw the coin over my shoulder, the noise of it hitting the water lost in the echo of voices and the sound of the waterfall.

I wish to fall in love.

It's a silly thing, wishing for love on a coin in an airport luggage claim, but I'm ready for it. For years, I've been reading romance books and watching sappy movies, deliberately

71

hiding it from my parents. How did wanting to be happy and fall in love become a shameful, lesser desire?

I'm so tired of being lonely, and previous entanglement (and regrettable attraction) with my employer aside, this could be when I finally find that connection I've been craving for much longer than I realized.

I watch as Zoe squeezes her eyes shut and mimics my action. It hits the water with a tiny splash, and I tap her shoulder, pointing to where it's glinting at the bottom. "When I was your age, I used to wish I could climb into the water and fish out all the coins. They're so pretty, aren't they?"

"Very pretty."

I do a double take, heart shooting into my throat as I stare in wonder at the girl beside me. Granted, we haven't spent a ton of time together yet, but up until now I've only heard her say *"Papa"* and *"no"* a few times on the plane. Her voice is sweet and clear, as though she's completely capable of using it, but chooses to save it for special occasions.

My eyes sting. "You have such a beautiful voice, Zoe. Thank you for letting me hear it."

"I believe this is everything." We look around to find Ellis approaching, pushing a trolly that's stacked high with all the bags we brought. He glances at the fountain. "Did you make wishes?"

Zoe takes my hand without me asking. "We did," I tell him, smiling at the little girl beside me. "We can't tell you, though. Sorry."

Ellis chuckles. "I understand. Come on, the car rentals are this way."

The crowds thankfully grow thinner as we move away from the luggage claim and my eyes catch on everything from license plates to electrical outlets, noting the differences from home. Zoe keeps switching between my hand and her father's, before finally realizing she can hold on to us both.

It's such a sweet, innocent moment, but something about it makes my chest ache. Has Ellis been on his own for so long that Zoe doesn't know how to be supported by two people at once? That leads to another question, one that's been lingering since we met for the second time in my mom's office.

What happened to Zoe's mother?

All my mom mentioned was that he was divorced, has an excellent professional reputation, and she suspected he was struggling as a single father. Not the kind of intel I was hoping for. I wanted to ask more, but experience has taught me that the fewer questions with Mom, the better. The woman is too smart, and will sniff out the tiniest hint of something you'd rather hide.

In this case, there's *a lot* I'd rather hide.

It's none of my business, but I can't stop myself from wondering. Even if he's divorced, wouldn't his ex-wife want to be involved in their daughter's life? Considering Ellis could take Zoe and swoop off to France at a moment's notice, there's no shared custody to worry about.

We reach the car rental business. Zoe and I busy ourselves with taking a copy of every single travel pamphlet from the display, while Ellis sorts out the reservation in rapid French.

Why is that so wildly, undeniably hot?

Maybe it's because of the *way* he speaks it. In English, his words are so deliberate and clean, it's as though he's spent years polishing them to perfection. The moment he switches to French, there is an ease and confidence that I haven't heard before. Listening to him chat and laugh with the man behind the counter, it's like he's lit up from the inside.

Ellis looks pleased as he crosses back to me and Zoe, holding up a set of keys. "Got us a free upgrade," he reports with such obvious enthusiasm it makes me giggle. "What?" he questions me, bemused.

I shake my head, trying to hold back my smile. "You're such a *dad*. How did I not see it immediately?"

His eyebrows lift in surprise for half a second, and I know it's because, apart from our tense encounter at *Monkey Do* a few days ago, this is the first time I've made reference to the first time we met. Shrugging it off, he laughs. "Would it *upset* you to get a nicer car than expected?"

Shaking my head and trying to keep my smile in check, I open the door for him to push the trolly through, and Zoe trudges after him. She's obviously beginning to lose her enthusiasm for this whole traveling business. "I'd be happy! I just don't think I would be *this* happy."

The rental car parking lot seems endless, but we finally find our small SUV. Zoe has to be bribed with screen time to get into the car seat, but eventually concedes, and then we're off again. This trip is starting to feel endless, but my heart lifts as we make our way out of the airport complex and into the outskirts of Paris.

"Where in France are you from, exactly?" I ask Ellis once the GPS has guided us out of traffic. He seems to know where he's going, putting his blinker on to switch lanes even before the phone indicates he should.

His expression is far away. "A small town outside of Dijon. My mother still lives there, but my father passed away when I was a teenager."

"I'm sorry."

Not taking his eyes off the road, Ellis takes Zoe's pink glittery water bottle from the center console between us and twists his arm to pass it back. "He was ill for years. It wasn't a surprise."

The GPS doesn't have us turning for several kilometers, but unexpectedly, he pulls off the main road and into a bustling downtown shopping area. I peer over at him curiously, but before I can ask where we're going, he parks the car beside a yellow brick building. There's a blue striped awning, and tall glass windows which frame a display of jewel bright pastries and cakes.

I gasp, whipping around to face Ellis, who is definitely trying not to look too pleased with himself. "*Pastries*?"

"You're in France, Josephine," he replies wryly, turning off the car. "*Pâtisserie*."

I laugh, delighted, and turn to the backseat to find Zoe craning her neck, trying to get a better look at the selection. "Will you convince your Papa to let us buy one of everything?"

In the end, we don't really buy one of everything, but we get pretty close. When the three of us get back in the car, my arms are laden with two big white boxes of treats, and by the time Ellis has finished buckling Zoe into her booster seat, I have the chocolate creation she was excited about ready to go on a napkin. Not that it will save us. There is going to be crumbs everywhere.

"Which one should I pick?" I debate out loud as we pull back out onto the road. The car smells like sugar and bread, and my stomach—which still hasn't wholly recovered from the supposed pork chops—growls.

From the back seat, there's a contented sigh.

"Try the almond," Ellis advises as he takes a napkin from the cupholder, helping himself to one.

While a tiny part of me wants to pick something else just to exert my independence, it does look particularly good. As I take the first bite, my eyes flutter shut and I sink back into the seat with a rapturous moan. "Oh my god," I mumble, already checking to see how many more we have. "That's incredible."

When I open my eyes again, in the corner of my vision, I see Ellis's hand drift down, subtly adjusting his pants.

Oh.

Heat pools between my thighs and I cross my legs, staring out the window so he can't see my burning cheeks. He's hard. Is it because of me? Is he hard because I moaned over a croissant?

No way. I'm not going there. Even if it *was* about me, which it isn't—I've been reliably informed that guys sometimes just get random boners—he's probably just reminded of the last time we sat side by side in a car. Which started with an impromptu date at the grocery store and ended in me riding his cock in the backseat.

Attempting to dismiss the memory of Ellis's hands roaming over my body or the things he whispered in my ear, I keep my eyes trained on the landscape flashing by outside. It's not a good distraction. Everything has happened so fast. I never quite had time to process, and now it's hitting me all at once. *I actually did it.* I told Mom I wanted to take time off, I had sex with a stranger, I got on a plane to a foreign country where I don't speak the language, and my only connection will be that same stranger and his six-year-old.

Okay, so there have been bumps in the road, but overall, *I'm on a roll.*

It's getting dark out, and it doesn't take Zoe long to pass out in the back seat, covered in croissant crumbs. I twist around to remove her shoes and tuck the knitted blanket Ellis brought around her shoulders. Her nose wrinkles in her sleep, and I experience the same tug of affection I did when we made wishes at the airport.

This kid is going to own my ass. Calling it right now.

"Thank you," Ellis says softly when I turn back around.

On the dashboard, the GPS pings, and he turns the car onto a more sparsely populated road. It's beginning to appear more like the country. The large street signs and chain restaurants have vanished, giving way to fields and clusters of small businesses.

"Is it weird? Coming back, I mean," I ask after a long stretch of silence, peeking over at him.

The corners of Ellis's lips lift. "A little. I haven't lived here since college. The last few years, I've found myself beginning to think in English."

"My condolences." I shift the partly empty box of pastries —*pâtisserie*—to the floor and cross my sore legs on the seat. "I hope I can learn some French while we're here."

"You will," he assures me. "Faster than you'd expect. And I'll help you, of course."

If he could stop being so darn likeable, it would really help my resolve to dismiss this attraction.

We fall silent again as the sun falls lower beyond the rolling fields, painting the sky bright orange and pink. My eyelids are beginning to grow heavy, and I keep almost drifting off. While it's mid-afternoon at home, the long day of traveling has worn me down and I know stopping for coffee would risk waking Zoe.

"Go to sleep, Josephine," Ellis assures me after a while, his tone amused. "I'm fine. I had coffee on the plane."

I try futilely to stifle my yawn. "Are you sure?"

"Quite." His lips twitch. "I guarantee Zoe won't let either of us sleep in tomorrow. Rest while you can."

Curling my legs beside me, my head drops onto the window, and I let my eyes close with a sigh of relief.

* * *

There are gates. Actual wrought iron, ten foot tall gates, fashioned into the shape of ivy that mimics the actual plant growing up on the stone pillars on either side of the drive.

Ellis and I glance at each other. "Uh, is somebody supposed to meet us?" I ask, because the chain securing them closed does *not* look decorative.

He leans forward, squinting through the windshield. It's pitch black outside. Our headlights shine a little way up a long drive, but not far enough to illuminate any kind of structure.

"There's a groundskeeper, supposedly. My assistant sent him our travel details." Ellis glances at the clock on the dashboard.

A moment passes and I lean forward to eye the gate, speculating. "I could probably climb that. Maybe there's a shed or something with bolt cutters."

"You are not climbing the gate and going nosing around in the dark for bolt cutters," Ellis huffs out, his tone making it clear this isn't up for discussion. "If anything, I—" A knock on his window makes both of us yelp, and my heart shoots into my throat.

"Shit," I hiss, clutching my chest, as Ellis rolls down the window. The man standing there looks about fifty, with a weathered, tan face and hair that's mostly gone.

"*Bonjour, monsieur,*" the stranger grunts, and those are the last two words I'm able to pick up on before the two men exchange words in French.

In the backseat, there's a little whine and I turn to see Zoe blinking at me blearily. "We're here, honey girl," I say, attempting to keep my voice gentle and bright, because she's writhing against the seatbelt, done with being constrained. I glance at Ellis, who's just closing the window, an envelope in his lap. The groundskeeper moves through the headlights, unlocking the gate with a key so big it can be seen from here. "I'm going to let her out of her seat, if we're just going on the drive."

Ellis nods his agreement once his glance in the rearview mirror seems to confirm a breakdown is imminent. No sooner have I released Zoe from her seatbelt than she's clambering up between the seats and into my lap, whimpering.

"If you hold her and rock her, it will help," Ellis advises me quietly, just as the chains give way and the groundskeeper pushes the great gate open, waving us through with an impatient scowl. "*Merci!*" he calls through the crack in the window, and the car inches forward.

"We are going to have so much fun exploring tomorrow," I tell the little girl in my arms, holding her close and rocking back and forth as Ellis suggested.

It's too dark to see much, but it's clear there are no other structures in sight apart from the massive house looming ahead of us at the end of the drive.

When we get close enough to make out more than the general shape, I hear myself gasp.

It looks like something out of a fairy tale. Surrounded by nothing but nature, the *Le Château Perdu* appears to be centuries old. The building is constructed in roughly cut stone, but there's an elegance to the architecture that takes my breath away. Massive windows line the front of the house, and all of them are dark.

"The groundskeeper says there's a housekeeper who comes up from the village twice a week. She set up three bedrooms in the east wing," Ellis tells me as we get out of the car, a symphony of crickets serenading us as we walk up to the heavy wood front door. Zoe is in my arms, her head nestled beneath my chin, and we hang back as Ellis takes a huge, iron key from the envelope the groundskeeper gave him, and fits it into the ancient lock.

The metal grinds, and then the door opens easily. Ellis goes first, turning the lights on, and I gasp when I see what we're walking into. The entryway beyond it is so big we could have parked inside it. An eclectic mix of art covers the walls, and a grand, flagstone staircase curves around the edge of the room, leading to the upper floors.

"It's amazing," I whisper, my heart suddenly soaring because *I get to live here?*

Ellis lifts a hand to guide me toward the stairs, but his fingers have barely made contact with my lower back before they've fallen back to his side.

He clears his throat, not looking at me. "We'll explore in the morning. Let's all try to get some sleep, and then..." His words trail away as he gazes into a darkened doorway leading off the foyer.

Then, without another word, he's striding off toward it. Zoe and I watch as he plunges into the darkness. A moment later, lights flicker on inside, and another gasp catches in my throat.

It's the library.

The late Monsieur Perdue was rumored to be an avid collector, but it appears *"avid"* was an understatement. The room is massive, with twenty-foot walls and an actual balcony that wraps around the top half of the room, accessing a second set of shelves. While it must have once served as a ballroom, now, it's stuffed with more books than any one person could ever hope to read in their lifetime.

Holy shit.

"Well." Ellis steps back and closes the door. When he turns back to us, he's brimming with enthusiasm. "I think six months might be inadequate after all."

It doesn't take us long to find the East Wing, or the bedrooms the housekeeper made up. "Goodnight," I whisper to Ellis as we transfer a very groggy Zoe from my arms to his.

My stomach flutters as his arms brush mine and, to add insult to injury, my heart follows suit as I watch my new employer lay a gentle kiss on his daughter's hair.

"Goodnight." Ellis's eyes meet mine for a fraction of a second before we've both turned toward our rooms.

Despite my exhaustion, I feel strangely restless as I close

the door quietly behind me, looking around the warm, cozy space. Pale floral wallpaper covers the high walls, and gauzy curtains flutter in the breeze from the open windows, catching on the carved wood bed.

All I have is my small overnight bag, too worn out to reject Ellis's offer to bring all the other luggage up in the morning. I change into an oversized t-shirt and brush my teeth, gazing at my reflection in the mirror of the surprisingly modern bathroom. It's still so surreal that I'm here, thousands of miles away from the life I'm supposed to be living.

I didn't like my life, so I changed it. That's the kind of thing that other people do, stronger, braver, more resilient people. That's what I always thought, anyway. If I was able to do this, maybe I can be like that too. Maybe this time next year, I won't even recognize my life.

My heart full to bursting, I wander back into the bedroom and notice a door facing the same direction as the large windows. Curiosity getting the better of me, I cross to open it and suck in a startled breath.

It's a balcony, supported by elegantly carved marble columns and by the looks of it, stretches along the entire top floor of the chateau.

I'm in a trance as I step barefoot onto the cold stone ground and move to the edge, my hands finding the marble railing.

Beyond the chateau's sprawling, walled garden, there's a moonlit meadow, swaying gently in the summer breeze. A pond occupies the far corner of the property, and a little stream winds through the bordering trees to feed it.

"Wow." I start, whipping around to find Ellis standing the doorway to the right of mine, looking out at the same view I was just enjoying. "Sorry." He winces, holding up a hand in apology. "Zoe is asleep in my room. She didn't want to be on her own tonight. I just wanted some air."

"It's fine," I whisper, watching as he comes to stand beside me, separated by ten feet of railing.

We stand together in silence for a long time, staring out at the grounds. I let out a long, rocky breath. "Six months really doesn't feel like enough time."

Ellis's now-familiar, throaty chuckle greets my words. "It could be longer. You saw that library."

I turn, bracing my forearms against the railing, and look at him properly for the first time since he came out here. He's changed into a white t-shirt and sweatpants, and his feet are bare on the stone floor.

Sensing my gaze, his eyes meet mine and—in a flash—rake over my body. I'm wearing my usual bedtime attire, but how did it never occur to me how thin it is? There's no way he can't see my nipples, pebbled from the cool evening breeze, or fail to notice how much of my legs are bare.

Ellis turns back to the meadow, his throat working.

My heart sinks.

"I'll see you in the morning." I push off the railing and slip back through the door to my bedroom. The moment it's closed, I lean against the cool wood, the knob digging into my lower back, and my pulse racing.

That first night, I was surprised I had an *older man thing*. Now it seems fairly obvious I have an *Ellis Delvaux thing*, and it's no use pretending I'm not attracted to him when we were together for all of two minutes, and my panties are damp. Denial isn't going to help anybody here.

What *will* help is the unwelcome reminder I just received, that even if Ellis Delvaux is nice, a good dad, and easy to get along with, he's still a man who has proven the only thing he wants from me is unattached sex.

While that sounds pretty appealing right now, I can't go there again. Hard nope. We might be in the most beautiful, romantic place in the world, but this isn't a fairy tale. I thought it might be that first night back home, but I can't let myself forget that if it weren't for my mother, I probably never would have seen him again.

Getting thrown together like this doesn't change the fact that he didn't call, and I deserve someone who does.

That's it. End of story.

Eight

ELLIS

"*MERDE**," I curse under my breath, clicking the *connect* button on my computer for the third time in a row. As if moving two feet to the right will make any difference to the fact this building has stone walls. While I'm hardly an expert in technology, it seems obvious that four-hundred-year-old chateaus were not designed for their occupants to enjoy reliable internet connection.

Jean-Luc Perdue, the late owner of this estate, seemed to have strange priorities when it came to modernization of his ancient home. For example, the mirror in my en-suite comes equipped with adjustable LEDs, to provide the user with the most flattering light possible while brushing their teeth. Meanwhile, the stove appears to be at least a century old, and was filled with terra-cotta pots when Josephine went looking for a pan this morning.

Frustrated as I currently am, my lips twitch as I remember her bemused expression when she turned to face me, gesturing

---

* Shit

helplessly to the contents while Zoe and I picked at stale croissants.

That was the last I saw of them today, having headed straight for the library and didn't emerge for lunch. It's a comment on how well Josephine handled the trip with Zoe that I'm not anxious about leaving the two of them alone for long periods of time. I'm confident they'll be fine.

I, however, seem likely to begin tearing my hair out before the week is out.

Not having a stable internet connection will be a problem and considerably slow down the process. I pride myself on knowing rather a lot about rare books, but I'm not such an expert I can make determinations based on memory and opinion alone. I need to *research* dammit, and by the looks of it, I'll spend half my days going back and forth to the pantry— which Perdue evidently considered an optimal location for the wireless router.

When the *failed to connect* alert pops up yet again, I curse and snap my laptop closed, looking around the massive room with—not the first—stirrings of panic. I'm scheduled to present my preliminary findings to Weston's board of directors at their Monday morning meeting. I was hoping to have some progress to report, but all I can honestly say I accomplished today was fantasizing about fucking President Sutton's daughter over every surface in the room.

I really need to get that under control.

Casting one more desperate glance around, I redirect my focus towards the door. I need to send an email to Weston's technology director for her recommendation, but the jet lag has been brutal. As the day has progressed, I've found myself staring at the same things for god-knows how long, my brain lapsing into some kind of exhaustion induced hibernation.

Even if I stand here for another three hours, nothing else is going to get done today, and I really ought to check on Zoe and Josephine. The upset in her sleep schedule, combined with a drastic change in routine and the addition of a new person in her life, is bound to have made today a little rocky. It's only our first day here, and I'd rather not send her nanny running for the hills so soon.

Strolling down the carpeted hall which stretches across the center of the house, I shove my hands deep in my pockets, scanning the eclectic mix of contemporary and antique art hung in ornate, gilded frames. Most of the rooms are closed up, their furniture covered in canvas cloths and curtains drawn. Thankfully, the housekeeper took the time to clear out one of the living rooms across from the kitchen, and that's where I expect to find Josephine and Zoe. But when I pause in the doorway, I find it's empty.

Frowning, I'm on the point of going to check the gardens, when I hear warm female laughter coming from the kitchen. I freeze, listening.

"Oh no!" comes Jo's playful exclamation a moment later, her voice lifted with amusement. "Careful, honey girl."

Zoe's familiar humming follows this, and then the sound of a mixing spoon gently tapping the side of a bowl.

Regaining control of my limbs, I move in a trance toward the kitchen.

The girls don't see me at first. Zoe is standing on a chair at the counter, her face, arms and hair all covered in flour, and something sticky on her shirt. Standing at her side, Jo is in much the same state, and her smile is wide as she leans forward, holding the large mixing bowl in place so it doesn't go flying as Zoe stirs.

As I watch, my daughter gets a little overzealous and a portion of batter spills over the edge, splattering on the countertop. Immediately, she looks at Jo, wide eyed in alarm, but the nanny only smiles, wiping away the mess. "No big deal," she assures Zoe brightly. "There's still plenty. Do you think Papa will be surprised you made him dinner?"

There are times I'm not sure Zoe is engaged at all with what we're doing, or what's going on around her. Often, she seems lost to her own world, one I'm not privy to, but that isn't the case now. At Josephine's words, she smiles toothily, bobbing her head as she resumes stirring. Enjoyment and excitement are evident in every corner of her face.

Behind them, a pot is simmering on the stove, filling the entire kitchen with a mouthwatering, savory scent.

"I think he will be *very* impressed," Jo continues, and her hand hovers behind Zoe's back to ensure she doesn't fall in the few seconds it takes her to lean away and retrieve the salt shaker. "Will you cook with me every night? It's so much more fun with your help."

If someone offered me a million dollars to look away, I'm not confident I could do it. The way she talks to my girl... *Merde*.

Zoe notices me first, her eyes catching on me in the doorway and instantly going wide with excitement. With a happy yell, she hops off the chair and I kneel as she races across the kitchen, throwing her arms around my neck.

"Did you have a good day, *mon coeur*?" I murmur, kissing her hair, and inhaling her familiar scent. "Have you been a good help to Jo?"

Looking up, I see the nanny hurriedly wiping off the counter, her cheeks pink. "I'm so sorry, it's a mess in here. I was going to clean up before you finished up for the day."

"Don't apologize." I'll never let her apologize for a single thing as long as she keeps being so good to my child. Zoe untangles herself from my embrace and bounds back to Josephine's side as I straighten up. Hovering in the doorway, I watch Zoe retake the spoon with enthusiasm. "Do you want me to take over? You must be exhausted."

She shakes her head, smiling at me reassuringly. "We're fine! Almost done here."

"What are we having?" I edge closer to them, hands buried in my pockets.

"Oh!" For some reason, Jo isn't looking at me now, busying herself with gathering up items to return to the pantry. "It's crepes. With chicken and vegetables. I'm not really familiar with French cooking, but I found a recipe book —" She hazards a glance up at me, and her words trail away.

What must I look like right now? Shocked? Awed?

"If it's terrible, there's pasta in the pantry." Jo breaks the silence with a nervous laugh. "I have Zoe's chicken nuggets on standby, too, just in case this doesn't go over well. They're the French brand, but I let her pick them out. I just remembered what you said about not eating many home-cooked meals, so I thought—"

"It's wonderful," I cut across her worried rambling. Something is happening inside me, a growing warmth that has absolutely nothing to do with her lovely face or the curves of her body, and everything to do with her heart. Her heart, which I now suspect is somehow—miraculously—even more beautiful than the woman it rests inside.

Oh, for Christ's sake. It's been *one day* and any of my earlier hopes that living with her would prove we aren't compatible have already been thrown to the wind.

"I'll set the table." Still, even after I've made the offer, I don't move, watching the two at work.

Zoe's occupational therapist is always reminding me to do the fine motor skill exercises she provided, but it's an intensive, exhausting process just to get through a single set. Zoe hates it, I hate it, and by the end we're both close to tears.

Right now, she's cheerful and engaged, performing the same movements which have been such a struggle to teach her. Jo holds out her hand with a few tablespoons of flour resting in her palm and Zoe reaches out to put it, pinch by pinch, into the batter. The exchange is so casual, anyone would think the two had done it a thousand times before.

Moving further into the kitchen, I pass behind the girls to take some mismatched plates out of the cabinet. As I turn, however, I nearly run into Josephine.

Small, feminine hands come out, pressing against my chest to steady us both. "Sorry!" she squeaks, and seconds later, the whole thing is over. She's gone, and I'm moving in the direction I intended, half wondering if I just hallucinated. The warmth where her hands touched my chest seems to suggest not.

I'm also hard. Painfully so.

As I set the plates on the table, I pause, closing my eyes and attempting to exercise some control over my body. It's futile, and my mind is flooded with memories of her body moving with mine, *taking mine*. What is wrong with me? I'm not a damn animal. Surely I have more control over myself than this.

Opening my eyes, I look over my shoulder, and my gaze drops like a stone to the curve of my nanny's ass through her leggings. Apparently, no, I do not have more control over myself than this.

I gripped that ass as she ground herself over my cock. It was weeks ago now, and I can still feel the tight, hot grip of her cunt surrounding me, hear her breathy moans in my ear, taste —*stop it*. I grit my teeth, despising myself for my weakness.

I need some air.

"Would you mind if I stepped away for a shower?"

Jo turns to look at me, smiling reassuringly and oblivious to my inappropriate preoccupation. "Of course. We weren't expecting you to be done so early, so dinner won't be ready for a bit. Take your time. I promised Zoe we could walk back to the stream tonight, but you're welcome to take her if you'd like some family time." Her comment is offhand, but I can

89

tell she's trying to gauge where she stands in this new dynamic.

I wish I knew the answer.

While keeping professional boundaries seems vital considering my reaction to this woman, it isn't lost on me that Zoe and I are Josephine's only connections in a foreign country. How could I not, at least, treat her as a friend? Especially given how good she's proving to be with Zoe.

Hands tighten on my shoulders as she begins to ride me, our foreheads pressed together, stealing kisses— "Please join us," I hear myself say, and warmth spreads through me as she brightens.

Jo tucks a dark curl behind her ear and glances up at me as she moves to wipe the flour from Zoe's neck. "You're sure?"

As if I could change my mind seeing how happy it made her. I back toward the door, nodding. "Absolutely." *Absolutely not.* "I'll be back shortly. I just want to get rid of the dust." Fleeing when she makes me hard is not a viable long-term strategy to getting past this, but it will have to do for now.

As soon as I'm out of earshot of Jo and Zoe, I break into a jog, taking the grand staircase two stairs at a time and striding down the thickly carpeted east corridor to my room. I'm frustrated beyond belief, my cock hard as stone and unable to think of anything but the young woman cooking with my daughter just downstairs.

What is happening to me?

Yes, she's a wonderful person. Yes, she's excellent with Zoe and turns me on like no one has in my entire life. She's also twenty-two years old and the daughter of a woman who could end my career with a single signature. Before we came here, I swore this would end. Now, one day in, and I've somehow found myself in deeper than I was before.

If I ever had a chance with Josephine, it's gone now, and even if it weren't, *nothing has changed*, except the fact that I'm her employer now, too. She's not interested, and I refuse to be the sort of man who objectifies his much younger, very beautiful employee.

I don't need to shower, but it would look strange if I walked back down to dinner with dry hair. For the sake of appearances, I stride into the bathroom, glowering at myself in the bathroom mirror as I undress. As though I can intimidate myself into not jerking off to the memory of Josephine coming on my cock.

I'm only half paying attention to what I'm doing, but as I go to set my phone on the bathroom vanity, all it takes is a quick glance at the screen for me to go hurdling back to reality.

Incoming Call: Miranda Perkins

Well, on the bright side, my cock isn't hard anymore. Though even the most extreme case of blue balls seems like a good trade-off for not having to answer this call.

Gritting my teeth, I turn off the water and accept the call. "What do you want?"

Through the phone, I hear the distant sound of traffic before a cool female voice responds, one that was once so familiar to me but now only turns my stomach. "Hello to you, too."

"You're not calling me to make pleasantries. Either you tell me what you want, or I'll hang up." I pace out into the bedroom and pull the curtains, staring out at the grounds.

Miranda sighs. "I'm just checking in. I got your email about taking Zoe to France. How long will you guys be staying?"

The email I sent over a week ago? "A while," I reply vaguely.

Movement catches my eye at the edge of the garden, and I watch as Zoe bounds into sight, her hair shining in the afternoon sunlight. Jo follows a moment later, and I can see her smile from here.

More traffic sounds in the background when Miranda finally responds. "I'd like to visit while you're over there. I'll be in Brussels in a few months for the UN convention. Are you staying with your mother?"

"No."

A quiet noise of frustration follows this. "Okay. Thanks for the clarification. How is she?"

Birdsong filters in through the open windows. It's warm today, but not overly sticky and hot. I've been working to get a reliable internet connection all day, and have been struck dumb with lust for my nanny. The last thing I want to do right now is talk to the woman who set my life on fire and walked away.

Jo and Zoe kneel beside one of the raised garden beds, Jo pointing to things, her mouth moving in words I wish I could hear. "She's wonderful," I admit, wishing I could throw the phone at the wall and it would dismiss Miranda Perkins from my life forever. "I think the country will suit her. She seems to like it here. The transition hasn't been difficult so far."

Miranda laughs airily. "The land of her people. She always was a lot more like you than me."

"How would you know?" I lash out, unable to contain the sudden rise of bitter frustration. "You left when she was three years old."

It's unnecessary to be this hostile. I know that. So much tension could be avoided if I simply *got over it* and learned to live with the knowledge that neither I, nor our daughter, was enough for my ex-wife. How can I, though? When she insists on keeping one foot in our life and the other out, neither staying for good nor leaving forever.

For a moment, I think she's going to hang up, and it fills me with a surge of vicious pleasure that I've hurt her even a fraction of how much she's hurt me. Then, "Well. It was a pleasure as always, Ellis," Miranda says, sounding more weary than anything else. "I'll be in touch when my travel plans become a little more concrete."

"You're not coming to see her," I snap, watching Jo show Zoe how to cut what must be herbs from the raised garden bed. My daughter looks so happy, so carefree as the pair head back to the chateau, racing ahead with her hair streaming in the breeze.

How could her own mother not see how incredible she is? What a miracle? My heart wrenches and, before Miranda can do more than make a noise of protest, I end the call.

Below, Josephine has paused, looking back across the grounds. Her head falls back, enjoying a few seconds of sunshine on her face, and my breath catches in my throat. How could any man look at her and not be struck dumb? Is it any wonder I can't keep it together when she looks like *that* in leggings?

The breeze ruffles the ends of her hair as she looks up, and, as though she can sense my gaze, her eyes turn up toward the house. I freeze, suddenly conscious that I've stripped down to my briefs and that getting caught staring at my twenty-two-year-old nanny while barely clothed is hardly a display of the professionalism I promised her.

The sun is bright, though, and I relax slightly as she turns back toward the house, following Zoe without any indication I've been caught.

I groan, staring down at my erection, which is straining and just as viciously hard as it was before I got Miranda's call. *God help me.*

Turning on my heel, I stride toward the bathroom. Before I get in the shower, I turn on the water as cold as it will go.

Nine

JOSEPHINE

IT TAKES about a week for me to get nosey.

I'm not bored. There's plenty to do around here, and Zoe keeps me busy, but you can only live in an actual French chateau that was once owned by an eccentric millionaire for so long before you start to get curious. So, while honey girl is occupied with her daily allotment of screen time, I sneak off to the back staircase which must have once been used by members of staff.

While the main one in the foyer only goes up to the second floor, this one goes to a third. Ellis and Zoe discovered it a few days ago, but obviously hadn't felt the same burning curiosity that I did, because all I got out of him was; *"there's an attic"*.

Though, I'm coming to realize Ellis might be a little weird across the board. When I pointed out it was like he'd never seen the movie *"National Treasure"*, he only stared at me bemusedly. After dinner, I begged him and Zoe to watch it with me, and the man spent the entire time making comments about the historical inaccuracies while Zoe painted our toe nails.

It would make my life so much easier if I didn't find the

weird so freaking charming. Back in Connecticut, we were drawn together by nothing but chemistry and attraction. Spending this much time together is all the more dangerous now that I have confirmation our connection doesn't just exist in the one night we spent together back home.

Now, I know he's an incredible father, can be so sweet when he wants to be, and what his voice sounds like—all gravely and rough—when he first wakes up and hasn't gotten to the coffee pot yet. In fact, every new fact I learn about Ellis Delvaux makes me like him more, and I really wish he would stop acting as though he likes me too, because it's getting really hard to keep my heart out of this mess.

I'm supposed to be here for *me*, and I haven't spent a single evening alone since we got here, nor have I planned any trips away for my coming weekends off. It's hard to motivate myself to leave the chateau when I'm happier here than I have been in a long time. The place is beautiful, but it's more than that. For the first time, my days aren't scheduled. There are no classes to study for or volunteer hours to attend. When I cook dinner, there are people to eat it with me. It's such a small, ordinary thing. Ellis and Zoe probably don't think anything of it, but every time they pull out chairs at the table, setting down plates and cutlery, I'm beaming.

As I climb the stairs to the attic, it occurs to me that I don't know quite what I'm looking for, but there has to be something to distract me from these dangerous feelings in a dead rich guy's attic.

My thighs are burning when I finally arrive at a small landing, which is lit by the late afternoon sun spilling through the tiny window across from a heavy wood door. The knob turns without resistance, and I poke my head inside, instantly hit by a wall of heat and humidity that's risen from the lower floors and gotten trapped.

It's big, but not terribly interesting at first glance.

Edging over the wide plank floors, I cross my arms tightly over my chest, staring around at the dusty crates, flimsy cardboard boxes and the occasional piece of broken furniture. There's a shelf laden with grimy champagne flutes and an ugly painting of a baby. Beside it is a chipped marble pedestal.

It looks like the attic at my parent's house in Connecticut. Pretty disappointing, considering Ellis is wading through tens of thousands of rare books as we speak. It seems Monsieur Perdue's extravagant tastes didn't extend past the library.

The room is also feeling more unbearably hot by the minute, and my t-shirt is already sticking to my back. Letting out a heavy sigh of defeat, I turn to go, but my eyes catch on a machine sitting idle on a faded wood tabletop, and my heart lifts.

It's a sewing machine.

When she was still alive, my father's mother, Granny Georgia, was an avid sewer. She made everything from my Christmas stocking to elaborate quilts, and during the weeks I spent at her house every summer, she taught me too.

I'm not good, and the machine I learned on was a lot newer than this dinosaur, but I can figure it out, right? There must be somebody out there making YouTube videos on how to operate a sewing machine from the 1800's. It would be fun to have a project, and good to have something to focus on other than my hot as sin but very off limits employer.

Being out in the country like this has taken its toll on Zoe's Target wardrobe. We've only been here a week, and she's already torn through two dresses, a t-shirt and a pair of shorts. I can think of worse ways to spend my time than to make her new ones.

It's not easy to haul the thing downstairs without breaking a limb or any of the walls. I manage it, though, and Zoe is temporarily distracted from her tablet, watching as I waddle into the room with the heavy table digging into my stomach.

We've taken over one of the living rooms furthest from the library so we don't disturb Ellis during the day. It's cozy and decorated in floral blue wallpaper that laughably contrasts the squashy, bright pink couch and mismatched chairs. It also has the benefit of being located just across the hall from the pantry Wi-Fi router. This is fortunate, because I've been doing a lot of googling, as my student isn't exactly cooperative with the kindergarten lesson plans I downloaded before leaving. Technically, we're still on summer break, but I'm hoping to get a good routine going so she doesn't fall behind in the fall.

"It's a sewing machine," I say brightly as I set it down against a free stretch of wall. "I thought we could make you some new dresses together."

Zoe hums, scooting off the couch to come have a look. "Okay."

I suppress a smile, trying not to make a big deal out of it. Over the last few days, she seems to have become much more willing to speak in my presence. I'm not sure I've ever been so happy to hear someone tell me *"no"* twenty times a day.

Dusting my hands off on my cotton skirt, I stand back, examining the machine. It looks as though it's composed of pure iron and has to be about a hundred years old, but when I turn the knobs, everything seems to move smoothly.

"I bet we can persuade Papa to let us walk into the village for ice cream after dinner," I tell her, thinking of the small display of mending supplies I spotted at the market yesterday.

A deep voice comes from behind me. "Papa is easily persuaded."

Zoe brightens instantly, and skips across the room to give Ellis a perfunctory hug, before heading straight back to her tablet. I catch his eye, and my heart flutters at the crooked smile he gives me. "Done for the day?"

He sighs, smile slipping away into thoughtfulness. "Not

quite yet. I've discovered something rather odd. Waiting for emails back from a few colleagues."

"Odd?"

There's a glimmer of excitement in his eyes as he nods. "Come look."

I follow him back through the house, our footsteps echoing on the flagstone floors. The library is firmly Ellis's domain, and I do my best to keep Zoe out of here in fear of her disordering something he's worked on. It looks much the same as it did the last time I saw it, except the makeshift office set up at a glossy wood table in the center of the room. An orange extension cord winds over the motheaten rug from his laptop, and music is playing quietly from a wireless speaker sitting on a shelf nearby.

"Wait a moment," says Ellis, obviously brimming with excitement. I hover in the doorway, watching as he moves around the room, selecting books apparently at random from shelves in different areas, and sets the stack on the table.

For some reason, it's difficult to breathe as I move to his side, our elbows brushing when he opens to the title page of the first book and points to a line printed in English—*Second Edition*. Setting it aside, he flips open the next, showing me the same set of words in French.

"They're all like this," he explains. "At first, I thought I had simply stumbled upon a section of second editions, but no."

My jaw drops. "All of them?" I gesture at the massive room, at the thousands and thousands of books towering above our heads and even more sitting in crates. "Is that... is that *normal*?"

Ellis shakes his head, and his eyes are bright with excitement when he turns to look at me. "I've never seen anything like it. Collectors like this typically try for first editions, if anything. More prestigious."

"So why did Monsieur Perdue only collect seconds? He could afford firsts by the look of it." I gesture around at the magnificent old house with a weak laugh.

"Your guess is as good as mine." He drags a hand through his hair, staring around the room in wonder. His passion is contagious, and though I know next to nothing about this, I feel my heart beating faster. "This has to be one of the largest collections of second edition books in the world."

My mouth falls open in disbelief. "That's insane."

"Indeed." He reached over to pick up a few slips of paper, stacked neatly beside his computer. "That's not all. I've been finding *these* as I go." I take them curiously, and stare down at the elegant stationary, emblazoned with the initials "JLP" at the top.

Mari,

Do you remember that trip we took to New York? I was reminiscing about it the other day. You had all these plans for things you wanted to show me, and we barely left the hotel room.

I still haven't seen New York, and I regret nothing.

Your Luc

Then, the next.

Mari,

Happy birthday, my love. I've been thinking of you all week. I do hope that you have chocolate cake wherever you are (extra frosting, of course).

Your Luc

There are three more, and they're more of the same, idle reflections on memories or the writer's day to day life, all addressed to the same woman. I look up at Ellis, who was watching me read. "Luc was Jean-Luc Perdue? Was Mari his wife?"

"He was never married. I checked." Ellis takes the notes and sets the back down beside his computer. "You know as much as I do. It's curious, though, don't you think?"

Yeah, I do. "I wonder if he was collecting the books for her." That possibility makes the idea of Weston splitting it up and selling what they don't want to the highest bidder kind of tragic. "I don't suppose the school would keep the collection intact?" I ask, and my breath catches in my throat as brilliant, pale blue eyes meet mine.

Ellis's answering smile is sad. "I doubt it. Weston isn't in the business of sentimentality. Only a small portion of these books will make it into the school's collection. Most will be sold, donated, or auctioned off if they're valuable enough. I've already found at least three that are worth about ten thousand dollars. We're looking at millions of dollars in this room."

Millions? My jaw drops. "Holy crap. Does my mother know, yet?"

I wish I could shove the question back into my mouth the moment it comes out. At the mention of his boss, Ellis's back straightens and—on the pretense of checking his phone—inches away from me. "I have a virtual meeting with the board Monday night, and I believe President Sutton will be in attendance." He glances at me. "I'll be requesting an additional grant to stay here for longer if need be. Honestly, I have no idea how long this will take, nor would any of my colleagues. Each book needs to be photographed, catalogued, its value researched and then appraised..." He trails off, and there's an unspoken question hanging between us.

It's not really a question, though. Not to me. "I'll stay. As long as you and Zoe are here."

"Just like that?"

I shrug. "You pay well."

Ellis snorts and turns to lean against the table, smiling wryly. "No. I certainly don't."

"Well, you can't beat the office." I gesture around at the beautiful room we're in. "And Zoe would hunt me down with "Hungry, Hungry Hippos" anyway, so I might as well stay and save her the trouble."

He stares at me a moment, as though he'd like to say more, but finally smiles slightly and nods. "It's appreciated. Truly, Josephine. You're doing wonderfully with her. I've never seen her take to anyone so quickly."

My chest warms at the compliment and I turn away, looking around so he can't see my smile. I didn't know quite what I was getting into when I took the job. For all I knew, Zoe could have been a brat who would have made the next six months miserable. She isn't, though. She's sweet and intelligent, constantly looking to me with questions about the world around her and makes her point clearly with no need to speak more than a few words.

By Zoe's age, I'd been molded into a mini adult, very aware of social etiquette and trained not to get grass stains on my white pants. I never thought much about it, but spending my days watching Zoe romp through fields and stick her hands in puddles of mud, it's clear how stiff and lonely my upbringing was. My parents aren't bad people. They loved me, and each other, but there wasn't a lot of laughter in our house.

"I kind of love her already," I admit, feeling my heart swell with affection toward the little girl who's become such a big part of my life in such a short amount of time. "She's such a good kid, Ellis. Seriously. I know her being on the spectrum must have made it a rough go for you guys, but she's amazing. You've done such a good job."

Ellis stares at his shoes, his expression unreadable. "You're becoming something of an expert at giving me pep talks, aren't you?" He sounds pained, or embarrassed maybe.

Without thinking, I nudge him with my elbow, and instantly know I shouldn't have. There was nothing inappropriate about it. The gesture was friendly and perfectly benign, but it also crossed some invisible line I didn't even realize existed we'd drawn until now. It's the first time we've touched since that moment at *Monkey Do*, when he grabbed my wrist as I went to leave.

"Maybe I'm angling for a pay raise." I laugh, trying to cut the sudden tension.

The handsome man beside me scoffs and looks over, brilliant blue eyes glinting with amusement and something else I can't quite identify. "You'll be disappointed, I'm afraid."

Heat curls through my pelvis, a slow, heady spread that makes my stomach flip and my thighs feel loose. Yeah. *This* is why I lost my virginity to this man after two hours.

I push off the table, heading toward the door when Ellis calls after me. "You've been cooking dinner for all of us since we got here, which is not part of your job by the way. There's a little bistro in the village, why don't we all walk down tonight. My treat."

Pausing in the doorway, I look back over my shoulder, a smile tugging at the corners of my lips. "That's okay. I like it."

Ten

ELLIS

"THE PROJECT IS CONSIDERABLY MORE extensive than we were led to believe. Monsieur Perdue was something of a hoarder, I'm afraid. A significant number of the books are all-but worthless, but they're pushed in beside rare editions. There's no rhyme or reason to it. It's as if he was collecting them for the sake of it."

The Weston University board of directors stare back at me from my computer screen, each in their own respective box, often framed by what looks like an oak paneled study behind them. On the far right is a frowning President Sutton. She leans forward slightly, and even with three thousand miles between us, I get the sense that this woman is seeing far more than I'd like her to. "When you say valuable," she says, "do you believe the books you've seen so far are worth enough to justify your salary, and the salary of your temporary replacement at Montgomery?"

"Ah," I scratch my chin, letting out an uncomfortable laugh. "Madam President, this morning I found four books worth at least ten thousand US dollars. Each." This statement is greeted by stunned silence, so I hurry on. "I think it's safe to say there are millions of dollars in rare books in this house. I've already contacted several appraisal experts to examine some of them to verify my preliminary findings, but I'm confident that I'm in the right ballpark in terms of value."

There's no mistaking the excited, hungry glint in the eyes of the board. The only one among them who doesn't appear pleased is President Sutton. Is it because this news could very well mean her daughter will be gone longer? "Thank you for your work on this, Mr. Delvaux. Please keep us updated on your findings." She shuffles some papers on the desk in front of her, lips pursed.

"I will," I agree, and with a flurry of pleasantries, I sign off.

Leaning back in the kitchen chair where I took the call, I find myself grinning. Finally, at long last, my life seems to be moving in the right direction—a *positive* direction. My work is fascinating, challenging and valuable to the university. As far as I'm aware, I'm the only French-speaking member of the library staff, and my progress won't be slowed down by procurement of a work visa thanks to my citizenship status. *They need me,* and the knowledge that my job is safe lifts a heavy weight from my back.

Not only is work going well, but Zoe is thriving. I didn't expect it. Truthfully, I anticipated that the sudden, brutal upheaval of her routine would be catastrophic. Even after Josephine assured me that she would be coming along, there were a few sleepless nights, considering what I would do if the job was just too much for her to handle. My mother lives only a few hours from here, but she is diabetic and tires easily. While she could probably handle a few days with her grand-daughter here and there, it wouldn't be a long-term solution.

Now, just over a week and a half in, it's becoming clear that I won't need one.

Zoe is sleeping better, eating better, and I can't remember the last time we went so many consecutive days without a meltdown. Perhaps she's picked up on the uptick in my mood, or—more likely—I have Josephine to thank. The woman is endlessly patient, and seems to have taken it upon herself to involve my daughter in virtually every part of her day, from watering the vegetable seeds they planted in the garden to cooking dinner.

Instead of being dragged between school, a hodge podge of babysitters, the library and therapies, my girl finally has a chance to slow down a little. She spends her days exploring the chateau grounds, playing in the stream, walking into the village and doing school lessons on a blanket beneath the great oak tree out back. *She's happy* and now, all I need to worry about is what I'll do when we need to return to reality.

That time is a long way off, though, and I'm permitting myself a brief break from worrying.

Thanks to the time difference, this meeting with the board fell right at Zoe's usual bedtime. When I hesitantly asked Josephine if she would be willing to handle the nightly routine, she'd only smiled and turned to Zoe, cheerfully asking if that was okay with her. Zoe had brightened, bobbing her head, and judging by the lack of screaming I heard from the upper floors, everything worked out.

Now, it's not even eight o'clock, and I still have the energy to do more than heat up a microwave meal, shovel it down my throat and pass out on the couch. I'm tempted to find a book or watch one of the three dozen or so tv-shows my colleagues have recommended. Or, better yet, I could knock on Josephine's door and offer her a game of chess or—I stop the thought in its tracks, embarrassed. I'm desperately attracted to the woman, and my first thought is to invite her to play *chess* with me? Good god, have I been single for that long?

Instead of all that, I pick up my phone. While relaxation of any kind sounds appealing, I clearly have some energy to burn off.

> Ellis: Did she go down alright?

> Josephine: We played tag in the garden after teeth brushing and I had to carry her up haha. There were some half-asleep mumbled requests for Papa, but other than that, no complaints.

> Ellis: Thank you so much. I promise I won't make a habit of asking you to work during your off time. Since she's down, would you mind if I go for a run? I won't be out long.

Hopefully. If the sudden attempt to take care of myself doesn't result in a heart attack.

> Josephine: NP! I'm just reading. Watch out for Sean.

> Ellis: Sean?

> Josephine: The white rooster from the farm across the street. Total dick.

Chuckling, I jog up to my bedroom, pausing only to poke my head in to check on Zoe. Packing my running shoes was awfully optimistic of me, but now I'm glad I did, even if I'm dreading what is about to occur. Considering how long it's been since I went out of my way to do any kind of exercise, this won't be pretty.

If the rapid increase of gray in my hair is any indication, I'm not getting any younger, and it certainly wouldn't hurt to lose a few pounds. The unexpected urge has nothing to do with the beautiful woman living just one room over from mine. If my first thought was to ask her to play chess with me, I'm sure that impressing Josephine would take a great deal more than improving my cardiovascular health.

Just as I promised myself before leaving Connecticut, I've been trying my best not to think about our night together. As much as I'd like to, however, I just can't shake it. Memories keep intruding on everyday moments... I've never had such trouble controlling my thoughts.

Meanwhile, Josephine seems to have no problem putting the whole thing behind her. Now that she's seen first-hand what a mess my life is and the mountain of baggage I would bring with me into any relationship, surely she's lost any interest she once had. What twenty-two-year-old would sign up for a graying librarian and his stubborn daughter? Enough is enough. I'm driving myself mad, and I need to find a way to get over this fixation.

I change quickly and head back out, careful not to look at the crack beneath Josephine's door, or strain my hearing as I pass. How she's spending her night is none of my business.

I'm resolved to at least make it to the end of the dirt road leading to the chateau, but, as I expected, running is a special kind of torture. By the time I reach the gates, my lungs are aching and the muscles in my legs protest every step. I have to slow to a walk twice, but I manage the goal I set for myself—if one counts doubling over and gasping for breath on the side of the road as managing the goal. When I finally make it back, the last traces of sunset are vanishing behind the forest, and the back of my t-shirt is sticky with sweat.

I pause only to down a glass of water in the kitchen before limping upstairs, silently cursing the dust covered treadmill in the garage of my house in Connecticut. *Would it have killed me to use it more than twice?*

Forgetting my earlier resolution, my eyes are drawn, as if magnetized, to the bottom of Josephine's door. It's dark, and I'm gripped by an irrational twinge of disappointment. Of course she's asleep after chasing Zoe around all day, and even if she weren't, the balcony has been empty every night since our first here. If the fact I'd noticed at all isn't proof of my obsession with this woman, I don't know what is.

As I shoulder the door closed behind me, I strip off my damp t-shirt, cursing the stifling heat in my room.

The balcony being occupied doesn't even occur to me as I throw open the door, and my heart jolts when I catch sight of a pair of bare feet propped up on the stone railing.

My heartbeat had only just begun to slow, and now it's hammering against my ribcage just as hard as it was a few minutes ago.

"Sorry." I grimace, stepping outside, acutely aware of my lack of shirt and cursing myself for my lack of caution.

Josephine is seated in one of the old metal chairs, a lamp balanced in the open window frame and a book in her hands. She's dressed in the same oversized t-shirt I saw her in the other night.

It's so large it falls to her mid-thigh, and I feel a sick, twist of jealousy. Where did it come from? An old boyfriend? It has to be. Surely I'm not the only man on the planet tied in knots over Josephine Sutton. Hell, she's been going into the village with Zoe every day now, so I'm probably not even the only man in a five-mile radius.

If another man turned up at the chateau's door to take her away... *Jesus Christ*. I'm not sure what I'd do, but it wouldn't be pretty.

"Ellis! Hi!" She shoves the book into the chair beside her, cheeks much pinker than usual as she looks anywhere but at me, panic rolling off her in waves.

She's not the only one.

Seeing her like this, as though she just crawled out of bed —or is about to crawl *into* bed—is more than a little *affecting*. Ten minutes ago I was close to dry heaving, and now, just imagining myself peeling that shirt up to expose the rest of her creamy thighs is enough to make my cock throb viciously. All I can think about is laying my stunning, off-limits nanny over my bed and worshiping her until the sun comes up.

I've had weeks to come up with a *long* list of things I would do to her if given the opportunity.

"Um. Good run?"

"Very," I lie, praying I don't still sound winded.

God. I'm wearing thin gray running shorts, and my cock is all-but tenting them. How have I stepped back in time to coming up with creative ways to hide my erections? Pretending to be interested in the moonlit gardens, I move casually to the marble railing, willing my body to calm down.

I clear my throat, searching for something to say, and my eyes land on the book she's shoved into the chair beside her. "Good book?"

"Very!" Her voice is an octave higher than usual. "Awesome. Fabulous. Super... Super good."

I look over at her grinning, careful to keep my lower half turned toward the railing. "What an excellent selection of synonyms. I'll have to check it out."

Her answering smile is coy. "You're awfully cheeky for a man who couldn't remember the word for measuring cup this morning."

"I remembered it in French!" I object with a laugh. In some far corner of my mind, I know I should go back in. Just an hour ago, I was determined to move past this infatuation, and now I'm standing with her under the stars, shirtless. It's an unnecessary temptation. Why am I doing this to myself and, more importantly; *how is it possible I'm more attracted to her now than the night we met?*

Josephine's eyes are sparkling as she stands, stretching. "That's a big help to the English-speaking women you live with."

It takes every ounce of willpower I possess to stop myself from looking at her bare legs. Unfortunately, while my attention is focused on controlling my gaze, my mouth takes liberties of its own. "I did promise to teach you," I say, bracing my forearms on the rail. "We can start with cooking implements."

"Practical, in this household." She giggles, teeth catching on her plump bottom lip.

The night gets heavier as quiet stretches a beat too long between us. Josephine clears her throat, stepping backwards toward her open door. "Well, I should say goodnight."

"Yes," I agree unnecessarily, bobbing my head like an idiot. "Goodnight."

As she slips into her room, closing the door behind her, my eyes fall to the book she wedged beside the faded cushion of the lounge chair. Curiosity getting the better of me, I cross to pick it up, my eyebrows lifting at the unfamiliar cover.

I open it to the page her bookmark is on.

"Oh god," I cry, the aftershocks of my orgasm still surging through my body as he pulls out and flips me over, reentering me with a low groan of pleasure. He's so handsome that just looking at him steals my breath all over again, and I reach up to grab his tux, dragging him down to kiss me greedily.

Three days ago, I'd never had an orgasm, and now I'm naked beneath a fully dressed, much older man, my pussy stretched around his thick cock.

"You like it when Daddy takes you rough, don't you, sweetheart? Like feeling me use your little hole?" Judah growls in my ear, his pace faltering slightly when I clench the muscles of my sex to make myself tighter for him. "Tell me."

"Good book, Ellis?"

I was so absorbed in what I was reading, caught somewhere between being turned on and shocked, that I didn't notice Josephine reemerging from her room. At the sound of her voice, I jump, letting the paperback flip closed.

Merde.

"I'm sorry." It's not true, but I *should* be sorry. As soon as I saw the cover, I knew what type of book this was, and I opened it anyway.

Josephine moves forward to snatch it out of my hands. "You can read it after I'm done, if you want," she says cooly.

"I think I know how it ends," I reply with an uncomfortable chuckle, rubbing my stubble absent mindedly. "I really am sorry. It was none of my business."

Josephine gazes at me for a moment, then gives a little nod, her expression softening. "It's fine. You probably didn't expect —" She lets out an uncomfortable little laugh, her cheeks glowing pink in the light from her window. Seeming to shake herself, she looks up at me again, smiling valiantly through the embarrassment. "Okay. Well. I really should get to bed. There are strawberries in the field, and I told Zoe we can pick them tomorrow and make jam."

My chest warms. "You know how to make jam?"

She snorts. "God, no. Google always knows. I mean, probably. At least, that's what Google wants us to think."

A summer breeze raises goosebumps on my skin and catches the ends of Josephine's hair. I swallow, and I know the way I'm staring at her is a little too intense for the circumstances. "There are some recipe books in the library. If you stop by tomorrow, I'll help you find one that's helpful." I eye the book under her arm, filled with a new type of curiosity.

Is that what turns her on?

Does she hold a vibrator in one hand and the book in the other, making herself come to the words on the page? I shouldn't be thinking like this, but I have a habit of being weak where this woman is concerned and—*damn me*—the possibility alone is ruinous enough.

When she rode my cock in the back seat of my car, did she want to call me daddy?

Josephine pauses in the doorway, obviously regaining some of her composure, and the warm summer night seems to grow hotter. "Will I need a library card to check that out, Monsieur Delvaux?"

It's as if all the air has been sucked from my lungs, leaving me lightheaded and off kilter. She's flirting with me. For a moment, I allow myself to succumb to the fantasy, imagining crossing the distance between us, fisting the curtain of dark curls and kissing her until neither of us can breathe. I could walk her backward into my room, pull that damned t-shirt away and see her properly.

Never in my life have I wanted anything more.

"I can make an exception," I say at last, and the corners of her lips curl in a pleased little smile. By now, I've been looking —staring—at her for far too long, but I can't help myself.

Neither of us moves.

Something is happening here, but pausing to examine it seems akin to poking a sleeping beast. It might be fine, or it might awake with a vengeance and destroy everything in its path. Until now, I didn't allow myself to hope that I wasn't alone in this. Just as it did that faithful night we met, her wanting me has seemed far too good to be true.

Here we are, though. Thousands of miles away from where we started, wanting each other.

"I should go in and shower," I croak, praying it's too shadowy for her to tell how goddamn hard she's made me.

Jo nods hurriedly, already turning back toward her room. "Goodnight, Ellis."

It's not until the door has closed behind her for a second time that I manage to speak. "Goodnight, Josephine."

Eleven

JOSEPHINE

I HAD A FEELING the honeymoon wouldn't last.

Until now, Zoe has been nothing short of an angel for me. I'm not sure if I'm a novelty, or she's simply been too distracted and overwhelmed by the change of our environment to kick up a fuss about having a nanny, but whatever the case, it's over now.

"Zoe, *please*," I beg, my throat tight and my eyes burning. We're standing in the middle of the tree-lined lane that leads back to the chateau. Or, *I'm* standing. Zoe is sitting on the dusty road, crying her eyes out.

Wincing, I shift the heavy basket of groceries to my other arm and crouch down. "Do you want to hold my hand? We can have a bowl of ice cream together when we get back!"

This offer has absolutely no effect. I didn't really expect it to, but I've officially run out of tools at my disposal and we've arrived at bribery. Tears stream down her face, and she rocks back and forth, shaking her head furiously. "*Up!*" she sobs, kicking at the road to vent her frustration.

My temples throb. It's taken us half an hour to make it this far. Trouble began as we were leaving the market, a full load of groceries stuffed in the basket I found in the kitchen. My shoulders were aching before we'd even reached the edge of town. Which was when Zoe requested *"up"* for the first time.

Normally, I wouldn't have a problem with that. In fact, I love getting the snuggles. It was probably stupid of me to let her get used to it, but hindsight is twenty, twenty. My explanations of *"the basket is too heavy, I can't lift you too"* fell flat, and soon whimpering gave way to a full-blown meltdown, attracting disapproving looks and mutterings from a group of senior citizens that passed us on the road five minutes ago.

Now, my feet hurt, my arms hurt, my head hurts, it's about a million degrees out, and I'm close to crying too. Ellis won't be done working for hours, which means he won't be looking for us. I could try to call him, but with the spotty reception I likely wouldn't get through, and if I did, what would I say? My job is to take care of her, even when it's hard. This is the first really tough moment we've had, and I can't just bail out. Zoe needs to know I'm here for her when she's struggling. I am *not* a fair weather nanny.

Taking long, even breaths through my nose, I look around and spot a cluster of bushes shaded by a large tree. Marching over, I shove the basket into it and return to Zoe, lifting her into my weak, aching arms. Small limbs loop around me and almost immediately, her crying begins to calm, giving way to hiccups and the occasional little sob. I wish I could let go of my shame and frustration as easily. It's not her fault, and it's not mine either, but that doesn't make the situation any better.

My whole body hurts as the gates to the chateau come into view, but I force myself to keep going, praying Ellis doesn't spot us through the library windows. My goal is to handle this on my own, get Zoe calmed down, and tell him about it after the fact. Unfortunately, nothing about today seems to be going to plan. No sooner have I made it past the towering iron gate then Ellis steps out of the front door. Even from here, I can see his frown.

"Is everything okay?" he calls as we approach but must be able to make out the look on my face, because I haven't even opened my mouth to reply before he's jogging toward us.

I was doing okay. The frustration, shame and exhaustion were bottled up, but something about the sight of Ellis's concerned frown makes it all come back up.

"I've got her," I assure him, my voice high and strained as I try to hold back the feelings threatening to burst out of me at any moment. He must hear it though, because he ignores me, brow furrowed as he slows to a walk. "She got upset because I couldn't carry her and the shopping," I explain, wishing I could get myself to sound normal.

My arms flop to my sides like limp noodles when Ellis takes Zoe from me. He kisses her forehead, frowning. "Do you need some cool down time, *mon coeur*?"

As soon as they're gone, I collapse onto the front steps and bury my face in my arms, trying to get it together before Ellis sees. I don't want him to think I can't handle this, because *I did*. I handled it, and pretty darn well.

The tears have mostly dried on my face when footsteps echo from within the house, stopping just behind me in the open doorway. "I just need a second," I promise, wiping my eyes with the back of my hand. "Seriously, you can get back to work. I'll be fine."

"Jo." A hand touches my shoulder lightly, and my head whips around to find Ellis kneeling just behind me, his expression unbearably kind. "What happened?"

I sniff. "She was probably tired. We played by the stream almost all morning. When it came time to head back home after we went to the store, she wanted me to carry her. We got milk and juice, so the bag was really heavy. It's not like I didn't want..." I shake my head miserably.

Ellis sighs and straightens up, only to move forward and sit down beside me. "I'm sorry."

"Don't be." I attempt a smile, hating he's seeing me like this. It's *too much*. Being friendly and cohabitating is one thing, emotional vulnerability is another. I'm still tangled up about the other night on the balcony. The last thing I need is to cry all over him. "It's part of the deal. I knew it could happen."

"That doesn't make it any easier," he states gently. When I don't respond, choosing instead to stare at my shoes, Ellis nudges my shoulder with his own. "You did great, Josephine. You stayed calm, didn't you?"

Yeah, I guess I did, but it doesn't seem enough. "There were these old people, giving us dirty looks," I admit, my voice thick with hysterical indignation. "As if I wasn't doing everything I could, and Zoe was being spoiled or bratty, not tired and overwhelmed."

Ellis is silent for a long time, and when I hazard a look at him, his expression is wooden. Our gazes connect, and sitting this close, I can make out the tiny flecks of silver amidst the pale blue of his eyes. "I wish I could say that nobody's ever given me that look, but they have. Many times."

Grief expands inside me as I think of all the times Ellis must have felt like I did on that dirt road, struggling to keep my head and do the right thing for her while Zoe's emotions rage out of control. The difference is that I could have called someone for help. Ellis has been on his own for years now.

Some of my sadness must show, because the man beside me smiles gently.

"They can think what they like, Jo. It doesn't matter. What *does* matter is that the little girl in there knows she can count on you. In a year, or two, or five, Zoe won't remember a few judgmental strangers. She will remember the kind nanny who cared for her when she was living in a strange place, and how calm you were when her feelings were so big she couldn't contain them."

My eyes sting with more tears and despite my best efforts, a few of them manage to slip free. "You're not so bad at the pep talks, either." My bottom lip trembles as I wipe them away, sniffing. "Thank you. Really. I'll be okay, now. You don't have to stay."

Ellis doesn't move. "I'll just sit here for a moment, if that's okay with you. We don't have to talk."

I nod, and even through my misgivings about letting him see me so vulnerable, it's kind of nice to not be alone. A breeze plays across my skin, ruffling the ends of my hair, and we watch as a cat wanders across the drive, pausing to look at us before continuing on its way.

"Did you find anything cool today?" I ask finally, when my eyes are safely dry and the invisible ropes that constricted around my chest have loosened.

Ellis's now familiar quiet laugh makes my heart squeeze. "I found multiple cool things. The school is putting rather a lot of trust in me, considering I'm handling tens of thousands of dollars in books every day, unsupervised."

My lips twitch. "Maybe I've been placed here as a spy. To surveil you and make sure you aren't stealing rare books."

"That would be very clever." A quick peek over confirms he's smiling. "Though, somehow, I can't imagine you being a particularly good spy."

"Maybe that's what I want you to think. So, in reality, I'm excellent."

"I stand corrected." He gets to his feet, grinning down at me and then, after a quick glance around, frowns. "Where are the groceries?"

I groan. "Oh, god. I totally forgot. I shoved the basket in a patch of bushes so I could carry her. The milk is done for, but everything else was nonperishable."

He holds out a hand to help me up, and after the briefest pause I take it, nearly stumbling into his chest with how weak my muscles are. God, he's so much taller than me. No wonder my arms feel like jelly from carrying his kid around. If the long legs are anything to go by, Zoe will be outpacing me height-wise this time next year.

"We'll go back out after dinner to get it, or Zoe and I will if you'd like some time to yourself."

"I'm okay now," I promise as we walk, side by side, back into the house. I'm tired, yes, but also happy with how I handled this. "Just needed to breathe for a moment. Where is she?"

Ellis nods toward the living room. "I rubbed her back for all of two minutes and she fell asleep on the couch. She'll probably be out until dinner now. Meltdowns take a lot out of her."

We pause at the bottom of the stairs, and as I turn to face him, something in the air between us seems to shift. The change is palpable and comes on as suddenly as someone flipping on the lights. One moment it's not there, and the next...

Neither of us move, waiting for the other to break the spell. Ellis is looking at me, and I'm looking back. The air in the room has grown thinner, or maybe I've just forgotten to breathe, because all those very good reasons I have for not throwing myself at this man are nowhere to be found.

It's so easy to imagine closing the distance between us to wrap my arms around his neck, to drag him down to kiss me, and I *know* I can't do it. I know that. But when I suck in a long, shallow breath, trying to steady myself, we're standing close enough that the scent of him invades my senses, further muddling my thoughts. By now, I'm intimately familiar with the way Ellis Delvaux smells; like cinnamon, coffee and old books. Catching little hints of it when we pass too close to one another in the kitchen or when he takes Zoe from my arms isn't enough.

I want to be surrounded by him.

It isn't just a bad idea, it's catastrophic, but the consequences seem downright unimportant at this moment. Wanting someone this way feels like *too much*. Whatever is responsible for this pull between us has been there since the beginning, and it's only getting stronger.

Or I'm just getting weaker.

Ellis steps forward, those intense, pale eyes searching my face and I make a low noise somewhere between whimper and gasp when he lifts his hands to cradle my jaw. He's in control, tilting my face up, and I know exactly what's about to happen.

He's going to kiss me.

I want him to.

Every muscle in my body has gone soft, warmth spreading outward from my core, and when his lips brush over mine in the ghost of a kiss, I feel it everywhere. I don't realize I've reached out until my hands are on his chest and at my touch, Ellis groans deep and masculine and—god—*he still isn't kissing me.*

"We shouldn't," his voice is an octave lower than usual.

I nod, even as I stand on my toes, stretching to bring our lips together in something more than the unsatisfying phantom kiss. "Ellis," I plead, and the sound of me saying his name seems to break the tether he has on his self-control.

My back hits the wall at the base of the steps, and then he's everywhere, his larger body surrounding me, pressing me into the ancient plaster.

"Josephine." He still doesn't kiss me. Instead, Ellis's lips skim over my cheek and down my jaw, breathing me in as though he's as desperate to gather every piece of me he can. When he finds the soft skin beneath my ear, it takes all my focus to keep myself from crumpling. "There?" he murmurs, his thumb stroking the same place on the opposite side.

I'm putty in his hands, and the quiet, keening cry I make in response is all I'm capable of.

Ellis groans, pressing closer, ensuring I can't miss the hard length of his cock against my stomach, showing me what I've done to him. "You have me aching every hour of the day. *Merde*, you feel incredible. *Please mon amour*, let me take you to bed. Let me make you feel good."

His teeth skim over my pulse point, and a leg slides between mine, giving me the friction I didn't realize I was craving. Unthinking, I rock against him. My panties are so wet that I glide easily over his hard thigh, my quiet, broken moans muffled by the hand that comes up to cover my mouth.

"*Shhh,*" Ellis murmurs, still busy showering attention on the place below my ear, alternating between worshipful kisses and sucking hard enough to leave a mark. *I hope it does.* "That's it. Take what you need from me. That's a good girl."

His free hand finds my hip, guiding my pace as I start to grind faster, my swollen clit growing more sensitive with every pass. Vaguely, I know this might be something I regret. I know this is bad, but the *why* is elusive. I also know it feels *really, really* good and the need I have for this man wrapped around me seems so much bigger than the reasons I shouldn't.

My head falls back against the wall with an audible thud. I have no concept of how long we've been here, but it doesn't feel like long, and I'm already shaking with how hard he's going to make me come.

Before Ellis, I didn't know what it felt like to be with someone like this or want anyone this much. Now my associations of sex are inexorably tied to him. I tried to fight it, tried to hold on to some shred of self-preservation, and where did it get me? Dry humping his leg in the foyer.

"I need your come, *mon amour,*" he pleads, lifting his

thigh to increase the pressure on my sex. Seconds later, the hand over my mouth is gone, replaced almost instantly by his lips.

Finally.

There's no finesse or control to the way we kiss. It's bruising and messy and—*god*—so hot. We claw at each other, frantic and out of control. He grinds his erection against my stomach, leaving no question of whether he's as affected by this as I am. If we were anywhere else, I'm positive I would be naked beneath him by now, and the thought makes my inner muscles tighten, empty and aching to be filled. As one of Ellis's hands finds its way under my shirt, dragging my bra out of the way to tease and cup my breast, the added jolt of pleasure is all I need.

My orgasm rips through me, as violent and explosive as the incident that brought it on. Ellis's kiss muffles my cries, and just as I begin to come down, he groans.

"*Josephine.*" His forehead drops to my shoulder as he rocks against me in a short, grinding rhythm, his body shaking. It takes me a moment to realize what's happening, but my body floods with a fresh wave of need as I become aware of the damp heat spreading over my t-shirt.

Then, as the urgency drains away, both of us still.

Did we just...

Through the hormonal fog, the reality of what just happened is setting in, and even as we stay tangled together, our breaths slowing, it's like cold is spreading through the warm room. My pulse thuds unevenly as we untangle ourselves.

I don't want to look up, don't want confirmation of his regret, but I need to know. Sure enough, Ellis is staring at me as though I'm dangerous, as if I'm a bomb that just went off and destroyed all his careful control.

Neither of us speaks.

"I'm sorry," I whisper, not knowing why.

Ellis shakes his head, lifting his hands to scrub them over his face. "No," he finally says, lowering them to look at me with obvious regret. "That was me. I started it."

He *did* start it, but I didn't say no. Ellis might not want the same things that I do, but it's quickly becoming clear this attraction is very mutual and it isn't going to fade away.

This is going to happen again, and again, and if I don't keep it together, I'm going to end up going home with a broken heart. Ellis has made it clear where he stands, and I refuse to be the girl who thinks she can change his mind. I need to find a way around catching feelings, and fast.

For god's sake, try *not* falling for someone when every corner of this property is the most romantic place imaginable. You could get kissed in the hall closet to our right, and it would be a moment worthy of a glamorous black and white film.

It doesn't help that in the time we've been here, it's become clear Ellis Delvaux is exactly the man I thought he was the first night we met. He's kind, funny and noble. He speaks like he's reading from an old English novel and when he looks at me, he makes me feel like all those things I'm insecure about don't matter quite so much.

I like him—*too much*—and now, a horrible idea is beginning to develop in my mind, one with about a million pitfalls that I shouldn't even consider. The longer we stand here, lost in our shock, the more it feels like it's my only option.

Saying the words seems like a wall that I won't be able to get past. I must be braver than I realized, though, because when open my mouth—fully expecting to bail out before the first word—I say *it*.

"We should just have sex."

Ellis stares at me, obviously taken aback, and it seems to take him a full thirty seconds to process what I've just said.

"I'm not sure that's such a good idea," he chokes out at last, dragging a hand through his untidy hair.

I swallow, staring back. "Maybe it is a good idea." I keep my expression impassive, my tone calm and reasonable, even if I'm screaming internally. "It seems kind of silly to pretend we're not attracted to each other. That night wasn't an accident and this," I gesture to the wall we just defiled, "will probably happen again if we don't come up with some kind of solution. You... You want to, right?"

It's a little gratifying to see the shock on Ellis's face, and watch him struggle to compose himself. "I'm *ah*—" He coughs, looking around, as if someone will walk in and scold us, then edges closer to me, lowering his voice. "I'm not sure I should admit to that."

I feel myself smile. "You just did."

He winces. "So I did."

"I'm just saying," I continue, "we can approach this two ways. Either we live in mutual, sexually repressed misery for the next six months. Or..." I lift my chin, refusing to look embarrassed. "Or, we could come to an agreement."

"An agreement?" he echoes flatly, but despite his dubious tone, there's something darkening behind his eyes.

I nod slowly, savoring the dark thrill that comes from knowing he wants me so badly. "Yes. No strings attached sex. You're not interested in a relationship, right? So this is the next best thing. You can fuck me, and I won't expect anything else. I'll know you don't want me falling in love with you."

For the first time since we began this conversation, there's a flicker of pain in his expression.

"We can have rules," I press on, "boundaries. Actually, yeah. That would be a good idea." I nod to myself. "To make it clear that we're not in a relationship. So the lines don't get muddled."

"Josephine, I—" His words falter. "You deserve a good deal better than me."

That's not what I was expecting him to say, and it's suddenly difficult to swallow. How could he possibly think that? This man is good all the way through. The realization he doesn't see himself as I do makes my heart ache. It's not my business, though. He doesn't want me to be his girlfriend, he just wants to sleep with me, and I can be okay with that. *I can.*

I lift my eyebrows defiantly. "So, you don't think you could make me come?" His eyes flash. Right at this moment, I'm positive he's remembering the way I've come on his fingers, his cock and now his leg, and is itching to remind me. "That's what this is about, Ellis. Sex. Just sex."

He leans back, eyes searching my face, and I can practically hear the thoughts spinning through his mind. Suggesting this was impulsive, but the longer I think about it, the more sure I become that it's the only solution. We can't run from each other, or the attraction that is still very alive. Either we can vent that into screwing each other's brains out, or I'm going to get caught up in all the hopeless longing and desperate hookups, likely developing feelings that would end up hurting me.

Nothing could be a better reminder than the feelings of rejection that will inevitably come every time he fucks me and walks away. I'll be purposely hurting myself, sure, but it will save me a lot more pain in the long run. No strings attached sex is a vaccination against falling in love with Ellis Delvaux. And, if what just happened is any indication, I need it.

I let out a rocky breath. "Listen," I begin after the silence stretches for so long that it becomes clear that Ellis is too shocked to form any kind of coherent speech. "I'll leave my balcony door open tonight. If you decide you want to... well. If you want to discuss it, we can."

Twelve

ELLIS

AS HAS OFTEN BEEN the case these days, I'm distracted throughout the rest of the afternoon.

There is an appraiser from one of the largest auction houses in the country coming to the chateau in a few weeks to evaluate the first set of books to be auctioned off. I'm hoping to have a larger selection to show him, but that desire is looking increasingly improbable thanks to what happened in the foyer and my nanny's indecent proposal.

I must be mad. A certified, absolute lunatic for considering it, and yet considering it is all I can seem to do.

Josephine was right when she said this will happen again. It's all but inevitable. All she had to do was look at me and I forgot myself entirely, pinning her to the wall and grinding against her, coming in my pants like a teenage boy. After weeks of trying to pretend that what was happening between us *wasn't* happening, this was a brutal wake up call.

It was also an unnecessary reminder of how good she feels in my arms.

When I give up on getting anything accomplished for the day, I find Jo and Zoe in the kitchen, adding herbs to a pot of spaghetti sauce. Both are in good spirits despite their trying afternoon. The only sign what happened afterward wasn't a figment of my depraved imagination is a faint color that rises in Jo's cheeks as I enter the room.

After dinner, for the first time since we arrived, she didn't join Zoe and I for our evening walk. The two of us retrieve the basket of abandoned groceries from its hiding place, and I can tell by the slump in Zoe's shoulders that she isn't oblivious to the impact her meltdown had on Jo.

"I made Jojo sad." She drags her shoes over the dirt road as we turn back toward the chateau.

My heart twists and I stop in the middle of the road, kneeling so I'm eye level with my daughter. She doesn't meet my gaze, but she's listening. "Jojo knows you were upset and didn't hurt her feelings on purpose. She loves spending time with you very much, *mon cœur*."

Zoe rocks back on her heels, lips pulled flat and, for about the dozenth time today alone, I wish I could see into her mind and know the exact right things to say.

"You were an excellent help to her with dinner too, weren't you?" I press on hopefully, and Zoe's expression relaxes a bit as she seems to accept the truth of this. "When I came in, she had a big smile. You were making her very happy."

Another few seconds pass before Zoe hums to herself and pulls away from my hand, skipping off toward home.

Straightening up, I follow, feeling another deep pull of gratitude toward Jo for handling the whole business so gracefully. Meltdowns are brutal for even the most experienced of parents, and I'm certainly guilty of losing my cool once or twice. I can only imagine how trying it was for both of them, but as far as I can tell, Josephine didn't allow herself to cry until Zoe couldn't see it.

As if I needed further evidence she's the most incredible woman alive.

Dusk is settling by the time we arrive back at the chateau, and I allow Zoe a few more minutes of chasing fireflies in the meadow as I allow my mind to wander—yet again—to the nanny who seems to occupy the vast majority of my thoughts these days.

I should let this go. *I should.*

Having sex with her the first time was bad, this afternoon was worse, but to consider an arrangement with my boss's twenty-two-year-old daughter, a woman who also happens to be in my employ, now? It's beyond messy, an unquestionably terrible idea, but I can't quite convince myself to say no.

For one thing... God, I want her so badly. Despite what I promised myself when she agreed to come to France, it's obscene the amount of times I've given into the temptation to jerk myself off to thoughts of Josephine. That alone should be enough to throw up red flags, and it does, but they're not big enough to stop me from charging past them.

Just like the first night we met, I'm overcome by the temptation to allow myself to enjoy something that isn't right, but *feels* good. And of anyone in my life apart from my daughter, nobody makes me feel better than her beautiful, kind hearted nanny. In a matter of weeks, she has become the calm, warm center of my otherwise stressful existence. For the life of me, I have no idea how I managed so long without her, and I'm dreading the day we get back on a plane to Connecticut.

In another life, I'd have fallen in love with her. It would be easy to, even now. It's all the more evidence for me being out of my mind, because what kind of man looks at a woman like Josephine and sees her as a one-night-stand?

If I'd known what fate had in store for us, I hope that I'd have stopped myself, but in my heart I know it wasn't true. I was so sure that those few desperate moments with Josephine Sutton would be all I ever had. Now, she's offering me more of herself? More pieces? More stolen moments from a different version of my life?

Even if it's the most foolish, irresponsible thing I've ever done, how could I possibly say no? I'm thirty-six years old, and I've never experienced this kind of attraction before. Every single thing the woman does makes my blood boil. How am I supposed to work or think or breathe when she's around me?

As I've gotten to know her, I've found myself wishing that I *could* offer her more. Nothing has changed, though. I'm still in the situation I was in when we were in Connecticut. Her mother is still my boss, and if she returns to Weston, our relationship would be prohibited. Then there's the humiliating, gut wrenching truth that I couldn't keep my wife happy or my family together, so what chance could I have with a beautiful, much younger woman?

It will be hard enough to say goodbye to her when our time in France is over. What if I dated her and it didn't work out? What if she left me too? I would never forgive myself if I put Zoe in the position to lose another mother figure. The risks of pursuing a relationship with her are too high to consider.

Josephine's bedroom door is closed, but a light is shining beneath it as I lead Zoe upstairs to brush her teeth and get ready for bed. She's already rubbing her eyes, and sure enough, we only make it halfway through her favorite princess book before her breathing grows deep and slow.

My heart is pounding as I cross to my room and close the door quietly behind me, staring at the wall which separates my bedroom from Josephine's. She's over there now. Is she wondering if I'll come through the balcony and tell her I want her? Is she regretting making the offer at all when our emotions were high?

I don't sit down or get undressed. I stand there, my back

pressed to the door, willing myself not to do what I *know* I'm going to.

A better man would tell her no, or—better, yet—pretend the whole thing didn't happen. I can't, though. Not while I'm trapped in this house with the woman of my dreams who I can no longer deny wants me. There's nowhere to hide. Not anymore.

Even if I say no now, stand on my morals and muster up enough willpower to keep myself from walking outside and into her room. What happened today... *it will happen again.* It's only a matter of time before my willpower breaks, or hers does, and things get much more complicated. I can't stand the idea of hurting her again. This way, at least, there will be no misunderstandings.

I don't know how long I stand there, thinking in circles, or what finally prompts me to move. Once I do, though, I don't falter. I keep going straight out onto the balcony, where the last traces of sunset have gone, and the night sky is scattered in an impossible number of stars.

Lamplight is coming from within Josephine's room, shining like a beacon through the door that she left ajar and my heart pounds as I draw forward, pushing it open.

I find her laying on the bed, her head propped on her hand and a book on the quilt before her. She looks up when I step inside. For a moment, we just stare at each other, the implications of my presence hanging in the air between us.

She's done away with the clothes she was wearing earlier, and in their place is a tank top and small, cotton shorts that leave most of her legs bare. My cock throbs.

"Hey." Her honeyed voice is cautious as she sits up, curling her legs beneath her. "Did Zoe go down okay?"

I nod. "Yes. Tired."

She smiles weakly. "Long day."

"Yes."

Silence falls between us again, and, desperate for something to do other than lunge at her, I peer around. Her room is more or less the same as mine, decorated in pale florals and furnished in antique wood. The bed she's sitting on is the most notable feature of the space, with its four ornately carved posts and the canopy which frames her in gauzy, white wisps of material.

Will I fuck her in that bed? I want to.

Tearing my eyes away from the beautiful woman before me, I look around, my gaze falling on an upholstered chair sitting on the wall across from her. Grateful for the extra distance, I cross to it and sit, wracking my brain for what the hell I'm supposed to say here.

Even as a young man, I was a serial monogamist. I didn't have lovers, I had girlfriends, and now I'm sorry for it. She's younger than me—*much* younger—yet here, I'm the one out of my depth. Both at the prospect of unattached sex, and at the sudden urge to punch a hole in the wall at the thought of Josephine having other men in her bed.

"Can I ask what you had in mind?" I question, unable to stand the silence a moment longer, and gesture helplessly between us. "For this, I mean. If you're not regretting it now."

"I'm not regretting it," she assures me, nibbling on her bottom lip, looking far more hesitant and abashed than she did earlier when she made the proposition. *Maybe I'm not the only one who's nervous here.* "And, um, besides the obvious?"

The tension in my shoulders lessens incrementally. Reaching up, I rub the back of my neck, a little embarrassed myself. "Yes." I let out a short, strained laugh. "Besides the obvious."

God, help me.

"Well," she begins, a little hesitant, "I thought we should probably discuss the rules." I nod in agreement, and she thankfully saves me from making the first suggestion. "Like, we don't tell anyone."

"Agreed," I reply easily. This is so surreal. Are we truly having this conversation? I realize she's waiting for me to suggest something, and it's a struggle to turn my mind toward a single thing other than getting between her thighs. "*Ah,* no sleeping over? Zoe often wakes up early and comes looking for me."

"That makes sense." Her eyes search my face. "Um. We probably shouldn't do anything during the day when she's awake, then. She's sneaky."

I chuckle, acknowledging the truth in that. "That she is. So, set hours then, and nothing beyond them?"

"Eight to twelve?"

"That sounds... fine." *Incredible also comes to mind.*

"Um." She looks down. "I'm not jealous or anything. I just don't want to be... one of the many." I blink, shocked to silence as she continues in a rush. "You're single, and, you, um, look like that... I'd extend you the same courtesy."

One of the many?

Look like that?

My answering laugh is choked with disbelief. "You don't need to worry about that. There won't be anyone else."

As if anyone could compare to her.

As if I was capable of looking at anyone but her.

As if it was possible for a single other woman on the planet to consume me the way Josephine Sutton has.

"You can't know that," she argues weakly, hands twisting in her lap.

Maybe it should bother me that she's concerned about my other partners when this is supposed to be a casual arrangement, but I'm sure as hell worried about hers. The idea of another man laying a hand on her in the past is difficult, but *now*? I'd end up behind bars.

"I *do*," I insist, using the same authoritative tone I often employ during staff meetings at Montgomery. "I separated from my wife three years ago, and at that time, there's only been you. By now, you've seen first-hand that I have my hands full. Sex wasn't a priority."

Until I find myself before my twenty-two-year-old nanny perched on her bed in tiny cotton pajamas, laying down conditions for me to have sex with her. Forget a *priority*. Now I'd likely agree to chop off a finger or two for the honor.

Josephine seems to accept that and I can tell she's waiting, prepared to make a concession. There's only one I know that needs to be said, but knowing it doesn't make it any easier to say it.

I swallow with difficulty, my eyes following the warm glow of the lamplight over her slim shoulders. "This ends when we go home." My voice is dark. Flat. Dead. "I can't risk my professional reputation and possibly my employment. Zoe depends on me. I need to be responsible."

Or as close to responsible as I can be where Josephine Sutton is concerned. While she technically isn't a Weston University student at the moment, somehow I doubt her mother will care for the nuances of the situation if she ever discovers how we intend to spend the next five months.

Josephine nods in understanding, her expression unreadable. "Okay. That... that makes sense."

It *does* make sense, but that does nothing to help the hollow ache expanding inside me as we discuss it. "It's not a commentary of how highly I think of you, or even—"

She cuts me off with a pained grimace and shake of her head. "I get it, Ellis. Really. I don't expect anything from you beyond this."

There's no way to pretend that comment doesn't bother me, but there's nothing to be done about it. This is the situation we're in, and even unattached sex is more than I thought

I'd have of her. I can't be greedy here, not when there's more than my job at stake.

It's vital I keep myself in check for Zoe's sake, but I know that if it were for anyone but my daughter, I wouldn't be able to.

I'm so lost in my preoccupation that my heart leaps when I notice Josephine getting to her feet. We're only a few meters apart, and even in well-worn pajamas, she's almost too perfect to be real. Her full lips curve. "So that's it then."

That quiet voice cuts through my swirling thoughts like a knife, centering me in the present. For fuck's sake. I've been good and responsible all my life. I've followed every damn rule, and where did it get me? Divorced, raising my daughter alone, and struggling just to keep my job and pay the mortgage on an overpriced house I didn't want.

Pourquoi pas putain?*

"That's it," I finally agree, not bothering to conceal the way my gaze roams over her body. Christ, it feels good to look at her freely after restraining myself for so long.

My blood has turned heated, and a tension has coiled in my every muscle as the implications of what we just agreed to begins to set in. I get to put my hands on her. I get to feel the hot, tight grip of her cunt and hear her sweet moans in my ear.

Now, I know what she wants, and I'll be damned if she has to ask for it.

Blowing out a heavy breath, I finally drag my eyes away from her body to meet her heated gaze. My cock hardens. "Will you let me see you?"

It's all I've been able to think about for weeks now, hating myself for not finding a way to get her naked in the one chance I had. If I was going to spend the rest of my life pining, then I at least wanted to know what her tits looked like.

---

* Why the fuck not?

Who knows what the future holds, and I'm not taking any chances.

Josephine's teeth find her lip again, and she raises her hands to trail the tips of her fingers over the straps of her tank top. "I'm not wearing anything under this."

"*Good.*" The word bursts out of me, brusque and impatient. The air in the room has become stifling.

I watch, rapt, as Josephine fiddles with the hem of her shirt and—so slowly it's agonizing—lifts it over her head.

The noise I make when my eyes lock on her plump, rose tipped breasts can only be described as a snarl. "The shorts too. Now."

It's been driving me mad, the urgency I had when we were together. Why didn't I slow down? There were a million things I wanted to do and try, and all of them required more time, space and privacy than the back seat of my car allowed.

Now, we have hours and hours stretching before us, weeks, months, and for that time, *she's mine.* I should be stopping to savor her, but as she pushes her shorts and panties over her hips and they fall to the ground with a quiet rustle, I'm not entirely in control of my actions.

She's completely naked now, and the most exquisite thing I've ever seen.

"Get on the bed, Josephine," I tell her, my voice deathly calm and controlled. "On all fours. Spread your legs wide. I need to see you."

I'm being bossy, but she doesn't seem to mind. In fact, at my words, I'm sure I can hear her breath hitch. My hands curl over the arms of the chair, anchoring myself in place as she turns, providing me a beautiful view of the ass that's been the star of fantasies so filthy I didn't think myself capable of them.

Not for the first time, the book I caught her reading last week comes to mind. *Would she like to call me that?*

As she crawls onto the bed, I groan as I get my first look at her bare cunt, already glistening with arousal. My cock throbs, growing impossibly harder as I stare.

"Ellis," she whispers, her voice high with need. "I need you to fuck me."

I'm barely aware of getting to my feet until I'm standing behind her. We both jerk with surprise as my hands move to her hips. "I have one more rule," I tell her, my voice like gravel as I palm her ass, pulling her wide so I can see every inch.

I've never been this hard.

She squirms under my touch. "What—what is it?"

Releasing one cheek, my hand comes down on her ass in a sharp slap, making her gasp. "You get my cock when I say, sweetheart, and not a moment before. Between the hours of eight and midnight, I own this beautiful body, and I'll use it as I see fit."

Another spank, and *I can see* how wet she is from me talking to her like this. "Ellis..." she moans, and I'm positive I've never loved the sound of my name before this moment.

Ellis.

"Yes, that's right, *mon amour.*" My lip curls as I spank her again, harder than before. Her yelp of surprise turns to a wanton moan as the same hand which delivered her punishment moves between her thighs to cup her sex. "I'm the one making you so wet you're dripping down your thighs. Now, do you agree?"

"Agree?" she echoes, her voice strained as she squirms against the pressure of my hand, her fists curling on the sheets.

This time, the spank comes down on her cunt and even as her cry shatters the quiet of the dark room, fresh arousal glistens on her slit, confirming every theory I've had about her needs. My sweet little nanny likes it rough and dirty, and I'm fighting second to second to keep myself from ripping my belt open and fucking her as hard as I can.

135

"My last rule, Josephine," I grit out, dragging two fingers through the creamy mess she's making for me.

She bucks into my touch, and now her breaths are coming in desperate little pants. "Yes, anything—"

I press my fingers inside her tight opening, fucking her too lightly to give her any satisfaction, while relishing the tightness and heat of her, and the promise of what she will feel like wrapped around my cock.

"This is mine," I murmur, scissoring my fingers, stretching her to illustrate the point. "And this." They move to her clit, circling the swollen bud teasingly.

"Ellis." She hiccups, her thighs trembling as my hand moves back, circling the tight, puckered hole between her cheeks that I know instinctively has never been touched like this before.

Leaning forward, I kiss the base of her spine, holding her steady as I dip just the tip of my finger into her ass. "I'm going to fuck you here, too. Don't worry, *mon amour*. It's in my best interest to ensure you enjoy the experience."

Jesus. The things I'm saying out loud have only ever existed in the darkest corners of my imagination. Sex was never like this for me. Not with my ex-wife, or any of my partners before her. There's no experimentation here, or questioning whether Josephine likes what I'm doing to her. I've spent weeks of my life thinking about what she needs, and exactly how I'd give it to her.

I've never felt as sure of myself as I do now.

My free hand comes down to free my cock, and it's only when I've fisted my base, preparing to press inside her, that the alarm bells sound.

"Protection," I mutter, looking around helplessly, as though a condom will appear within reach.

Josephine gasps, turning to look at me, her gaze pleading. "Oh no. Please tell me you have something in your room!"

I don't. *I fucking don't*. Somehow, it didn't occur to me to pack condoms in the hurried rush to prepare for this trip, which I would be taking with my six-year-old daughter and a woman I thought would hate me until the end of time.

Cursing under my breath, I shake my head. "I'll go to the pharmacy in town tomorrow."

The lust hasn't drained away, though. Frantic need is burning through me, demanding I fuck her anyway. I must not have lost all control of myself, however, because I hold back. There are other options, after all.

I drop to my knees.

Thirteen

JOSEPHINE

I'M NOT sure how *"procure birth control"* didn't enter my mind before propositioning my boss with a sex agreement, but I'm not exactly mad about my lack of preparation. Because as far as suitable alternatives go, *this* is a strong candidate. In fact, I might beg him to do this to me daily, because it feels like I might just dissolve into the mattress.

Like... *how?*

"Ellis!" My fists tighten on the head of graying hair between my thighs, my back snapping off the mattress as my fourth orgasm hits me out of nowhere. I'm so swollen and oversensitive it's almost painful, and I have to grit my teeth to keep myself from screaming.

I don't know how long we've been doing this, because time stopped meaning much after orgasm number two. Every cell in my body seems to be centered on the feeling of Ellis's tongue against my clit, and the burning stretch as he presses a third finger inside me, hell bent on pulling every possible ounce of pleasure from my body.

It's too much, though, and as I try to squirm away, Ellis's free hand presses into my lower belly, stopping me. When he parts with my pussy long enough to look at me properly, his eyes are sharp and hungry, his lips and chin shining with spit and arousal.

I'm quickly learning that it's one thing for a man to say *"you're mine"* before he fucks you, but it's a whole other to actually feel like he owns you. I do, though, and it feels *good*. I didn't think it was possible to top what we did in the car that night, or recreate the burning need we felt in the foyer earlier today, but nothing has ever felt this good, physically or emotionally. Every day, I spend most of my time thinking, planning, worrying... It's such a relief to let it all go and trust him. Even if it's only for a few hours.

"One more," Ellis growls, and my protests are nowhere to be found as his mouth descends on my throbbing sex once again, hand still pressed low on my belly to ensure I can't go anywhere.

I collapse back onto the bed, shaking. I've barely come down from my last orgasm, and every firm lap of his tongue or decadent suck of my clit between his lips makes me twitch. "Ellis, I can't," I whimper, pulling his hair.

Pale eyes glint up at me, but he doesn't stop. On the contrary, the fingers inside me press further apart—stretching me to my limit—and my body begins to shake. Despite what I told him, and what I believed, it's happening anyway. The man between my thighs is determined to make me come, even if it has to hurt a little to get there.

My broken cry shatters the quiet room again as I come a fifth time. Ellis drags it on and on, groaning in frustration when I finally stop writhing against his mouth, my sex so sensitive he could probably blow on it and make me cry.

He doesn't though, instead he sits back, staring down at me so intensely it's like he's trying to memorize every detail of this. And, god—Ellis Delvaux is devastatingly handsome just standing in the library, covered in dust and frowning at an old book. Now, he's sitting between my bare thighs with my arousal on his face, his bare chest heaving and his thick cock angled directly at the part of me he probably ruined for anyone else.

"Come here," I plead, reaching for him, and he crawls over me, his erection trailing pre-cum over my hip and stomach. Our lips meet without hesitation, and I can taste myself on his tongue as we kiss hungrily.

"*Tu es incroyable, putain**," he groans roughly. It's the same voice he used when I rode him in the backseat of his car back in Connecticut.

Reaching down, I wrap my hand around the base of his cock. "I want you so bad," I whisper as he drops his head to my shoulder, rolling his hips into my grasp.

"Tomorrow," Ellis promises with a low, masculine grunt. He shoves a hand between us too, and wraps it around mine, squeezing himself with my hand, harder than I would have expected. "I'll drive into the village before dinner. Yes—*ah, dammit*—like that. Good girl, *mon amour*. Hold it tight for me."

I let out a breathy laugh, loving the weight of him pressing me into the mattress and the way our skin is sticking together from the heat. He lost his shirt after orgasm number one, and everything else went after number three. "Those gossipy old ladies who work at the pharmacy are going to think you're fucking your nanny."

"I'm not fucking you yet," he growls, releasing his hold on my hand. Without warning, my stomach swoops as he rolls us to the side. I find myself straddling his thighs, my slick, swollen pussy only inches from his thick cock. Ellis groans, his eyes raking over my body. "You've been tested since your last partner?"

---

* Fuck, you're incredible

My mouth goes dry at the question. *He* is my last partner, my *only* partner, and I don't know if I'll ever be able to tell him that. It feels even more vulnerable to admit it now than it did before.

I swallow. "I had a physical a few months before we... Before the car."

Ellis nods, his expression pained. "You're safe with me. Now, move forward a little—*that's it.*" He guides my hips forward, and we both moan as I settle over him, the lips of my pussy parted over his shaft.

Oh god.

We both watch, panting, as I roll my hips experimentally.

"Keep going," he grits out, holding me tighter. "That's it. You're doing so well."

I whimper, squeezing my eyes shut, struggling to think straight with him looking at me like that and the friction of my overstimulated clit bumping the head of his cock. Beneath us, the antique bed squeaks in time with my movements, an erotic soundtrack that raises goosebumps over my damp skin.

"Josephine." My eyes snap open as Ellis shifts beneath me, sitting up so we're almost nose to nose, his light blue eyes boring into mine. A hand tangles in my hair, and I barely have time to gasp before his lips have found mine again. "You feel so good," he mumbles between feverish kisses, his free hand gripping my ass.

Our bodies are sealed together and I can't glide over him as smoothly as I was a moment ago, but it's worth it. Even the feeble, desperate little grinds we manage send pleasure curling through my pelvis and up my spine. When we break apart, panting, I'm not capable of looking anywhere but into his piercing eyes.

A noise that's part shock, part pleasure, falls from my lips. This is too intimate, too erotic, *too much.* He's ruining me, and I don't ever want him to stop.

141

"I'm going to have you every night, *mon amour*. Your cunt will get wet whenever I walk into the room, because you'll remember how good I make it feel." He curses under his breath, tilting my body back so he can draw my nipple into his mouth, pulling it greedily between his teeth.

I'm so soaked that even his lower abdomen is coated now, and there will be a wet spot on the bed beneath us. Nothing, not even my spiciest books, could have prepared me for this man, and now I'm the only one who gets to see him this way. *Me*. Nobody else knows that beneath those buttoned up shirts and the appearance of a proper, sophisticated librarian, Ellis Delvaux is *dirty*.

"Ellis," I whine. At the sound of his name, he drags me back up and the hand still tangled in my hair forces me to meet his darkened gaze.

"Do you want to call me Daddy right now, *mon amour*?"

As caught up as I was in the moment's intensity, I didn't realize how close I'd gotten to coming until it's already happening. Pleasure shoots up my spine and I writhe over Ellis's cock, almost sobbing.

When I come down, I find him gazing at me in undisguised awe. One strong arm moves around my waist, dragging me closer, while the other is still pressed up along my spine, tangled in the hair at the nape of my neck.

Without pausing to second guess myself, I nod breathlessly, my pace increasing. *I want to make him come like this.* "Yes. *God*—" my voice breaks in a ragged cry. It feels like I'm floating, barely aware of our surroundings, my entire being focused on him. I'm a mess, a horny, dripping mess, and I've never felt more free.

"Say it," Ellis growls, his muscles tensed, and I can tell that he's doing everything he can to stop himself from coming. Even as his arm tightens around me, pulling me so close that I can feel every vein and ridge of his cock as I rub myself over him and the rasp of his chest hair on my nipples.

My nails are biting into his shoulders and I open my mouth to reply, but all that comes out is the same cry as before. "Daddy! *Oh!*"

The word has barely left my mouth before the world turns upside down. I blink, disoriented, as Ellis holds himself over me with one hand while the other fists his cock, pumping furiously.

I gasp at the first lash of cum on my belly, watching in fascination as Ellis covers me in his orgasm. It seems like so much, and I don't know why my first thought is to wonder what it would feel like inside me.

Holy bad ideas.

When it's over, Ellis sags sideways onto the bed, pressing a hand over his face, chest shaking in silent, incredulous laughter.

Yeah, nobody can understand the hysterical disbelief of what just happened better than I can. I feel myself grinning too as I look over at him. "Holy shit."

"Holy shit," He echoes, lowering his hand to meet my gaze. Like this, carefree and happy, he looks so much younger than I've ever seen him. For a few seconds, we stare at each other, still panting. Then, as if remembering the mess he left on my skin, Ellis sits up, looking around.

I watch, shamelessly enjoying the view, as he gets to his feet and crosses, totally naked, to the bathroom. Moments later, he returns, smirking when he catches me checking him out.

"I'm going to have my hands full with you." He chuckles, sitting on the edge of the bed and wiping away his release with a damp washcloth.

"Are you complaining?" I tease, tracing my fingers through the patch of light hair on his chest.

Ellis snorts, shaking his head. "If I ever say yes to that, I have developed a neurological condition of some sort. Seek medical attention immediately." As his eyes move to my face, the smile fades. "You're still alright with this? No regrets?"

"Nope." I smile, twining my arms around the back of his neck and dragging him back down to kiss me.

It's different from the other kisses we've shared, with the burning need I feel for him temporarily sated, but it still makes me warm all over. Ellis drags his thumb over my bottom lip when we pull away. "I should go." Some of my shock must show on my face because he sits back, looking unsure. "That's what we agreed on, yes? That's... I'm not sleeping here?"

A crack has developed right down the center of my chest, even as I hasten to nod in agreement. "Of course. Yes! That's fine!"

Feeling exposed, I snatch the crumpled sheet from beside me and pull it over myself as I scoot back against the headboard. I wanted this. It was my idea. I knew it would hurt, but somehow I expected preparation to dull the awful stab of rejection.

It doesn't.

Ellis watches me, his expression unreadable. Finally, he looks away and gets to his feet, beginning to collect the clothing he left scattered around the foot of the bed. Neither of us says anything as he dresses. All the effortless intimacy of a few moments ago has gone, and the crack in my chest seems to deepen by the second.

"I'll see you tomorrow," Ellis promises at last, sitting at the edge of the mattress and gazing at me through those intensely blue eyes.

"Okay," I whisper, empty of the happiness I'd felt only a few minutes ago. He doesn't leave yet. Reaching out, Ellis curves his hand around my face, cradling it, and I feel the strangest urge to cry. There's something so tender about the gesture, so devoted. He did the same thing our first night together, and I'd felt the same way then.

Him feeling nothing for me isn't compatible with him touching me like this.

Grave faced, he leans forward and kisses my chin, my jaw, my cheeks, my nose, my forehead. I can't breathe as he does it, torn between confusion and desperate, foolish hope.

"Josephine," Ellis murmurs my name as he pulls back to look down at me. He looks so handsome, tousled haired and so serious. It's like he's about to tell me something that will change my whole life. "If it's foolish to pretend we're not attracted to each other, it seems even more foolish to pretend that this means nothing." My heart stalls, and before I can respond to that, Ellis is getting back to his feet. "Goodnight, *mon amour.*"

Fourteen

ELLIS

IF I THOUGHT I was consumed by my thoughts of Josephine before today, I was sorely mistaken.

Last night was different from our first, and I'm still trying to work out whether this is a good thing or not. On one hand, my level of attraction toward this woman has—incredibly—increased. On the other, the chances of me getting any work done today have—wildly—decreased.

Unable to stomach the very-real chance I'd miss the village pharmacy's limited hours, I drove down after breakfast and bought condoms for the first time since college. The old woman who sold them to me pursed her lips, and as I walked back to the car, it occurred to me that Josephine was likely correct when she guessed keeping our relationship a secret might be impossible in this small community.

There's already been gossip about our presence in the chateau. Josephine and I have both had to fend off curious villagers who wanted to know if I was the late owner's distant relation or if Josephine was his illegitimate daughter with an American actress. In a slow, sleepy village like this one, Jo, Zoe and I are big news. My constant corrections that she is my nanny, not my wife, certainly won't be to my advantage now.

It says a lot about how desperate I am to be inside this woman that I find I don't particularly care. In fact, it's comforting to know she'll be seen as mine in this small corner of the world. At the least, now I won't have to contend with every handsome farmer in a fifty-mile radius turning up at the door of the chateau in the hopes of charming the beautiful, intelligent American staying here.

A beautiful, intelligent American who I brought to orgasm on my tongue over and over again and who ground her greedy little pussy all over my cock. Finishing all over her barely took the edge off, and even the distant sounds of her voice calling after Zoe outside the library windows, or catching the scent of her hair in the downstairs hall, is enough to destroy any feeble levels of concentration I've been able to muster up.

I take my lunch in the kitchen, hoping for a glimpse of her, but she and Zoe must be eating somewhere on the grounds because they're nowhere to be seen. By the time mid-afternoon rolls around, my brain has turned to sludge, and, in need of a break, I go in search of the women of the house.

Today is cooler than it has been since we arrived, and even the urgency to lay eyes on Josephine fades a little as I stroll through the chateau's quiet garden. The seeds Jo and Zoe planted are beginning to emerge, and I pause to water them, attempting to gather some composure before continuing on my way. The last thing I need is to take one look at her, lose my mind, and kiss her in front of Zoe.

It was difficult enough to see the two bruises that bloomed on her neck overnight, souvenirs from our encounter in the foyer, and not launch myself across the breakfast table to find out if I left some on her breasts too.

I was never like this with any of my previous partners. The

possessive, jealous monster that Josephine inspires in me is unprecedented and more than a little alarming. Even the first night we met—after I'd accepted it would be our *only* night—I couldn't stand the thought of another man's hands on her.

A few more minutes outside succeeds in lowering my blood pressure a bit. It's easy to be peaceful here, insulated from the pressures of academia and the constant stress of my day-to-day life.

Of course, the real world has a way of making itself known regardless of where you are. My reminder that life is not all rustling fields and rare books comes in the form of my ex-wife's name on my caller ID.

I consider not answering it, but Miranda's attempts to connect with me either end after the first call or continue on the daily until I work up the will to deal with her. While today does not feel like that day, I would rather address whatever she wants now, rather than risk Josephine becoming aware of the situation.

Gritting my teeth, I accept the call and bring the phone to my ear, staring hard at a nearby patch of strawberry plants. "*What?*"

She releases a frustrated sigh. "I'm trying to be civil, Ellis. You could make an effort to do the same. For Zoe's sake."

A sour taste fills my mouth at the sound of her voice, and it takes every ounce of willpower I possess not to throw my phone to the ground and stomp on it. How dare this woman, who all but abandoned her own child, lecture me about doing what's best for Zoe? As if every day of my life isn't spent running myself ragged to do just that, while the woman I thought I would grow old with floats freely through life.

Perhaps reading my silence as the exercise in willpower that it is, Miranda sighs. "I didn't call you to fight. I have the dates I'll be in Brussels in two months. You'll still be there, right?"

"Yes," I admit, knowing where this is going. "But Zoe is

just getting settled into the routine here. I don't want you coming up. It confuses her."

"I have a right to visit my daughter."

"*Your* daughter?" I let out a harsh, humorless laugh. "What size shoes does she wear, Miranda? What's her favorite color? She's a child, not a play thing for you to set on a shelf and come back to when you happen to be in the area. You haven't visited for six months, and before that, it was eight. Why bother at all? Is it for you, or for her?"

When she doesn't respond immediately, I begin to wonder if perhaps I've *finally* made my point. It's a foolish hope, and one that's proven wrong when Miranda grits out. "I have visitation rights, and I'm choosing to use them. You know I come when I can, so unless you'd like to take me back to court and drain whatever is left of your savings, then you'll give me your address and a good time to visit. Whenever it is, I'll make it happen."

I pinch the bridge of my nose, struggling to think straight through the anger and frustration this conversation has caused. How could I have married this woman? Is my judgement so terrible that I thought Miranda Perkins was the love of my life? Swallowing back the shame, I speak words that sound so hollow, they echo through my mind after I've spoken them. "I'll email you a list of dates."

"Thank you." Miranda states with a sigh, obviously relieved she's gotten her way. I'm on the point of hanging up when she speaks again. "Ellis?"

God, I can't stand the sound of my name coming out of her mouth. "What?"

"She's doing well?" There's a hopeful, slightly strained plea in her voice that takes me off guard. It doesn't dispel the loathing I hold for my former wife, but it does take the edge off the fury I was gripped by only moments ago.

Miranda cares, just not enough.

I sink down on a bench beside the freshly tilled garden and stare down into the dark earth without really seeing it. In truth, I'm years away, replaying the coldest, most desolate moments of my short-lived marriage. "She's good. Enjoying the country life."

Miranda laughs. "I bet. Do you remember when she was a baby? We'd lay her on her stomach in the grass and she was so fascinated by it?"

I don't reply. Yes, I remember that. I also remember the fights, the pleading, the hurt, the lies and, ultimately, watching Miranda walk out the door for the last time. A family of my own was something I always wanted, but once I got it, the happy moments were a few scattered stars amidst an otherwise dark sky.

The reality that I'd married the wrong woman had set in not long after the wedding, but I thought if I worked hard enough, dedicated myself... the ring on my finger meant something to me and I've never felt like more of a failure than the day I signed the papers, admitting defeat.

"I'll send you the dates," I finally say, and don't wait for her reply before I end the call, dropping my head into my hands and forcing air into my unwilling lungs.

Being the bitter, angry ex-husband isn't something I want, but I can't seem to help myself. If Miranda had shouldered her share of parenting Zoe, likely I would have been free to be more than the stressed, harassed shell of a man I've become. Maybe I would have called the beautiful young woman who I met at a party and not been weighed down by the pressure to protect my daughter from being abandoned a second time.

As if I didn't have cause before, how can I not hate Miranda even more now, when her actions mean I can't have Josephine?

Drained of any peace I found outside, I get to my feet and make my way into the meadow, heading toward a patch of trees which conceals the stream winding through the estate. I've only been out here a few times, but I know it's become a favorite haunt of Jo and Zoe's.

Sure enough, when I get close, I hear giggles and splashing amidst gently gurgling water. A bit of the tension in my shoulders fades away as I pick my way through the trees, listening to my child's happiness.

I find them easily.

Zoe is in her bathing suit, waist deep in the gentle stream, wearing a floaty vest and goggles half the size of her face. Upstream, Jo is standing in the water, a mesh bag of rubber ducks in her hand. "Are you ready?" she calls down to Zoe, who nods enthusiastically. Jo releases the duck. It bobs and weaves slowly over the stream until it reaches Zoe, who dives for it, splashing around theatrically and squealing in delight when she emerges from the water. The duck is held triumphantly over her head.

"I got it!" she squeals, eyes bright and the tips of her hair dripping. "I got it! I got it!"

Jo, who must have spotted me when Zoe was in pursuit of the duck, catches my eye. "Have you come to join us?" she calls, her face transformed by effortless joy.

As if I could ever say no to that.

The volume of Zoe's excitement rises considerably when she sees me pulling off my shoes and rolling my pants up over my knees. As I step into the cool water, wading over the rocky stream floor toward Josephine, it's as though the current is taking away the negative emotions I arrived with. Or, more likely, it's the woman I'm moving towards, who is looking at me with something in her eyes I don't dare name.

She's wearing cutoff jean shorts and a little white cotton blouse today, with her dark curls braided back out of her face. We exchange a slight, secretive smile, and it's a struggle to look away when I reach her side.

"Do you think you can catch two?" I call to Zoe, and her eyes brighten at the challenge.

As it turns out, she can. Jo and I erupt into applause, and Zoe beams, obviously pleased with the attention for her efforts. "We've been doing this for over an hour," Jo tells me with an easy laugh as we watch Zoe dive for another set of ducks. "It's the simple things, I guess."

Yes. It is.

I swallow, keeping my eyes trained forward before I can do something foolish. "Are we on for tonight?" I ask quietly, unable to stop myself or even pretend to play it cool. We haven't had the chance to talk about what happened last night, but a heated look I received over breakfast seemed like sufficient confirmation she didn't regret it.

It wasn't even twenty-four hours ago that my head was between this woman's legs, and I can't wait to do it again. The noises she made... *merde*. I'm a changed man. If all she wanted was for me to make her come, I'd still count myself lucky.

"If you want to," Josephine replies quietly, and I glance over at her, my blood heating at the way her teeth have caught on her bottom lip. She stares determinately forward, as if she's just as worried as I am that she'll throw caution and reason to the wind, if not careful.

Emboldened, I move closer on the pretense of reaching into the bag of rubber ducks hanging off her arm. My hand drifts up the back of her leg, fingers brushing the soft skin of her inner thigh for a fraction of a second before I pull it away. My cock leaps at the sharp gasp above me. "I want to."

I straighten up, pretty goddamn smug at how flustered she looks.

This woman makes me happier and more relaxed than I have in a long time. Ever, maybe. Once, I rolled my eyes at older men who found a new lease on life in the arms of a younger woman, now here I am among them and I couldn't give less of a damn. The last weeks of being close to her have been nothing short of torture. All I could think about is touching her and now that I can, I intend to take full advantage of our arrangement.

If this is all I can have of her, I'll take it and be grateful.

"Papa! Jojo!" Zoe's indignant squawk firmly ends the moment, and we continue the duck releases for another thirty minutes, Jo eventually wading downstream to join Zoe in the deeper water.

In the past, it's taken me hours or even days to get past the frustration and negative emotions that come from speaking with my ex-wife. Today, though, as the three of us traipse through the meadow back to the magnificent old house, tired and happy, the fading afternoon sun warming the damp clothes on our backs, I couldn't possibly feel anything but happiness.

"I'll make dinner tonight," I tell Josephine, catching her at the bottom of the great stone staircase as Zoe moves out of view at the top.

Her eyebrows lift in surprise. "Do you cook?"

Have I truly not made her dinner yet? Glancing at the second floor landing to make sure Zoe hasn't come back into view, I draw closer, lifting my hand to play with the ribbon securing the end of her braid. Keeping our arrangement within the set time we discussed is already proving to be impossible, and we're not even twenty-four hours in. I forget myself so easily with her.

"I know I've mainly survived off freezer meals, but I am a Frenchman, Josephine. I do have some of the associated talents." They might be a little rusty, but I'm determined.

Warm hands settle on my chest. "Well, then," she murmurs, and we're standing so close her breath brushes against my neck. "*Excusez-moi monsieur.*"

I chuckle, wrapping my hand around the back of her neck

and lowering my lips to brush hers. "Your accent was very good. I'm impressed."

"You should be."

Fuck, I love it when she gets smart with me. I steal one last heated kiss and force myself to step back. It's almost worth it when I see her hand move to the banister, steadying herself.

I grin. "Send Zoe down to me. Why don't you work on the dress you've been making?"

A faint blush crawls over her cheeks, and her gaze drops to the floor. "It's not very good. I don't know what I'm doing. I was going to ask you to help me get the machine back in the attic."

Nudging her chin, I force her to meet my eyes. "It makes you happy, doesn't it? Who cares if you're not good at it? Why don't you let Zoe and I drive you into the next town over this weekend? There's a shop there that sells sewing things."

I'd looked it up a few days ago, when I saw Josephine hunched over the ancient machine in the living room, her nose scrunched up in frustration. Now, I'm glad I did, because the most adorable, pleased little smile has spread over her face and I find myself swelling with pride at being able to make her happy.

She's going to ruin me.

"Okay," Josephine agrees, still pink cheeked. "If you're sure."

We're still standing so close together, and the urge to kiss her is almost overwhelming. "I'm sure. In fact, I'm rather looking forward to it and will be quite insulted if you back out now."

She giggles, backing away. "I wouldn't dare."

"See that you don't." I don't move until she's vanished after Zoe.

It's only after she's gone and I've turned toward the kitchen that it occurs to me we've just broken one of the rules.

Fifteen

JOSEPHINE

"TELL ME ABOUT THE HOUSE."

I lean my hip against the kitchen doorframe, staring out at the rows of flowers and shrubbery in the garden, all casting long shadows in the dying, evening light.

Ellis is visible in the distance, strolling along the tree line with Zoe occasionally popping in and out of sight at his side, her head barely visible above the high grass. Fireflies sparkle around them like stars and my chest aches with how badly I want to be there too. We had just finished dinner and were about to head out on our usual walk when a call from my mother forced me to send them off without me.

I haven't been avoiding her exactly, but I've certainly pushed off any kind of in-depth conversations, using the time difference as a convenient excuse. I'm not angry with her over the fight we had when I dropped out of school. She apologized, and arranged me being here as a sign of contrition, but our relationship isn't the same as it was. Or, I'm not the same as I was.

"It's beautiful," I tell her honestly. "The nearest village is about a twenty minute walk. Zoe does better with school work when she can get some energy out early in the day, so first thing we usually walk to the market to get what we need for dinner. There's a garden and a stream where it's deep enough to swim in places. My room has a balcony. It's magical."

Not to mention the handsome, older librarian who eats my pussy like he'll die if I don't come.

Mom hums thoughtfully. "You sound very settled with them."

Them, not *there*. A word choice that brings on a surge of anxiety. I watch Zoe hopping up and down, pointing, and clearly intent on drawing Ellis's attention to whatever it is she's discovered.

I swallow. "She's a really sweet kid."

Mom doesn't acknowledge this. "And her father?"

Ah. There it is.

I press the heel of my palm into one eye, suppressing the urge to chuck my phone into the nearest bush. "Ellis has been very kind to me."

The memory of his pale eyes boring into mine as I rubbed myself all over his hard cock comes to mind. God—did I actually call him *daddy*? Whenever I thought about it today, which was often, I couldn't decide whether to be mortified or turned on.

Who am I kidding? I'm so turned on that I can't think straight.

"He seems to have made some very interesting discoveries in the library. Have you seen them?"

"A few." I drag my sandal over the stone threshold. "Whenever I go in there I'm so stressed that I'll knock something over and destroy a priceless literary treasure, I try to stay out of his way."

"For the best," she says approvingly. "He's a nice man. I'm very glad he has your help, Jo. You have such a big heart, though, and I don't want you to get... overly attached."

The veiled suggestion isn't difficult to pick up on. Mom is starting to wonder, a little too late, whether it was ill advised to send her daughter off to a foreign country with an older, handsome divorcee.

"Don't worry. I'm focusing on me," I assure her, hoping she doesn't pick up on the lie. In reality, it's been a relief to not think about myself so much, and to have people who need me for things.

In the distance, Zoe and Ellis emerge from the woods, holding hands.

Mom chatters on about Dad's newest fellow, some charity gala they've been roped into attending, the neighbor's dog barking early in the morning and the unseasonably hot weather. She asks a few more questions about the house, about Zoe—whom she seems to adore despite having never met—and pretends to be enthusiastic when I reveal I've been relearning how to sew.

I'm barely listening, and when she finally tells me she needs to jump on another call, it's a relief to say goodbye. With any luck, a talk this long will have bought me another few weeks without further questioning, and considering how I intend to spend the rest of my night, I really don't need her nosing around.

Crickets are chirping in the long grass, and the sticky heat has been replaced with cool evening air. While my first instinct is to walk outside to join Ellis and Zoe, my common sense makes an unexpected visit, and has me turning toward the grand staircase instead. There's still an hour to go until eight— the hour I've mentally dubbed *"sex o'clock"*—and I'm grateful for the time to get my head on straight.

Last night was intense, and mind blowing, and will probably ruin me for anyone else for a good long while. I need to remove my heart from my vagina and enjoy this for what it is;

incredible sex with a much older, hot, French librarian who wants me to call him daddy.

Not one woman in the world is feeling sorry for me right now.

Just for something to do other than analyze the situation for the nine thousandth time, I sit down at the sewing machine and by the time the sky has turned from blue to black outside, I think I've figured out why the seams of Zoe's dresses have been coming out all lumpy.

I'm at the point of taking a seam ripper to one of the failed skirts, when a gentle knock on the balcony door makes me jump. A moment later, it cracks open and Ellis steps inside. The dark, hungry look he gives me is enough to wipe away all thoughts of children's dress patterns.

"Hi," I breathe, setting the fabric aside and getting to my feet, something warm and heavy settling in my pelvis.

Ellis closes the door behind him, and the air seems so much stiller than it did before he arrived. "I got almost nothing done today." He murmurs, eyes roaming unapologetically over my body.

"I—" I stammer, staring at him questioningly as I try to figure out where he's going with this. "I'm sorry?"

His lips twitch. "You should be."

Reaching into his pocket, he pulls out a small cardboard box, tossing it onto the bed. My stomach flips when I realize what it is. The atmosphere between us feels charged, like lightning is about to strike nearby. I barely recognize myself as I succumb to the pull, taking the first step toward him.

This is my choice. Even if it's a mistake, or something I'll live to regret, I'm not just sitting on the sidelines, following the rules and living my life for other people. It's terrifying and exhilarating and as I get close enough to twine my arms around Ellis's neck, lifting my chin in silent offering, I think I'm becoming someone new.

He doesn't make me wait. I barely have time to gasp as Ellis leans forward to capture my lips with his, a hand pressed flat against my lower back to pull me close. We sway on the spot, kissing, and wetness floods my panties when he presses his erection into my stomach.

Drawing back, Ellis's hands find the hem of my shirt, dragging it up and away from my body. "I'll never get tired of looking at you." His voice is quiet but rough as he smooths both hands over my waist and up to cup my breasts through the thin cotton bra I'm wearing. Without a word, he pulls the material aside, exposing me.

"I like it when you do," I admit, trembling as his thumbs brush back and forth over my pebbled nipples, sending a current of need directly to my pussy.

My shorts and panties go next. Ellis kneels before me, kissing and licking the skin just above my mound as he drags them down over my hips. "I wanted to take my time tonight, but you had to be a little cock tease, didn't you? You had to make me hard half the goddamn day?" He mumbles into my skin, hands wandering back to my ass and giving it a little squeeze.

The muscles below my bellybutton tighten. "I'm sorry, Daddy." My voice breaks, and I squeak in surprise as he lifts one hand to give my ass a firm smack.

Ellis grunts in approval, doing it again. Apparently losing patience with our games, he rolls back to his feet, disposing of my bunched up bra within seconds. My fingers move to his chest, trying to get the buttons free as we kiss, and his hands work my hair free from it's braid.

I'm rapidly becoming addicted to the feeling of his skin against mine and I moan when I can finally push the cotton away, arching my back so my nipples brush the surprisingly soft hair scattered over his chest. I've only just reached for the button of his pants, when Ellis pulls away, his eyes glinting as he stares down at me.

"Get on the bed." His voice is strained. "Sit on the edge. Spread your legs."

I rush to do as he asked, almost stumbling as I sit on the side of the mattress. My thighs part, and my heart is pounding as Ellis's fingers undo the button and zip of his pants, letting them fall to the ground. His cock juts out, long and hard, and somehow way more intimidating than it was yesterday. Probably because sex was off the table then, whereas now...

He's going to fuck me. Probably hard.

A soft whimper breaks free from my lips as Ellis reaches over to grab the box of condoms, tearing the cardboard open without hesitation. The crinkle of the wrapper makes the muscles in my core flutter, and I watch as he brings it to his tip, rolling the material down without taking his eyes off my pussy. It should make me self-conscious, like he's inspecting me, but my legs fall open wider, offering him a better view.

I want him.

"That's it. That's my good girl. Keep those legs open nice and wide," he leans over me, bracing one hand on the mattress beside my head and gripping the base of his cock with the other.

He doesn't pause to see if I'm wet or get me ready. We're moving as one, perfectly in sync as my legs wrap around his waist and he settles his thick tip against my opening. I think he's going to push further, but he doesn't. Instead, Ellis leans forward until his lips brush the shell of my ear. "I want you to call me Daddy when I'm inside you. Do you understand?"

My word of agreement is lost in a strangled cry as he drives forward, burying himself in my unprepared pussy. It's a stretch, I still feel like he's too much, but the pain is less than it was the first time. "Daddy," I cry, my back bowing off the bed, trying to find more room for him.

I'm so full.

Ellis hums, taking one of my nipples in his mouth and sucking gently, giving me a moment to adjust. "You have the greediest little cunt, *mon amour.*" He switches to the other side, drawing the tight bud between his lips with a little more aggression than he used before. "I've been working my cock to it for weeks, thinking of all the things I'd like to do to it."

Without warning, he draws back, almost to the tip, and presses forward again, releasing a deep, masculine groan. "*Oh,*" I breathe, as pleasure begins to curl up my spine, my nails digging into his shoulders.

"We're going to go hard in a moment," he warns me, and the words send more wetness flooding over his shaft. "I'm going to put your legs up, just like this." He stands at the edge of the mattress, his cock still inside me, and lifts the back of my knees so the backs of my thighs are pressed against his stomach.

Experimentally, he leans forward, effectively bending me in half. "Ellis," I whisper, my voice breaking as he takes a few, shallow thrusts, hitting a deeper place than before.

The man inside me chuckles, his gaze burning as he looks down at me. "Arms around my neck, Josephine. That's it. You'll tell me if it's too much for you, yes?"

I nod, knowing full well it would take a lot for me to ask him to stop. The need to please him, to take whatever he gives me, to be *good* for him... "Yes, Daddy," I promise, and as I drag him down to kiss me Ellis groans, his tongue invading my mouth, consuming me with a ferocity that makes me dizzy. My unguarded sex clings to his as he pulls free and, just as quickly, drives back down.

He swallows my cry, and does it again, his tip bumping the deepest part of me. I can't move, or adjust, or even help, all I can do is lay still, letting him pound into me, using my pussy with a ruthless, unyielding pace.

"Good girl," Ellis growls against my lips, the room filling with the noise of him fucking me. "Jesus, you're so wet. You like this, don't you? Like driving me out of my mind with your hot little pussy?"

Holy hell, I do. I really do. It doesn't seem possible that I could come like this, but every thrust brings me closer to the edge, and I find myself begging him for more. "Daddy, please, fuck me harder," I cry, my nails biting into his back, hard enough to leave marks.

I hope they do.

Ellis must be thinking along the same lines, because he ducks down, sucking on the skin below my ear, leaving marks that anyone would be able to see. He's claiming me.

I explode, coming with a scream that Ellis muffles with his hand. He doesn't stop fucking me, doesn't slow or let up even for a second. If anything, his relentless pace grows faster, harder, more aggressive. "Someday, I'm going to take your ass this way. You're going to beg me to, mark my words."

Shaking, sore and half out of my mind with what he's doing to me, I nod. "I want you to, I want it everywhere—"

"I know. I know you do, *mon amour*. You're such a good girl for me, so tight and wet and willing." His pace stutters. "*Dammit*, I'm close. Hold still and let me fill you."

Seconds later, Ellis's forehead drops to my shoulder and his pace finally becomes uneven and shallow. I hear myself moan as he presses deep, his entire body shaking with how hard he's coming. It goes on for so long, as this older, more experienced man is overcome by the pleasure he took from me.

After an age, Ellis lifts his head and kisses me so deeply it makes my heart lurch.

Oh, god.

"*Mon amour*," he groans weakly, letting my legs slip back to his sides. "You're incredible."

I wince as he pulls back, dragging his softened cock from

my tender sex. "Stay there," he orders me, and chucks the condom in the little trash can beside the desk, striding naked into the bathroom.

As I watch him go, my face splits into a smile, and I scoot backward onto the bed, giggling to myself.

"What's so funny?" Ellis asks, grinning as he reemerges from the bathroom a few seconds later, a wet cloth in his hand.

"Not funny," I admit, sighing as he sits beside me and cleans away the mess I made, looking relaxed. "Just checking out your butt. I haven't had such a good view before."

Ellis snorts. "I'll admit, I haven't thought much about the pros and cons of my butt. It's been largely utilitarian until this moment." He tosses the cloth toward the laundry basket and follows me onto the mattress, kissing my shoulder.

It's strange, going from wild, rough sex to giggling and flirting within a few minutes, but I love it. "It's a very good butt," I assure him, humming happily as he lifts his arm, clearly indicating he wants me to curl into his side. "Bubb-licious."

He's still for a moment, clearly processing this. "Did you just say *bubblicious*?"

The word sounds even more ridiculous spoken with his accent and I break out into peels of giggles. Ellis exclaims over them, telling me why it is absolutely not a real word, and proposing adjectives he thinks more appropriate.

That night, we don't have sex again, but he doesn't leave my room until one.

Sixteen

ELLIS

> Mari,
>
> It's rained all week, and I feel myself becoming gloomy as winter gets nearer. Sometimes, I think of trying to meet someone, that having company might be nice. I'm not sure it would be fair to anyone.
>
> Are you happy? I hope someone is.
>
> Your Luc

I STARE DOWN at the slip of paper, written in the same craggy, uneven handwriting as I've seen on the others. By now, I have quite the collection going. A box sits beside my makeshift-desk in the center of the library, almost overflowing with scrawled missives from the former owner of these books to some unknown woman.

Josephine came in a few days ago to retrieve an escaped Zoe, and ended up sitting cross-legged on the floor for nearly twenty minutes, reading one after another. We talked about it later, when we lay tangled together on her bed, her cheek resting on my bare chest.

"I think he loved her, and she died. This must have been his way of grieving."

My opinion wasn't so concrete. *"It doesn't explain why they're all second editions."* I pointed out, but the discussion was forgotten as Josephine's hand drifted to my cock.

This note is the first to confirm that the intended recipient isn't—or wasn't at the time—dead. Still, it reveals none of Perdue's motives, and I find myself unable to shake the curiosity. The books themselves leave more than enough mystery to be concerning myself with, and yet these little missives are what keep me up at night wondering.

That is, when I'm not being kept up by Josephine Sutton.

In the weeks since our *collision* in the foyer, I've fucked her every night, sometimes twice. If I expected that having sex regularly for the first time in half a decade would more than satisfy me, I was mistaken. Every time we're together, every new memory of her hands on me and mine on her only makes me greedier for more.

With a speed that is more than a little alarming, it's become clear there is nothing casual about this so-called arrangement. It's a special kind of nightly torture when I'm forced to pull away from her, put my clothes back on and return to my cold, empty bed. Though it's nothing compared to the times when I catch a glimpse of the hurt she doesn't want me to see.

Our relationship now defies every instinct I have where she is concerned. It isn't right, and yet, there isn't a choice. *I can't keep her*, but reminding myself doesn't help. If my connection with Josephine could be reasoned away, we wouldn't be in this position to begin with. I'm a man obsessed, not just with her, but with the way she makes me feel.

In the wake of my divorce, I was too busy adjusting to the reality of becoming a single parent to recover from the emotional effects of Miranda's betrayal. How is it that I never noticed my low opinion of myself until Josephine made me feel good again?

The thought of my lover has my attention straying far from the task at hand. For a moment, my fingers only hover above my laptop's keyboard as I stare blindly into the screen, trying to return my concentration to the reason we're here at all—*my job*. It's Saturday, but I wanted to get some extra work in while Zoe was occupied with a puzzle.

Just as I've regained some semblance of productivity, however, there's a knock on the library door.

My heart lifts when I see who it is.

"I'm sorry to bother you," Josephine says gently, not moving further into the room. Her dark curls are braided back today as usual, but instead of her usual uniform of shorts and t-shirts, she's wearing a dress I've never seen before. I'm positive I would remember it.

"You're never bothering me. I'm not even supposed to be working today," I assure her, eyeing the white cotton without bothering to disguise my approval. I crook my finger and feel myself smirk. "Come here."

Her lips curve too as she moves closer, stopping beside me and leaning her hip against the table. I consciously have to stop myself from reaching out to touch the curve of her waist. God knows we don't always follow the rules, but Zoe could be anywhere right now. I need to keep my hands to myself.

"You look very beautiful today," I observe, my voice throaty. "I haven't seen you in this before."

She fiddles with one of the straps self-consciously. "Oh. Well, I just finished it this morning, so—"

"*You made this?*"

Nodding shyly, she pushes off the table, turning to give me

the full effect. The garment is simple but looks professionally made, and I'm stunned that it was sewn by the same woman who was asking me to put the ancient machine back in the attic only a few weeks ago.

There's a lump in my throat and a burning in my chest. It's always difficult maintaining the boundaries we set, but at moments like this, or when I see her adoration of Zoe, it's damned near impossible. How could any man on Earth not fall for this woman? She's incredible.

"It was pretty easy. I just followed the pattern I got online. What do you think?" Josephine questions, and there's a vulnerability in her voice that needs to be put to rest immediately.

I reach out to take her hand, and she allows herself to be pulled forward, stopping between my legs. This time, I don't hold myself back from touching her the way my body demands. I feel rather than hear her breath catch as my hands settle on her waist, feeling the familiar curves of her body through the cotton. "*Je ne me suis jamais senti comme ça avant.*" *

She touches my shoulders, a little line forming between her eyebrows as she gazes down at me. "What does that mean?"

I swallow. "It means you're stunning, and I can't believe how good you've gotten with that machine."

Josephine smiles in thanks, but there's something in her eyes that says my lie wasn't quite as believable as I'd like it to be. She draws away, and my hands fall back to my lap. "I just wanted to see if it was okay if I took the car today. It's in your name and everything, so I think you'd need to call the rental company to get me added to the insurance or whatever. If it's extra money, I can pay for it."

---

* I've never felt like this before.

"You're already on the car insurance, I had you added at the airport," I reply, surprised she didn't know. "And of course you can take it. Where—*ah*—do you have plans?"

What does it say about me that I don't want her off on her own? I'm not a controlling man. Nothing would make me happier than for her to have these new experiences, to see my home country and fall in love with this life she's forged for herself.

I just want to be at her side when she does.

"No plans." She draws her finger along the edge of the table. "I just wanted to do some shopping. Trying to change it up a little and since it takes me about two weeks to make a single dress..." She smiles wryly.

Throwing caution to the wind, I pull her into my lap, dragging her lips to mine before she even has time to gasp. My tongue darts out, parting her lips, and licking away the taste of the strawberries she must have just been eating. She tastes like summer and sin and *mine*. It's been less than twelve hours since the last time I was inside her, but I'm starving as if it's been weeks.

"What was that for?" Josephine asks breathlessly when our kiss ends, pupils wide and lips parted.

I tuck a stray curl behind her ear. "Let me take you shopping."

Josephine makes a noise of protest, but I silence it with another deep, searching kiss, keeping my hearing strained for the telltale sounds of Zoe approaching.

When we break apart again, she's frowning. "Do most fathers take their child's nanny shopping?" There's a disapproving, haughty quality to her voice that makes me grin.

"No, but men do their lovers." Another kiss, and, clearly against her own will, she melts into me. I'm determined to win this one. Maybe it's old-fashioned, but I like the idea of her wearing things I've bought her, and love the idea of spoiling this hardworking woman.

Jo goes above and beyond for Zoe and me every single day. She deserves to have everything she's ever wanted, and I'll make sure she does. Even if it means dragging her from store to store and buying women's clothing at random until she relents.

Then, because I still haven't gotten a response, my smile slips. "Unless you'd rather go on your own, of course."

Josephine is shaking her head before I've finished the sentence. "I'd love company, but I can buy my own clothes, Ellis!"

I hum, pretending to take this seriously. "We'll see."

The three of us are in the car thirty minutes later, driving past the village and out toward the small city a few kilometers south. Zoe is settled in her booster seat, brow furrowed and noise canceling headphones in place as she takes in the scenery.

"She's talking more than I've ever heard," I admit under my breath, heart full to bursting, when I peer in the rearview mirror and meet Zoe's bright gaze. She sticks her tongue out at me. I stick mine out back. Turning my attention back to the road, it takes an inordinate amount of concentration to keep myself from reaching out and taking the hand of the woman beside me. "I can't thank you enough. You're incredible with her."

Jo laughs. "You say that like it's some kind of burden for me. I love spending time with honey girl. I think I tell you how awesome she is at least once a day." She casts a fond look over her shoulder toward my daughter, who is now absorbed in attacking a coloring book with a neon pink marker. Then, "Have you noticed that you only call me Jo when in reference to Zoe?" she asks curiously. "But when it's just us, you call me Josephine?"

I hadn't realized I was doing that, but now that I think

about it, she's not wrong. "I suppose it's my way of keeping it separate," I muse, staring straight ahead. "Things are a bit... *muddled*."

Muddled is an understatement, but in the corner of my eye, I see Josephine nodding in silent understanding.

We don't speak for the rest of the drive, apart from idle commentary on the beautiful scenery flashing by outside the windows. Coming here means so much more to me than I thought it would. The last time I did, it was to visit my mother shortly after the divorce and I was too busy spiraling to enjoy it.

Now, it's good again. The chateau has been a dream, but it's more than that. The countryside, the slower, more family focused way of life, the wine—*God, I missed the wine*. This is my home, and if it weren't for getting my dream job, I'm positive I wouldn't have lasted so long in Connecticut.

The nearest city to us, *Moulins*, is crowded with visitors for the weekly street market. Zoe and Jo stare out the windows with round eyes, pointing out fountains, churches and other landmarks as we pass. Zoe snatches both of our hands the moment we're out of the car, squealing with delight when Jo and I lift her off her feet over and over again.

The three of us eat lunch beneath a striped awning at a little cafe, our chairs rocking over the cobblestones as we listen to a man playing a bright green piano across the square. Zoe, miraculously, doesn't throw a fit over her grilled cheese sandwich coming with white cheese instead of yellow and Josephine gives me a warning look when I lift my thumb to wipe a little spot of cream from above her lip.

I give her one right back when she offers to pay for her own meal.

Afterward, we stumble across a collection of women's clothing boutiques. Zoe has limited patience for watching Jo peruse racks of dresses, so I slip my credit card to the amused salesman before taking her across the street to watch fudge being made in a shop window.

There isn't a doubt in my mind that if Josephine knew I was paying, I'd be lucky if she allowed me to buy her a single pair of socks. It's gratifying when she emerges onto the street twenty minutes later with a sour expression and two full bags in her hands.

"I believe this is yours." She slaps the card down into my palm, glowering me. "Ellis, this is too much. You need to take it out of my pay."

God, do I want to kiss her.

Pleased with my underhanded victory, I scoff. "No."

She's adorable when she's flustered. "I spent like... a lot of money!"

"Good!" It's only catching sight of Zoe's curious expression that makes me step back from Josephine, clearing my throat. "Where next?"

We spend the next few hours wandering the city in search of more Zoe-friendly entertainment. The onslaught of new stimulation and walking begins getting to her just before dinner, and she rides on my shoulders back to the car. We've barely gotten on the road again before a quick glance in the rear-view mirror confirms she's passed out.

"Too much fun," Josephine giggles under her breath, reaching into a bag at her feet and producing a box of macaroons. She selects an almond one and hands it over to me, already knowing full well it's the one I'd pick myself.

I take a bite, filled with an unbridled, full body happiness that has nothing to do with the sugary treat melting over my tongue. "Did you have a good day?"

Josephine curls her legs up beside her and leans over the center console, resting her head on my shoulder. Her fingertips drift over the swell of my bicep. "I had a perfect day."

Emotion clogs my throat, and I reach across my chest to

catch her hand, dragging it up to kiss the delicate, translucent skin on the underside of her wrist.

As we drive, it occurs to me that from the beginning, I've been looking for reasons I shouldn't fall for this woman. How did it escape my notice that there were so many more reasons I should?

Seventeen

JOSEPHINE

"THE APPRAISAL TEAM will be here at nine," Ellis informs me, pressing a kiss to the top of Zoe's head as he moves past her to his usual chair at the end of the scrubbed wood table.

He looks very professional. Most days, when it's just the three of us at the chateau, Ellis can be found in jeans and t-shirts, or even shorts if it's particularly hot out. Today, he looks like the head of Montgomery Library I met back in Connecticut.

What is it about this man's forearms, when paired with rolled-up sleeves, that make me *weak*?

"Would it be a good morning for us to go into the village?" I ask, because no matter how hard I try to keep an eye on her, if Zoe wants her Papa, she will find a way to sneak off. On an ordinary day it's no big deal, but today, I can sense Ellis wants to be an expert in his field, not the doting father of a slightly clingy six-year-old.

The grateful look I get to this makes me laugh. "What do you say, honey girl?" I ask, turning my attention to the little girl beside me. "Should we take a walk into the village and play at the playground for a few hours? We can bring a picnic and do our lessons on the blanket."

Taking a walk, eating outside, and going to the playground are three of Zoe's favorite things. The wide-eyed look of excitement I get is perfectly predictable, and I smile as she flees in the direction of the stairs, undoubtedly going to select her stuffed animal companions for the day. Lately it's been Ducky Number One, Ducky Number Two and Kitty, but Ducky Number One has been on his way out, frequently replaced by Unicorn Number Three.

Zoe's taste in names leaves something to be desired.

"Thank you," Ellis says as her footsteps echo off, helping himself to some of the cut fruit I took out. "I wish I could tell you how long it will take. They're driving all the way from Paris for this, so I suspect they'll want to make a thing out of it."

"How many books are they appraising?"

He sighs. "There are twenty-four I want looked at. Two of which I can't get any information on at all."

My jaw goes slack. "*Twenty-Four?*"

"Twenty-four," he confirms gravely, stabbing his fork at a piece of sausage on his plate. "And god knows what else I'll find before the end of this. Perdue was mad. The man was using a complete set of Sherlock Holmes books, *signed* mind you, as a stand for a potted plant."

"Must have been some plant." I pop a raspberry into my mouth, biting back a smile at Ellis's obvious annoyance with the former owner of the chateau. If Perdue wasn't dead, he would be getting an earful from Weston University's rare book expert.

Pale blue eyes track my every movement as I bring another berry to my lips, fork suspended halfway between his plate and mouth. "I have plans for us later," Ellis tells me, and through his deceptively nonchalant, casual tone, I can detect a dangerous edge.

I bite my lip, my pulse suddenly racing as heat spreads between my thighs. Only a minute ago, the atmosphere in the kitchen was lazy and casual. Now... "Oh?"

Beneath the table, a familiar, large hand finds my thigh, inching higher to the edge of my panties. Ellis leans closer, "You—" His words falter at the sound of the ancient brass bell that hangs beside the front door. "Damn." Ellis shoots me an apologetic look. "They're early."

The hand on my leg vanishes as he gets to his feet, straightening the collar of his shirt.

Biting my lip to keep myself from smiling, I stand too, and do up the button he missed when he dressed this morning.

"Thank you," he murmurs, lowering his lips to my cheek, lingering for just long enough to make my breath catch.

"Good luck," I whisper back, not sure why we're keeping our voices down, but enjoying the cozy sense of companionship. As much as I'd like to avoid it, the truth is that our relationship feels different now. The rules are beginning to seem more like light suggestions that Ellis challenges at every opportunity, and I can sense we've crossed the point of no return.

There is nothing small about the feelings I have for him, and the question is whether I should try to distance myself now or stay the course and hope for the best. I know it's a bad idea, and that there are about a million red flags here, but in my heart, I know I'm not going anywhere.

My sense of self-preservation leaves a lot to be desired.

Zoe comes back into the kitchen through one door just as Ellis vanishes out the other. I point to her abandoned breakfast, clearing my throat significantly, and turn toward to the pantry to begin packing snacks and a lunch for our morning out.

"Papa has an important day today," I call to Zoe as I collect a selection of the limited foods she will consume without a meltdown. "Should we bring him a treat from the *patisserie* for all his hard work?"

I've said the magic words. Zoe nods eagerly, bouncing up and down in her seat. "One for me?"

"Well, I think we're owed a tip for delivery, don't you?" I open my mouth to say something else, but stop short, listening to the sound of raised voices from the foyer. Soon, they're moving toward us, and most definitely do not sound like a bunch of rare book experts.

"—can't just turn up. I have people coming to the house at any moment. I have a job to do."

"Oh, we speak English now?" comes a heavily accented woman's voice, dripping in sarcasm. "I don't need you to entertain me, Ellis. By all means, go do your job. I'm here for Zoe. She's much better company than you."

My mouth snaps shut just in time for Ellis to round the corner, looking flustered and followed closely by a round-faced older woman with iron colored hair and a bag thrown over her shoulder.

"*Grandmaman!*" Zoe squeals, throwing herself off her chair and toward the woman who can only be Ellis's mother.

"*Bonjour, ma petite fille**," coos Madame Delvaux, crouching down to hug Zoe. "I've brought you all the presents Papa didn't let Santa Claus deliver for Christmas."

Ellis drags a hand over his face. "*Maman*—"

"Don't you *Maman*, me." She gets back to her feet, and despite her being at least a foot shorter than him, he cowers. "You've been raising my granddaughter all the way in the States, and you come here then tell me to *wait*? Whatever for? Have I been such a terrible mother that you see fit to punish me?"

---

* Hello, my little girl,

Without waiting for an answer to her furious inquiries, Madame Delvaux begins riffling around in the overstuffed tote bag on her arm and produces what looks like a full gallon of bright pink, sparkly slime.

I wince. *God, lady. Think of the carpets.*

Zoe yips in delight, diving for the container, and over his mother's shoulder, Ellis points at the face of his watch, giving me a pleading look.

I step forward, putting on my brightest *university president's daughter* smile. "Hello, Madame Delvaux. I'm Jo Sutton, Zoe's nanny."

She turns, looks me up and down, and finally rounds on Ellis. "She's pretty."

"*Ah.*" He coughs, looking anywhere but at the three women in the room. "Yes?"

I'd be insulted by the reticence if he hadn't spent the better part of an hour with his head between my legs last night. The man is borderline obsessed with going down on me, which certainly suggests a certain degree of attraction.

Madame Delvaux huffs, her look of annoyance a mirror image of Ellis's, but doesn't comment further. She turns back to me, eyes narrowed. "If my son is too busy and important for me, perhaps you have time to show me around, Miss. Sutton."

"Of course! And Jo is fine." I begin gathering up the breakfast plates as his mother sits beside Zoe to help her open the tub of slime.

Ellis hastens to help, and as we stand side by side at the sink, he gives me a significant look. "Is it becoming clear why I moved three thousand miles away?" he asks in a low mutter, and I can't help but giggle.

"She is a little terrifying," I concede, glancing at the pair out of the corner of my eye.

The six-foot-something man beside me winces. "I'm so

sorry to leave you with this, *mon amour*. If it was any other day—"

The doorbell rings again, and his shoulders drop. "Don't worry. We'll be fine," I assure him and, with a quick glance over to make sure that nobody is paying attention, reach out to give his hand a quick squeeze. "You'll do great, Ellis. They'll be trying to poach you from Weston by the end of the day."

The soft, thankful look I get in response makes me wish desperately for eight o'clock, when we can be alone. There's hours to go, though, and when we turn back to Madame Delvaux and Zoe, the older woman is observing us a little too intently.

Crapping crapsicles.

"*Maman*, I will come find you when my meetings have finished," Ellis promises, already heading toward the door.

"Yes, yes." She watches him go before her sharp gaze lands on me. "Jo, you said?"

I nod. "*Oui**, *Madame Delvaux*."

"Maude will do, I think." She heaves herself out of her chair. "Come, Zoe. *Grandmaman* has been in the car all morning, and I'd like to stretch my legs."

Ellis's mother doesn't say much as we show her the garden. The peas and a few onions that we planted when we first arrived are the only thing I've been able to save from the rabbits, but she makes a good show of tasting one and complimenting Zoe on all her hard work.

Zoe's main contribution has been dumping out a miniature watering can about once a week, but her proud, toothy smile makes me more than happy to give her the credit for this one.

"How long will you be staying with them?" Maude asks as we cross the garden wall into the field beyond the chateau.

---

* Yes

I pause as she turns back to the magnificent old house. "Until the end. Ellis thinks it will take a few months longer than the university originally budgeted for, but the books are worth so much that nobody is complaining."

Except my mother, but even she wouldn't pressure one of her highly educated, qualified staff members to complete his work faster so she can shove her daughter back through the door of a physics classroom.

It won't make Elizabeth Sutton happy, but the unsubstantial future I saw when I first arrived here is growing more clear by the day. If nothing else, my time here has taught me I'm not cut out for academia. I'm sure I have the ability, but I'm equally sure it would eat my soul away piece by piece until there was nothing left. What I do like, the thing that makes me look forward to getting up every morning, is working through Zoe's lesson plans with her and finding creative ways to make the dry topics more interesting.

Zoe breaks away from us as we move further from the chateau, and I'm just trying to think of a benign small talk topic when Maude brutally ends the silence.

"So, how long have you been sleeping with my son?"

The noise I make in response is somewhere between a yelp and a choke. If Maude suspected something was going on before this, I might as well have just confirmed it. Still, I can't just tell her—"Oh, I'm just the nanny!" I squeak.

Maude's withering look confirms this isn't believable in the slightest. "Don't lie to me, dear. You're dreadful at it." Fair enough. My face is burning as I grapple to find the right words, unsure if I'm about to be threatened to leave Ellis alone or shoved into a wedding dress. Maude sighs. "He's a grown man, I've no business meddling in his love life. What I am concerned with is ensuring you're not like *the other one*."

Oh. "His ex-wife?"

Maude scoffs, making her distaste clear. "Who else?"

I lift my shoulder helplessly, because I don't want to admit it, but Ellis has only mentioned Zoe's mother in passing. She's alive, I know that much, but nothing about the circumstances which led her to leave her husband and daughter.

"He doesn't talk about it much," I admit, filled with the familiar sinking sensation that always comes after I've let my feelings run away with themselves a little too much, when I catch myself hoping and then get slapped with a reminder of why I shouldn't. Things might *feel* different, but are they really? Ellis has never opened up to me, or really let me in. Have I completely misread things between us?

My heart is in my shoes as Maude carries on, waving her hand dismissively. "That man." She shoots me a severe, side-long look. "You mustn't let him get away with it, Jo."

"We're not together," I blurt out, horrified that I have to admit this to Ellis's mother, of all people. "Not romantically. It's more, um, you know—"

"Carnal?" suggests Maude, ignoring my stammering. "I'm a sixty-five-year-old mother, Jo. There's little you can say that would shock me."

I believe her. "Is he your only child?" I have never heard Ellis mention any family members apart from Maude and his late father.

"He is. We had difficulties getting pregnant, or rather, staying pregnant." I turn to look at her, and the pain in Maude's face is horrible.

"I'm so sorry."

She waves me off, her expression softening. "By the time Ellis came along, we'd given up. He was worth the wait, though. While the other mothers were chasing their sons all over the county, getting calls from teachers and angry fathers, my Ellis was reading his books and focused on his studies."

Maude loops her hand through my arm, and high grass

brushes our elbows as Zoe clambers onto her favorite stretch of rock wall. We stop to watch her balance along it, nose wrinkled in concentration.

My heart squeezes with fondness as she jumps off the end, stumbling a little but popping back up in seconds. "Jojo! *Grandmaman!*" she calls, pointing to the patch of forest that conceals our little stream.

I nod, forcing myself to smile, and she darts off toward the trees. Maude and I follow as she continues her story. "My husband was sick for a long time before he passed, but it still hit Ellis hard. He was only fifteen at the time. He craved the big, loud family, the kind of love my husband and I shared. You can't rush these things, though, and when you do, you pay the price."

My eyes burn, and emotion clogs my throat, imagining a teenage Ellis shouldering that kind of grief. "He doesn't talk about his father, either."

Maude stares ahead of us, unsmiling. "I guessed as much. He's always been that way. Terribly noble. Convinced he has to carry his burdens and everyone else's."

The last of the long meadow grass tickles my legs as we follow Zoe over the tree line. Sunlight is streaming through the canopy of trees, sending shoots of light onto the clear forest floor.

Maude doesn't elaborate, and I fall silent, trying to ignore the hundred or so questions I have for her. There's only one that I can't hold back. "How did you know?" I ask. "That we're involved? You only saw us together for a few minutes."

"A few minutes is all it takes, dear. Seconds would have been sufficient. Some things can't be hidden, though my son certainly tries."

"What things?" I press, unable to help myself.

The older woman pats my hand. "Ellis is very like his

father, you know. The spitting image. I haven't seen it for twenty years now, but his expression when he looked at you was just the same as my Philip's when he looked at me."

Eighteen

ELLIS

THE LITTLE IMP is asking for it tonight.

She had to know I was coming. Josephine isn't one to lose track of time, and apart from a few incidents when Zoe was particularly difficult at bedtime, I've been in her room at 8:00 every single night for over a month now. Generally, I'm inside her by 8:05.

Which means that tonight, when I arrive to find a trail of clothes leading to the dimly lit bathroom, and the sound of the shower running, I'm sure it's not accidental. Prowling forward, my cock is already half hard as I pause in the doorway, enjoying the sight before me.

Josephine is standing beneath the spray of water, her head tilted back as she rinses shampoo from her hair. The bubbles flow freely down her body, forming rivers between her breasts and over her ass. I watch, reaching down to squeeze my erection through my pants.

The days have felt endless lately, and even juggling my dream job, spending time with Zoe and contemplating the mystery of Monsieur Perdue's notes, isn't enough to distract me from counting down the hours until she's in my arms again.

The unspoken rule that the limited block of time was to be used for the sole purpose of getting the sexual frustration out of our systems, has been dismissed. While there are certainly more nights than not spent doing just that, there are also times when we watch movies or read side by side, sometimes cuddling and talking. It feels as though I'm in a relationship that exists only between the hours of eight and twelve, and every day, it's getting harder to keep it that way.

Tonight, though, my only plans are to make the little tease scream.

She knows I'm here, and she's putting on a show for me. I watch, rapt, as she trails her fingertips over her breasts, tummy and mound. Leaning back against the wall, she rocks her hips into her own touch as a quiet moan echoes off the tile. Patience nowhere to be found, I reach for the hem of my t-shirt.

I've had enough.

It only takes a few seconds for everything I'm wearing to hit the floor and Josephine's lips curve into a pleased little smirk as I step under the water, watching her fingers circle her clit.

"What were you thinking about?" I brace my forearm on the wall above her head and reach down, my free hand covering hers, guiding the pace.

Josephine sighs, tilting her chin up, my cue to kiss her senseless. Instead, I lean forward, dragging my nose over the patch of skin I've developed a fondness for marking. Her body is covered in love bites, all the shape of my mouth and ranging from deep purple to pale yellow.

Between us, my hand slows hers to a sensual, slow pace. There's a frustrated little noise from above my head, making me smile into her skin. "I was thinking about you," she admits, and if I wasn't so close to her, the words would have been lost in the spraying water.

Good, but not enough. "What was I doing to you?"

She moans. "Daddy, *please*—"

I get so hard when she calls me that. It taps into the same depraved, possessive side she so often awakens in me. I guide her hand lower. She thinks I'm making her fuck her own pussy, but my fingers join hers, stretching her more than she expected. Josephine's sharp gasp of surprise goes right to my cock.

I lift my lips from her neck to swallow her cry as her inner walls clutch at the combined intrusion of my fingers and hers. "There you go," I murmur against her lips, setting a slow, teasing rhythm. "Does that feel good, sweetheart? This is what you needed, isn't it?"

"Yes," she whines, hitching her leg higher over my hip, trying to make room for more. "Ellis—*oh god*—Daddy, please fuck me."

"Not yet." I nip at her bottom lip and soothe the hurt with my tongue. "I want to know your fantasy."

I'm positive that if we weren't in this position, her face would have gone that adorable shade of pink it does when she's shocked. Right now, she's too worked up, too absorbed in what we're doing to get self-conscious. "I was thinking." Her voice breaks into a sob as I increase the pace of fingering her, eyes going wide. Judging by how her walls are fluttering and clutching over the intrusion, she's already close. "I was thinking about sucking you off."

"Yeah?" I grit out, and between her spread thighs comes the rapid slapping of wet flesh as I work her hand harder. This entire situation is impossibly erotic, and if she wraps her mouth around my cock, I'm going to blow in seconds.

Damn me, I have to make this last, and to that end...

Josephine cries out in protest when I pull back, but it

morphs into a gasp when my hands wrap around the back of her thighs, lifting her and holding her open, pinned to the shower wall by my body.

"Put me in." She does as I say, panting as she grips the base of my cock and guides my tip to fit against her slick, pink entrance.

I ease forward until I'm balls deep. "Such a tight pussy," I growl the vulgar words, enjoying the way her cunt clutches at me as I say them. Pulling back, I drive forward again in a vicious, hard thrust that sends her up the wall and tears a broken sob from her lips.

"You're not wearing a condom," she reminds me, hands buried in my hair as I find a deep, grinding rhythm.

Damn, I'm not. We've been terrible about that lately, but I've thankfully had the presence of mind to pull out. "You're making me lose my mind," I mutter and lean forward to claim her lips with my own, kissing her until she comes, then letting her drop to her knees, fucking her mouth for all of thirty seconds before I explode down the back of her throat.

I'm distracted as we get out and dry off, unable to shake the feeling that something ominous is approaching.

It's not a mystery why.

Nothing has changed, and yet, everything is different.

The pressure seems to be growing every day to make a decision, to commit to her or let her go, to find a way to keep my heart out of this mess while knowing it's too late. She has me, and I don't know how to get free, or if I even want to.

* * *

"You're not as discreet as you think you are."

I pause, a plate suspended beneath the flow of water from the sink. My mother takes it deftly from my hands, to wipe it with the dry cloth in her hands. She's been here for two days now, and other than a few pointed remarks over whether I was going to help Josephine into her chair at dinner or whether I knew when her birthday was, the meddling old crone has kept her opinions to herself.

Thirty-six years of experience with my mother have taught me always to expect the unexpected, however, and I had a feeling her silence wouldn't last.

Jo and Zoe are in the back garden, picking berries from the patch of gnarled old raspberry bushes. I can just make them out through the kitchen window, and regretfully, I tear my eyes away to give my mother a tired, dismissive look. It won't throw her off the scent, but I do have some pride. "You're seeing things."

Maude sighs, tossing her towel onto the counter and crossing to one of the kitchen chairs. "Is that what you're going with, dear son? That I'm losing my marbles? I thought you were more clever than that." She looks amused as she lowers herself into her seat. "Let's drop the pretense, shall we? Your *nanny* already fessed up."

I groan. If my mother had arrived with some notice, I'd have been able to prepare Josephine, but instead she was thrown to the meddling, nosy wolf with no warning at all. "What did you say to her, *maman*?"

"Nothing you shouldn't have said to her yourself."

Irritated, but not surprised, I shake my head. "Good god. Is it any wonder I'm already gray?"

This statement is met with an impatient *tutting*. "It certainly hasn't hindered you in finding a *twenty-two-year-old* girlfriend. I'd give you far more grief for that if I didn't like her so much."

Despite myself, I lean against the counter to look at her directly. "You like her?"

"I just said that, didn't I?" Maude waves off my answering noise of impatience with a laugh. "Oh, don't get your underpants in a twist. Of course I like her. She's lovely. Far too good for you, of course, but if she's willing to settle, I'll accept the wonderful daughter-in-law without complaint."

My gaze falls to the floor as her words fill me with something hot and bitter. "She won't be your daughter-in-law."

"Why not?"

"You *know* why not."

Looking satisfied she's gotten a rise out of me, my mother leans back in her chair, fixing me with a severe, unimpressed look. It's the same one I got when I was ten years old and she caught me skipping school to read under a tree, or when I was considering turning down my scholarship to Weston to stay close to her. "May I give you a piece of advice, Ellis?" She purses her lips.

"You will whether I want it or not, so I don't see why my response to that matters."

She continues on as if I haven't spoken at all. "Don't push the right woman away because you once chose the wrong one. You're giving Miranda far more power than she deserves."

Ice slides down my spine. "It has nothing to do with me. Or Miranda for that matter," I bite back, furious. "My feelings aren't the only thing to consider here. There are other factors. Seeing her publicly could cost me my job, and I can't put Zoe in the position to be abandoned again. Like it or not, I need to protect her."

"Protect her, or protect yourself?" I hiss in protest, and she scoffs. "Oh stop, Ellis. You've always been the same. So stubbornly noble. Sometimes, keeping one's word does more harm than good, my dear. Your dear ex-wife proved that."

"I don't want to discuss this with you anymore. It's absolutely none of your business."

Maude looks as though she's prepared to ignore this too, but turns her attention to be the back door as it opens, Jo and Zoe reentering the kitchen.

"Look, Papa!" Zoe gloats, thrusting a heaping basket of berries into my hands.

"We'll have to freeze them or something," Josephine muses aloud, crossing to wash her hands in the sink beside me. "There's no way we can eat them all before they go bad. Maude, you'll have to take some home with you, too."

My mother pulls Zoe into her lap, kissing her cheek fondly. "Oh, I'll never say no to that. I know how to appreciate a gift when I see one." She gives me a challenging look.

I ignore her, turning my attention to my daughter. "Come on, Zo. Bath time."

"I can do it, if you want," Jo offers as she turns off the sink, taking the towel I offer her with a gentle smile of thanks. It's only for a fraction of a second, but my heart still flips when my eyes meet hers. *God, she's so beautiful.* Every time I think I've gotten used to it, the realization will sneak up and hit me over the head all over again.

"*I'll* do it," Maude informs us. "Both of you have earned a break. Why don't you walk into the village? Or even drive into the next town for a drink? I'd be happy to—"

"*No.*"

The word came out too harsh, too fast, and too loud. For Zoe, who has only heard me raise my voice a handful of times in her entire life, it's alarming. In an instant, she's burst into tears, and throat thick with regret, I move forward to lift her into my arms.

"I'm sorry *mon coeur*," I tell her, sick with guilt. She clings to me, sniffling, and I rub her back. "I'm very sorry." Turning toward my mother and Josephine, my second round of apologies gets caught in my throat.

Josephine has turned back toward the door, and though I can't see her face, I can tell by the way her shoulders have bunched forward that she's upset. "I'm going for a quick walk!" she says in a rush over her shoulder, her voice falsely

189

cheery and bright. Seconds later, the door shuts behind her with a snap.

Maude glowers at me. "*Tu êtes un imbécile.*"*

Yes, I know very well what an idiot I am, but Zoe is still whimpering, and there's nothing I can do for Josephine. Not at this moment.

Turning my back on my mother without another word, I head toward the stairs, murmuring quiet, apologetic words to my daughter, even as I spiral further into guilt and misery. I feel like a bastard. Maude's questioning had me on the defensive, struggling to make sense of the tangled web of responsibilities, fears and feelings for the one woman in the world I shouldn't.

If I'm honest with myself, this has been building for weeks. This is a relationship, whether we label it as one or not, and it's happening, regardless of if I'm ready for it. For months now, I've been keeping this woman at arm's length, neither pushing her away, nor pulling her close, lashing out like a wounded animal when my mother tried to give me a push.

It was always going to come to a head, and now I've pushed us over the edge with a single word.

No.

One final attempt to pretend this woman doesn't mean everything to me, and I might have pushed her away for good.

If I had even a sliver of self-control left to my name, I would let it be. We'd grow apart. I wouldn't go to her room anymore, and she wouldn't fill my days with those tiny, precious moments of connection. My job would be safe, I wouldn't risk my daughter being abandoned a second time, and everything would go back to how it was before.

It won't work, though. If the last months have taught me

---

* You're an imbecile.

anything, it's that I can't run from this, and now, I'm done trying.

Thankfully, Zoe seems to have recovered from my momentary loss of temper, and cheerfully recounts how she helped Jojo cut fabric for her new princess dress as I get her bathed and ready for bed. I listen patiently, my battered heart swelling with pride at how well she's speaking now. The past year has brought a lot of progress, but it isn't in question that only a few months of consistent exercise, fresh food and one-on-one attention from Jo has done wonders for my girl.

When Zoe has finally settled down, I leave her room, heading straight for the balcony door.

Nineteen

JOSEPHINE

"MOM, why is this suddenly such an issue?"

Even from thousands of miles away, I can see my mother's pinched, disapproving expression. It's the one she uses when discussing ethics violations and making political commentaries. There have only been a handful of times when I've been on the receiving end of it, and why would I?

I didn't sneak out, pick fights or date boys with lip rings. What parent wouldn't want a physics nerd daughter with a 4.0 GPA and no sex life? Me stepping off the path I designed for myself—with her careful guidance, of course—is unprecedented. I can tell she's been trying to play it cool, but beneath that calm facade, Mom is panicking.

"Honey, we're just worried." She says *"we"* as if my father isn't so unobservant it didn't take him two months to notice Mom had traded in his car for a newer model (in a different color). I would be surprised if he's realized I'm not in the house, never mind that I've left the country. Since I left, the only communication I've received from him was a picture of his breakfast with an egg emoji.

It's an effort not to make a noise that betrays my impatience. "I'm healthy, and happier than I've ever been. Me coming to France was *your* idea, remember?"

Mom isn't as successful in holding back her sigh. "Frankly, I thought you would get bored by now, Jo. What do you do with your time apart from working with that little girl? You have such a brilliant mind, sweetheart. I'd hate to see you lose momentum and waste your potential."

We're going in circles. We've had this same discussion over and over again, and she still doesn't get it. I don't know what I want to be, or where I want to do it, or who I want to do it with. All I'm sure of is that I didn't like my life before, and I do now. Complicated relationship with Ellis and currently bruised heart aside, *I'm happy.*

Or maybe I'm not being clear enough. Maybe I'm tiptoeing around her feelings like I've always done, trying to make everyone happy. Except now, I'm including myself. It's starting to seem like a losing battle.

"I have to go, Mom," I tell her, my chest hollow.

"Jo—"

"We'll talk soon. Love you!" And, ignoring the answering noise of protest to this pronouncement, end the call.

I stare blankly at the darkening sky outside my bedroom window. My relationship with my mother used to be so easy. We never fought, never disagreed. I looked up to her. Now, it's like we're speaking different languages, and the only thing we get from talking is more frustrated.

Granted, I'm not exactly of sound mind to be managing this situation at the moment. After a day spent being tired and overly emotional about everything, my period arrived just after I fled from Ellis.

That, at least, I'm confident in being upset over, because the mixed signals are giving me whiplash.

One moment, it's like we're on the verge of our situation-ship turning into an actual relationship. The next, he's raising his voice to his mother because she tries to prod him into taking me on a date.

God forbid.

I didn't go down for dinner. About an hour after we typically eat, Zoe came up bearing a wrapped sandwich from the village's small patisserie, an obvious offering from Ellis. She crawled onto the bed with me and rested her head on my lap, accepting pieces of bread—ones untouched by meat, cheese, vegetable or any condiments—and humming with pleasure as I combed my fingers through her hair.

We talked quietly about what she wants to do next week, and when she informs me she wants to cuddle and sew with me, I can't even attribute the burning behind my eyes to the hormone cocktail I'm currently marinating in. Where her father twists me up in knots, my relationship with Zoe has always been easy. The two of us seem to move at a similar pace, and enjoy the same things. It's hard to believe how lonely I felt even a few months ago, when now I have a small, temperamental friend following me every minute of the day.

Zoe gets bored with me eventually and goes off to join her Papa. It's only when I hear their footsteps in the hall and the typical bedtime battle underway that I sneak downstairs and scavenge every last snack that I can from the kitchen, grateful not to encounter Maude.

I've been hiding ever since, and it's only the knowledge that Ellis will soon be turning up in hopes of having sex—which is firmly off the table tonight—that motivates me to pick up my phone again.

> Josephine: Hey, going to have to bail on tonight. I'm sorry. Not feeling great.

There. He doesn't need the gory details, and I can cry, eat and sulk in peace.

I toss my phone away, my bottom lip trembling. Knowing I'm being weepy and hormonal does nothing to help me rein it in. This thing with Ellis was timed horribly. The first day of my period is always the worst, and all I want to do is stay in bed, binge movies that make me cry and wear my favorite unflattering pair of Weston University sweatpants.

Thankfully, tomorrow is Saturday. Normally, I get up with Zoe and Ellis anyway, but this time I intend to take advantage of my day off and sleep until noon. They can entertain Maude on their own. I'm not a part of their family, and it's time I remembered my place.

I'm just on the point of selecting a sufficiently sappy movie from the pre-downloaded selection on my laptop, when a quiet knock sounds on the balcony door and Ellis appears a moment later, looking concerned. He looks even more handsome than usual, with his hair rumbled, and dressed in his own pair of Weston sweats.

"I wanted to check on you," he says gently, brow furrowed in concern as he sits on the edge of the mattress. "You're sick?"

"In a manner of speaking." I wrinkle my nose and gesture vaguely to my lower half. "Sorry."

If he's phased by this, there's no evidence of it in his expression as he eyes the snacks I assembled from the kitchen. "Don't apologize. Do you need anything?"

Pushing myself up a little more against the headboard, I fiddle with the hem of my ratty tank top. "I'm okay, I think."

He doesn't look convinced. "Are you sure? I have painkillers in my room, and—oh. Your water bottle is empty. Let me fill it for you." He goes to take the favorite blue bottle off the bed beside me, but I put my hand on it to stop him.

"I'm okay, Ellis. Seriously. You don't have to do this. I wasn't expecting you to... to lie here and spoon me or something. You signed up for fun and sexy, not hormonal and weepy." *As he made clear a few hours ago, I am not his girlfriend.*

Ellis gives me a withering look and tugs the water bottle free before turning on his heel and vanishing out into the hall. A few minutes later, he comes back with the bottle filled, ice and fresh lemon slices. He noticed that I like it that way?

"I had this in my room as well." He reaches into his pocket and produces a fancy looking French chocolate bar.

Though I'm determined to be difficult, my lips pull into an unwilling, sad little smile. "Do you have a secret stash? Have you been holding out on me?"

He tosses it into the pile of other snacks beside me and sits back on the edge of the bed. "It was just the one, I'm afraid. Though, now I'm curious if *you* have one."

"I'll never tell." I wince as I'm hit with another nasty cramp, pulling my knees up closer to my chest. Ellis stares at me for a long moment, expressionless, and finally gets to his feet. "Thank you for this. I'll see you tomorrow," I promise, knowing full well I'll only be emerging from this room for more food when the supply runs dry.

Ellis isn't leaving, though. He kicks off his shoes and, without a word of explanation, walks around to the other side of the bed.

As I blink at him, confused, he shoves the snack mountain down toward my feet. "What are you doing?"

"Sitting with you." He pulls back the covers and gets in beside me, fussing with the pillows behind his back and even reaching over to turn on the lamp on the bedside table.

I gape, opening and closing my mouth like a goldfish. "This is against the rules," I blurt out, heat rushing to my cheeks. It makes no sense. On a regular basis, this man walks into my room, tells me to take my panties off and bend over. I do it, call him daddy and beg for his cock without a second thought. Now, we're sitting side by side, fully clothed, and I feel so much more vulnerable.

He picks up a bowl of popcorn and helps himself to a handful, peering over at my laptop screen. "What are we watching?"

What is happening?

"Ellis," I snap, getting irritated. "If you're feeling obligated—"

"I'm not feeling obligated, Josephine." He takes another handful of popcorn and leans across to use the track pad on my computer to select *Little Women*.

I hit pause before the opening credits can begin, filled with the bizarre desire to laugh and cry at the same time—*freaking period*. "Why?" I demand. "The last time I checked, I'm not your girlfriend. That's why you snapped today, right? Because your mother thinks we're together?" I let out a hard laugh. "Well, now she knows that's not the case. You'd better leave before she comes in here to borrow a comb and gets confused about our relationship status."

The words are spilling out without pause. For as long as I can remember, I have been stuffing down my hurt or anger instead of making others uncomfortable. I don't remember ever just telling someone how I felt, or calling them on their crappy behavior. I have no idea what makes this different, or why I'm now capable of doing it, but *I'm proud of myself*.

"It's shitty, Ellis. Really freaking shitty. One minute you're telling me this means something, you're trying to get me to break the rules and being sweet to me, and *further* complicating this already *super* complicated situation. Then the next you're losing your temper when your mother tries to play matchmaker."

"Josephine—" he begins, an apologetic note to his voice, and *I don't want to hear it.*

"No. I'm not done," I snap, sitting sideways so I can glare

197

at him. "You've been giving me mixed signals from the first night we met. I know you have some stuff you're working through, and that you don't want a relationship, but if that's the case, you need to stop acting like we're in one when it suits you and pushing me away when it doesn't."

My tirade is fading away, replaced by a bone deep exhaustion that has nothing to do with running around after Zoe all day, and everything to with having feelings for a man who is pretty much the definition of emotionally unavailable.

Ellis's throat works, as though he's having difficulty swallowing, his expression crestfallen. For some reason, this show of emotion only makes the ache in my chest worse. He has feelings for me, but *he doesn't want to.*

Tentatively, he reaches out and takes my hand. "You're right." He nods to himself, as though confirming what he just said. "I'm so sorry, Josephine. This wasn't... I haven't handled this well."

I press my lips together, trying to keep myself from either crying or yelling at the beautiful man staring at me with regret in his eyes. Honestly, I have no idea what will come out if I try to open my mouth right now, but it won't help the situation.

Ellis continues, his hand still gripping mine. "I hate that I've hurt you, hate that I've become the sort of man who is so wrapped up in his own issues that he causes someone else's. I want to do better for you. You deserve better."

I shake my head miserably. "I can't keep doing this, Ellis. It's too much. Things have gotten way more intense than we meant them to, and I'm getting so mixed up over what's real and what isn't."

At my words, something ignites behind Ellis's pale eyes. "*We* are real, Josephine. When I said I wanted to do better, I didn't mean to go back to the arrangement we had. We both want more, so let's be more."

I still, replaying his words in my mind as if I've somehow

heard him wrong. I haven't, though, and now I'm torn between bursting with joy that he's offering me everything I've ever wanted from him, and building a ten foot, barbed wire topped fence around my heart. Even that might not be enough. At this stage, I might need to surgically remove him.

"I don't want to force you into a relationship." My voice is hollow with exhaustion. "This isn't an ultimatum."

His thumb smooths over my knuckles. "Of course it isn't *mon amour*. It isn't your nature. You are hardworking and kind and loyal. You treat my daughter as if she were your own and make friends with my cranky mother and make me feel more myself than I have in a long time." Tears fill my eyes as Ellis continues, his voice unbearably gentle. "*That* is why I want to be in a relationship with you, Josephine."

"You said you didn't have space in your life for me," I whisper brokenly, recalling the what he told me back in Connecticut, just before we came here.

Ellis smiles slightly. "In my defense, I had no idea you would make room for yourself. Nor did I realize how much of a burden is lifted when you have someone who cares as much as you do."

Damn it. *Damn it.* I don't want to be the girl who throws herself joyfully into his arms and tells him all is forgiven.

"Well, what about Weston?" I demand, fighting to keep ahold of all the reasons he had.

As if his job is of no real importance, Ellis shrugs. "We have *at least* four months to go until that becomes an issue. You were only a few credits shy of graduating, and I am not above sneaking around for a few more months if it avoids putting either of us in an uncomfortable position. And as for Zoe, because I'm sure you'll bring her up next, I'll just say that I would like to be sure we're on very solid footing before introducing her to our relationship. For what it's worth, though, I think she would be delighted to keep her Jojo."

Okay. That's... Well, that's fair. Really fair.

I'm just resuming the mental scramble for another thing to throw in our way when Ellis sighs. "Nothing needs to be resolved tonight, *mon amour*. I know I've given you quite enough reason to be wary." His gaze darkens, and my heart stalls. "That being said, I would like to make it clear that I have every intention of making you mine."

I nod—*because what else am I supposed to do*—and Ellis settles back against the pillows, apparently satisfied.

"You're not leaving?" I ask in surprise, still trying to work through the mess of emotions I'm feeling right now.

He shoots me a tired look. "Let me take care of you, Josephine. Please."

It's the *please* that does it for me.

I nod.

There are probably some really badass, strong women out there who could tell a man like Ellis Delvaux *"no"* but I am not one of them. Or, at least, I've exhausted my supply of denial for the night. Maybe it's just because I want him to stay.

Ellis leans over me and takes the computer, pulling it into his lap. "Come here," he murmurs.

I obey without complaint, scooting over the mattress to curl into his side, my head resting on his shoulder and his arm wrapped around my side. Ellis restarts the movie and my tension begins to drain away. It's so nice to be held like this.

"*Little Women*, huh?" I observe, cuddling closer. Warmth floods through me when he kisses my hair, dragging me more securely against him.

He chuckles. "I thought it was on theme."

We both watch as the character of Jo appears on screen. "Your dad jokes are getting worse."

Ellis only reaches for the closest snacks. "Salty or sweet?"

Twenty

ELLIS

IT'S BEEN a long time since I dated, or thought about dating, or considered potentially someday *maybe* dating.

Once, I was rather good at it. Most of my girlfriends were serious, intellectual and career minded. My "move" back in the day was to bring them to poetry readings or wine tastings, capitalizing heavily on my accent and knowledge of literature.

Josephine is different.

There's no impressing her with my culture or taste in wine. She knows me. We live together for heaven's sake, and she's already privy to many of the things about myself I'd rather hide. She knows I can't finish a movie without falling asleep, dirty every pot in the kitchen to make a simple dinner and has seen me grumpy, exhausted, joyful and everything in between. The woman spends her days taking care of my daughter, who thinks *her* Jojo is the greatest thing since sliced bread.

Despite the mess I've made of our early relationship, I know she has feelings for me. For the first time in my life, I'm trying to win the trust of a woman, not her heart.

In the week since the near end of our relationship, there's

been *some* progress. She's still guarded with me, but I can sense the ice thawing with each passing day. This morning, I brought her coffee in bed and keep catching myself grinning as I remember the pleased little smile and sweet words of thanks this got me.

I am not taking anything for granted. It's not lost on me how close I came to losing her for good, and have no intention of abandoning my campaign of shameless adoration for a long time. Possibly ever. Just to be safe.

Asking my mother to babysit so I'd have a few uninterrupted days to do this required sacrificing some dignity and suffering through a lot of smugness, but it was worth it. We need time together, just us, and now we'll have it. I've been bursting with excitement to tell her since the matter was resolved this morning, but haven't seen her all day.

The decision to stop running from this has been liberating. It's as though the world has been turning on the wrong axis for months, and suddenly righted itself. Giving myself permission to fall in love with Josephine Sutton was the most natural thing in the world.

Even the upcoming visit from Miranda isn't torturing me quite as much as it was before. It seems important to get our relationship on solid footing before I throw in yet another complication, but we're moving in the right direction.

There are still weeks to go, and somewhere in that time, I'll find a way to tell Josephine the truth. Even if I'm dreading it, I'm cautiously optimistic that she will understand, and we'll be able to get through the whole business with less drama than usually accompanies my ex-wife's self-serving visits.

Now, I want to focus on her—*us*—and spend the entirety of Friday struggling to make it through my work. By the end of the day I'm eager to leave the library, going in search of my mother, Jo and Zoe. The house is quiet, however, and so is the garden. I'm deciding whether to check the stream at the edge of the grounds or head toward the village, when my gaze catches on a square indentation in the high grass.

It's rare that I rely on my intuition, but some prickle of awareness has me moving through the garden and out into the field. It's a pleasantly warm day, as I stroll through the meadow toward the place I spotted from the garden, brushing past wildflowers and plump, pollen covered bees.

Sure enough, when I reach the place, I find myself standing at the edge of a blue checkered blanket nestled amongst the long grass, with a beautiful young woman spread out over it, a book in her hands. She's alone.

Josephine blinks up at me in surprise over the top of her paperback. "Hi," she says cautiously, propping herself up on her forearms as I lower myself onto the blanket across from her, our legs stretched out side by side. We're in our own world here, surrounded by a fortress of rippling grass and wildflowers, with only endless blue sky stretching above our heads.

My eyes catch on the container of strawberries resting beside her, and I smile. "Where are Maude and Zoe?"

She stretches, setting her book aside. "There's a children's event at the local library. I guess they're giving out free books and there will be a bounce house. I was planning to take Zoe, but your mother wanted to."

A light breeze carries over the meadow, making the walls of our fortress sway and ripple. "Marvelous places, libraries," I muse, reaching out to tuck a wayward dark curl back behind her ear. "Speaking of marvelous places, what would you say about a weekend in Paris?"

Josephine wrinkles her nose. "I mean, I would love it, but Zoe wouldn't. We'd probably spend half the time in the hotel room letting her decompress."

My chest warms. *We.* Such a small word, with such an enormous meaning behind it. "I meant the two of us," I correct her gently, reaching out to take her wrist in my hand, tracing the veins lightly with my thumb. "Maude is going to stay with Zoe. It'll only be two nights, but I thought you would enjoy it," I finish rather lamely, suddenly worried I might have overstepped.

The slow smile spreading over my girlfriend's face soon puts my fears to rest. "When would we go?"

I sag in relief, my heart full to bursting. "Tomorrow."

Her mouth pops open. "*Tomorrow?*"

Nodding, I lift her hand to my lips, kissing the back. "There's a train that leaves the village station at noon."

"Ellis." She laughs, delighted. "This is amazing. When's the last time you had a whole night off?"

Almost as soon as she asks, something shifts in the air between us. We both know, but I say it anyway. "It was the night we met."

We haven't slept together since our fight. I've been letting her take the lead, eager to make it clear that I want her for so much more than her body. Now, I can sense we've both had enough.

She hums, letting her thighs part a few inches. She's wearing her white summer dress today, the one she made. Holding her gaze, I reach out to run my hand up the inside of her leg, stopping when I encounter her damp panties.

"Have you missed my cock, sweetheart?" I ask, my voice strained.

Josephine's teeth find her plump bottom lip but release it almost instantly, her gasp lost in the sound of rustling grass as I cup her sex with my entire hand. Pale thighs inch further apart.

"Maybe," she admits coyly, letting out a soft, needy sigh as she shifts and squirms to get more of the friction she needs. The shy young woman who was once too embarrassed to tell me what she needs is gone. Now, my dirty little nanny spreads her legs and shows me.

God, she gets my cock so hard.

I swallow. "When will they be back?"

"Not for a few hours." Josephine falls back onto the blanket, her hair a dark, tangled halo around her. My heart stalls. Has there ever been a more perfect moment than the one we're living in right now? Releasing my hold on her pussy, I rise onto my knees, covering her body with my own.

Josephine's legs part in welcome, making room for me to settle my erection against her cunt. I trail my nose up her throat, greedily inhaling the fresh air on her skin, and when I kiss her, I can taste strawberries.

"Can I have you right here?" I murmur in between slow, deep kisses.

Josephine is nodding before I've finished speaking, and we work together to rid her of her dress, so she's laid out beneath me in only a tiny white thong. I leave it for now, reaching instead for the bowl of strawberries.

They're warmed by the sun and overly ripe, perfect for what I intended. She sucks in a startled breath as I bring the fruit to her nipples, circling them and leaving trails of jewel red juice over her delicate skin.

I suck it away, and my cock throbs at the way she arches her back, letting out a loud, shameless moan of pleasure. Pausing long enough to meet her heavily lidded eyes, I smirk. "Stay still for me, *mon amour*. Let me eat."

My greedy girl does nothing of the sort.

"Ellis," she whines, pulling my hair with both hands. "I need you."

"I know you do," I murmur, barely lifting my lips from the trail of strawberry juice that I've left on her other breast. "Be patient, Josephine. I'll fuck you in just a moment."

She whimpers, grinding her greedy little pussy on my abdomen. "Daddy—"

I sigh in feigned disappointment, lifting my head to look at her directly. "Who is in charge when we're together like this?"

She trembles. "You are."

"That's right." I curl my hand over her covered sex again, chuckling when I find she's soaked right through her panties. "You are worked up, aren't you?" I coo, and, with a quick glance up to make sure she's watching, I hook her panties to the side to drag the strawberry through her slit. Gathering as much of the creamy arousal as I can, I bring it to my mouth and bite down, groaning as the taste of fresh strawberries and Josephine's pussy explodes on my tongue.

"God, Ellis," she half laughs, have cries, gazing at me with undisguised desire as I shift down between her legs and lift them over my shoulders.

Without pause, I bury my face in her wet cunt, groaning at the familiar taste of her mixed with the sweetness of the strawberries. My cock is an iron rod in my pants, and I press my hips into the ground in an attempt to relieve some of the ache.

The possessive, primal need to make this woman mine is crackling to life inside me. Knowing I have this effect on her, that she needs this as badly as I do, is intoxicating.

"*Oh my god, oh my god, oh my god,*" Josephine chants, panting and mindless of anything but the need to come. Her hands are tangled in my hair, pulling me closer, wanton and needy.

I press two fingers into her slick center, groaning at how wet she already is, anticipating the relief her tight, slick hole will give my aching cock. This wasn't my intention when I came out here, but the moment she spread her thighs, I knew how this would end.

"There you go," I groan as the pads of my fingers brush

the spot I *know* will make her crazy and Josephine's back bows off the blanket, the fingers in my hair tightening. Her body is a bow, ready to snap, and I pull her swollen clit between my lips, sucking it harder than I normally would in my desperation.

She comes with a feeble cry, her warm thighs pressed to my ears as I lick her through it, drawing out her pleasure. I could do this all day, could happily eat her pussy all over again and make her come until the sky above us turns black.

That's not what either of us need, though.

"You're so beautiful," I tell her as I sit back, ripping my t-shirt over my head and falling back over her body, meeting her lips in a kiss that makes me think of forever. It's always been like this between us. Every time we're together, I lose myself in this woman, and yet *this*...

Her hands are between us, working to free my cock, and we both make noises of relief when my length bobs into the warm summer air between us. Without even looking up, I reach down to grip my base and guide my tip to her slick opening.

"This is mine," I grunt, relishing the way her body arches off the ground as I bottom out, her lips falling open in a cry. I do it again, the force of my thrust sending her a few inches up the blanket. It's not enough. I'm as deep as I can go, and *it's not enough.* "The thought of you with anyone else makes me insane. If I ask you the name of your other lovers, don't tell me, Josephine. I've decided to kill them."

Maybe not kill, but I wouldn't walk away without an assault charge.

Her expression flickers. "There's no one else," she breathes, pulling me closer to kiss my jaw. "Only you." My pulse stutters and I still, staring down at her. Is she just saying that, or—"I'm sorry I didn't tell you then." She gazes up at me, vulnerable and unsure. "I thought you'd stop and I... I'd never felt that way before. I wanted you."

God. My heart twists as I start to move again, my hands framing her face so she can't look away. Devotion and adoration are exploding inside me, and I want her eyes on me. "It will only be me, do you understand?" A choked sob escapes her lips as she nods. "I'll be so good to you, *mon amour*, but it will only ever be me. You'll only know my touch, my cock, my body. *You're mine.*"

My thrusts become rough again as urge to claim this woman burrows under my skin. Growling in impatience, I grip the back of her knee, dragging one leg over my shoulder.

This isn't lovemaking.

This is *primal.*

Not one word passes between us as I fuck her harder, filling the warm afternoon air with the crude sound of my hips slapping against hers and the wet noises of her cunt taking me. I want her to speak, want to hear her break, beg, plead.

Leaning down, I nip at her bottom lip and immediately soothe it with my tongue. By now, I can't count the number of times I've felt like a changed man between this woman's thighs, but this is different.

I drive forward faster as my free hand finds her throat, pressing hard enough for her eyes to go wide with shock. We've never done this before, but the flood of wetness over my cock leaves me no doubt of how she feels about it.

"That's it, take it," I grit out between kisses, and the hand on her throat tightens. "You're doing so well—*merde.* You're always such a good girl for me."

At my words, the volume of her cries increases.

I, quite literally, can't stop fucking her. *Jesus Christ,* she turns me on. My kind-hearted, patient girl who sews princess dresses and makes sure everyone in the house has a home cooked meal, also likes to be choked, taken rough and call me daddy.

That I'm the only one to see this side of her, the only one

who has ever seen her this way, is beyond satisfying to the dark, possessive side of me she's awoken. I'm overcome by the brand new knowledge that, if I play my cards right, I could be the only one *ever*.

Growling, I redouble my pace, half out of my mind with the need to make her come. We've only been at it a few minutes, and already my balls have drawn up tight, throbbing and full. Never, not once, have I failed to get her off before myself, and I won't be starting tonight.

Nails dig painfully into my back, hard enough to leave marks, as her mouth falls open in a choked scream. Beneath me, her entire body convulses, shaking as I fuck her through her orgasm, drawing it out as long as I can as I bite my tongue to keep myself from coming.

When Josephine sags back onto the blanket, her cheeks flushed and her eyes dazed. One look at her is enough to finish me off.

I come like a freight train, grinding helplessly into the swollen hole I've fucked harder than even my fist. My cock swells and throbs inside her, cum flooding out of me. It's all I can do not to collapse, and Josephine kisses my neck and jaw, her whimpers muffled in my skin as her hips lift up my body, letting me spill deeper.

"Was that too much?" I rasp when the last of my orgasm dies away.

Josephine's head shakes against my cheek, still panting. "It was perfect."

It's not until I pull out that I realize what I've done. Cursing, I look down at my half-hard cock shining with our combined releases.

She sits up, eyes widening in shock. "I'm sorry. I don't know what I was thinking," I croak, numb with disbelief. How could I not have thought about it? I was so lost in the moment—in *her*—that it didn't even cross my mind.

My heart hammers against my ribcage as the consequences of what I just did sink in, and I stare between us at her bare cunt. Her bare cunt that's not on contraceptives and is currently full of my cum.

"It's okay." Josephine whispers. "It's a bad time of the month. I couldn't... We should be fine."

My relief is minimal, and it takes me a moment to place the emotion settling inside me; disappointment.

What is wrong with me?

Getting her pregnant would be a disaster of epic proportions. Yet as I move two fingers down, spreading her sex to allow myself to see the first drop of my release escape, I'm not worried in the slightest.

God help me.

I swallow. "Well, the damage is done. We might as well enjoy this, yes?"

"Enjoy it?" comes Josephine's ragged response, and I drag my eyes up from my release leaking out of her.

My fingers dip down to collect what's escaped, and we both inhale sharply as they press it back inside her. "Can I do it again?"

Twenty-One

JOSEPHINE

THE ALARM GOES off when the light in my bedroom is still blue and hazy. Behind me, Ellis grumbles indistinctly, and the arm wrapped around me tightens, stopping me from reaching over to turn off the chiming noise.

"Don't shut it off. I'll go back to sleep," his mumbled words are barely audible through the pillow.

We're still naked, and the insides of my thighs are sticky with his cum. Yesterday, we lay together in the meadow, talking, until the sky started to darken and we walked hand in hand back to the chateau. Ellis only released me when we came within view of the kitchen windows, but not before dragging me behind a garden wall and silencing my giggles with a kiss that made me hot and restless all over again.

We haven't stopped to discuss the specifics of our new relationship status. While I'm pretty tired of the sneaking around, keeping it from Zoe seems like the right thing to do, at least for now. We're making progress, but there are so many questions for me left unanswered and fears left untouched. This feels new and fragile, and I'm still not convinced it won't all go to hell before we go home.

Ellis crept back into my room after bedtime. We had sex twice, him coming inside me each time, before finally falling asleep. When I woke up, I half expected him to be gone, but he's still here holding me.

I smile into my arm as the alarm chimes louder and, with obvious reluctance, Ellis releases me to reach over and turn it off himself. With a quiet groan, he leans back into the pillows, scrubbing his hands over his face. "*Merde*, I'm exhausted."

"Should I send you to bed early tonight?" I tease, sleepily tracing the dusting of light hair on his chest.

I feel rather than hear Ellis's answering chuckle. "God, no."

Rolling over, I check my phone, and smile when I see he's set the alarm an hour before Zoe's usual wake up time.

We have time. Not a lot, but enough.

My hand drifts down his abdomen, finding his softened cock easily. Ellis blows out a rocky breath when I sit up, watching myself stroke him. My clit throbs as he grows hard and long under my touch. A bead of pre-cum appears at his tip and I don't hesitate to lean forward and lick it away.

We've been sleeping together for almost two months now, and I've only sucked his cock a handful of times. I've learned that Ellis is far more interested in giving me pleasure than taking any of his own, but that makes me all the more determined.

Sure enough, his hands weave through my hair, pulling me up just as I've wrapped my lips around him. "I want to," I plead, panting. Ellis relents, his hold on my hair relaxing, and lets out a low curse as I take him in my mouth eagerly.

"I want to come in your pussy. You have one minute," he warns, voice strained.

Challenge accepted.

Using the saliva that's dripped down, I fist his base, stroking what I can't fit in my mouth.

Ellis must guess what I'm up to, though, because my head is yanked up again seconds later, forcing me to meet a pair of heavily lidded blue eyes. "Sit on my face, and you can keep sucking me. How's that?"

Even after all we've done and all the times he's had his face between my legs, it's a whole other level to sling my leg over Ellis's face hovering over him with his cock inches from my lips.

I'm so sensitive and sore from last night, and the teasing blow of air against my clit makes me gasp.

"I said sit, Josephine," he growls, and the hands on my thighs drag me down, sealing my sex against his mouth. His hold on me is firm, and even if I wanted to, I couldn't move.

His long, thick cock is right in my face, but I've barely gotten it together to wrap my lips around his head when the overwhelming sensations between my legs make me cry out. Ellis is fucking me with his tongue, probing my opening with teasing licks and searching, hungry thrusts while he holds me firmly in place. Even if I'm on top, I'm completely at his mercy.

It's the mirror above my dresser, which is tilted at exactly the right angle to show a complete view of the erotic act being committed in the center of my mattress. Heat floods my core as I see the way Ellis's fingers dig into my thighs, only his mussed hair visible.

I watch myself come, my smaller, softer body convulsing atop his larger, harder one, so far gone I can barely keep my eyes open.

Nearly the moment I've recovered, I scramble off him and turn, slinging a leg over his hips. Ellis watches, his jaw strained, as I lower myself onto his cock. I'm still tender and swollen from the rough sex we had yesterday, but the edge of pain somehow heightens the pleasure as I ride him.

"Look," I murmur, nodding to the mirror.

Ellis's eyes flash when he realizes, and his breathing changes as he watches us, growing heavier.

"Jesus. *Mon amour*," he mutters, eyes still locked on the mirror, watching the slow roll of my hips. "*Yes*—just like that. Use my cock."

I moan, grinding my oversensitive, swollen clit against the wiry hair at his base. The friction is perfect, and I'm just beginning to chase my orgasm, when an unexpected pressure against my other hole makes me suck in a startled breath.

"Relax for me," Ellis coos, using my arousal as lube as he presses a single fingertip into my ass. "That's a good girl. Do you like it?"

My eyelids flutter. I think so? The foreign intrusion is strange and almost violating. I fall forward, my forehead pressed to his as he wraps his free arm around my lower back, keeping him in place as he fucks my pussy from below and the single finger on my ass probes deeper, circling and stretching my entrance.

"Words, Josephine," Ellis reminds me, his voice a dangerous, low purr in my ear.

I'm going to come so hard. My muscles are coiled tight, ready for the fall, and it's only the knowledge that Ellis will absolutely stop if I don't answer that makes me open my mouth. "I like it," I whimper, shamelessly arching into his touch. "I like it so much, Daddy."

"I know you do." He chuckles, and the addition of a second finger makes me explode, gasping and bucking as pleasure courses through every nerve in my body.

Ellis keeps up the pace he's set until I've calmed down, collapsing into his chest, sticky and weak. Even though I'm pretty sure another orgasm would finish me off, I moan in protest when he pulls his fingers from my ass.

He fumbles blindly for the drawer of the bedside table,

yanking it open. I know what he's looking for, and my walls clench on his cock when I see the long, slim vibrator.

"We'll take this nice and slow. Lay on top of me just like this and try to relax."

I tremble, turned on, and worried at the same time. "What are you going to do?"

A low, buzz fills the quiet room as he turns on the vibrator. Ellis doesn't reply at first, drawing the device over the place where we're connected, gathering the slickness of my orgasm. "I'm going to put this in your naughty little ass, and you're going to bounce up and down on my cock like a good girl. It will make both of us feel good."

The tip of the toy finds my entrance, circling slowly.

"Ellis," I breathe out, the vibrations traveling through my pelvis, making my pussy clench around him.

He groans in approval, dragging my lips to his and kissing me hungrily. "Deep breath." He swallows my gasp as the vibrator presses past the ring of resistance, slipping smoothly inside me.

I come instantly.

One moment I'm focused on the brand new sensation of being filled in two places at once. The next, I'm being swallowed whole by an orgasm that's almost painful in its intensity. It's everywhere, swelling through my whole body, and Ellis has to swallow my scream with a frenzied kiss.

"That was the sexiest thing I've ever seen," he growls against my lips, fucking me steadily from below as I come down from the high, panting and trembling. The arm he has wrapped around my waist tightens. "Tell me whose cunt this is."

"Yours, Daddy," I moan, listening to the sloppy, wet noises of his thick cock pumping in and out of me.

"And this ass?" The vibrator presses deeper, the intensity notching higher. Ellis groans into our kiss, his pace stuttering.

He's overwhelming me with sensations, but I'm not the only one being affected by them.

I whimper. "Yours, Daddy."

This is the right answer, because a moment later, the arm on my waist loosens. I know what he wants. Pressing my hands to his chest, I sit up, my lips parting in surprise at how full I am.

Our eyes meet as I start to move over him, fucking myself on his cock and the vibrator at once. "Is it good for you, too?" I breathe.

Ellis makes a noise somewhere between a laugh and a groan. "It's incredible. God, look at you." His jaw strains, watching my small breasts bounce with each rise and fall of my body over his. "Ride me. That's it. Ah, *merde*, just like that—" My thighs are burning and my pussy is throbbing and so oversensitive it's painful, but I still don't want this to end.

I don't want *this* to end.

I don't want to say goodbye to him. *Ever*. How could I go out and date, knowing that there's a man walking around somewhere else who makes me feel strong and sexy and adored, a man who gives me room to grow while supporting me all the while? Despite my best intentions, I've tumbled head first into wanting Ellis Delvaux for the rest of my life.

"Come inside me," I plead, praying he doesn't notice the sheen of tears in my eyes. "Please, Daddy. *Please*—"

Ellis's free hand clamps down on my hip, holding me down and sealing my body against his as his cock twitches inside me. I'm still not used to the sensation of the wet heat from his release coating the deepest part of me. It's not something I would have expected to like, but suddenly, locating a clinic where I can get a birth control prescription has gone straight to the top of my priority list because I want to feel this every time.

I fall forward over him, and Ellis drags the vibrator slowly from my ass. A dull thud beside the bed tells me what he did with it, and I smile into his damp skin as his arms curl around me.

"You're incredible." He groans, kissing my neck.

The burning behind my eyes has thankfully faded away, but I still keep my face buried in his neck, letting my breathing slow as his cock softens inside me and Ellis strokes up and down my spine.

How is this moment more intimate than what we just did?

"What are you thinking about?" he murmurs, kissing my temple, and I lift my head to see him.

My heart stalls. Will I ever get over how handsome he is? "I'm excited to go to Paris."

Ellis's expression is soft as he brushes the hair back from my face with a tenderness that makes me ache. I never imagined that falling for someone would be like this, intense and scary and all-consuming. Already I'm so close to loving this man, the faintest breeze could blow me over the edge. Two days alone with him in the most romantic city in the world would certainly do the trick.

Our lips meet and we kiss slowly, as though we're trying to savor this moment for as long as we can.

"God, *mon amour*," he whispers as we break apart. "I've never felt this way before. I didn't even know it was possible. All my life, I've thought the poets were just being dramatic." A reluctant little giggle escapes my lips and I lift off him, falling to the mattress at his side. Ellis reaches over me to check the time on my phone and groans. "Zoe will be up soon."

He steals one last kiss before pulling away from me and swinging his legs over the side of the bed. "I can take her down and do breakfast, if you want," I tell him, stretching luxuriously over the crumpled sheets. There's an ache between my legs that will probably get much worse after we make it to our hotel tonight, but I'm beaming at the prospect.

Ellis smiles at me gratefully. "That would be helpful, actually. I need to tie up a few minor projects in the library before we leave." He pulls his briefs back on and turns in search of his sweatpants. When he finds them, though, he makes no move to put them on. Peering over at me, he frowns. "Are you offering as my girlfriend, or as my nanny?"

"Oh, definitely girlfriend," I reply airily. "Your nanny is off this weekend."

He grins as he dresses quickly, but pauses on his way out the balcony door to kiss me one more time. "Thank you."

"For the world class sex?" I tease, twining my arms loosely up around his neck.

Ellis chuckles, but shakes his head. "Thank you for being you, *mon amour.*"

He leaves, and I take a few more minutes to lie there, wondering at the brand new sense of fullness in my heart. For the first time since we got here, I'm allowing myself to hope.

Twenty-Two

ELLIS

I'VE GOTTEN out of the habit of keeping my phone on me. The service at the chateau is spotty at best, and there's really not much point unless one happens to be sitting two feet from with Wi-Fi router. My staff back at Weston has learned to expect a wait when they contact me, and I've found myself checking it less and less.

This morning, as I step back into my bedroom from the balcony, exhausted but more rejuvenated than I've felt in years, I bypass the device completely. It's Saturday morning. Nobody needs anything urgently from me. I intend to squeeze in a rapid shower, but before I can even enter the bathroom, the knob on my bedroom door rattles and Zoe shuffles in.

My heart, already so full, seems to expand at the sight of her.

It's only been a few months since we arrived in France, and I can't stop marveling over the change I've seen in my daughter. For so long, the two of us were in survival mode, struggling just to make it through the day, but lately I've been able to enjoy being a parent and spending time with my child.

"Good morning, *mon cœur*." I beam, sitting on the bed so

she can crawl into my arms and snuffle into my chest. "Did you sleep well?"

Zoe nods, picking at a small hole in my t-shirt. "You smell like Jojo."

I still, and with an ear pressed against my chest, she's undoubtedly able to hear the sudden increase in my heartbeat. "*Ah.*" I cough, completely taken off guard. She's a perceptive child. It hadn't occurred to me how difficult it would be to keep this from her long term. "I gave her a hug."

It's not technically a lie. I lost count of the number of times I crushed Josephine's body against mine in the last twenty-four hours.

Thankfully, Zoe seems to accept this and we move on to the discussion of my upcoming trip, which I first broached to her last night. The promise of two days of unlimited time with *grandmaman* was received with great enthusiasm, and she chatters nonstop about all the things they're going to do together as we head downstairs.

I hear Jo in the kitchen already, and I send Zoe off to her, making a detour into the library. The rest of the morning passes in a blur of packing, stolen kisses with Josephine whenever we happen to be in the same room as each other, and lots of hugs for Zoe.

It's only when we're about to leave and I realize I have no way of checking in later that I go back upstairs in search of my phone. The device is where I left it, and I pause to scroll through a few texts I missed. When I see the name at the bottom of the list, my stomach drops like a stone.

> Miranda: I've tried calling you three times in the last two days. My schedule was moved around, so I'll be there tomorrow instead of the 7th. If this is your way of trying to get me not to come, it won't work. I gave notice, just like it says in the custody arrangement, I'm getting on the train in the morning.

My blood is rushing in my ears, and for a moment, I think I might vomit. Dimly, I'm aware of my phone hitting the floor with a dull thud. Never in my life have I had a panic attack, but that must be what this is. The walls are closing in on me and my breaths are coming in shallow, rapid gasps that don't quite fill my lungs. I feel like I'm drowning, and *I can't think.*

Miranda is coming here. Today.

Josephine and I are finally on solid ground, we're scheduled to leave any minute. I've had no time to prepare Zoe, or myself, for that matter. Even my mother will probably be an issue, as she hasn't seen Miranda since the divorce and might well make good on her old threats to stab her. My ex-wife's sporadic visits are always stressful and emotionally exhausting for both me and Zoe, but this is something else entirely.

The room spins around me, needles piercing my lungs with each breath.

Grasping at straws, I lunge forward, grasping the phone as I reread her message in the off chance I've misunderstood the message. I haven't. *Of course I haven't.* If Miranda is good at anything, it's ruining my life, and today might be her greatest victory in the game of emotional warfare she's been playing for years.

I stare at my screen until it goes dark. I can't think, never mind decide what to do next, and I have no idea how long I stand there trying. My only hope—and it's a feeble one—is that I can talk Miranda into not coming. Perhaps I can offer to take Zoe to see her, or meet half way in a neutral place... *Anything* that will stop this from happening.

I should have known she might switch the date. Miranda once rescheduled my birthday when it interfered with a bachelorette party. My hand shakes as I press my ex-wife's contact, bringing it to my ear and listening to it ring.

"Hey," Miranda answers, her tone impatient.

I squeeze my eyes shut. "I'm sorry I didn't get back to you sooner. The service around here is spotty and I've gotten in the habit of leaving my phone behind."

A hard laugh greets my words. "Sure thing."

"Listen, Miranda." I cut to the chase, scrubbing a hand over my face. "I haven't had time to talk to Zoe. My mother is here. I'm supposed to be going away for the weekend. It's a really bad time. Is there any way I can take Zoe up to see you next week? That way, you won't need to make the trip at all?"

There's a beat of silence. "You actually expect me to believe that? There is a zero percent chance you're going to bring her to Brussels, Ellis." Miranda scoffs. "I'm already at the train station. I get in at half-past twelve."

The line goes dead.

The plastic of my case creaks ominously under the pressure of my hand, and I toss it away onto the mattress. "*Shit*," I hiss, just as there's a quick knock on the door. Before I can call out to whoever's there to *give me a damn moment*, it opens.

"Hey," Josephine greets me cheerfully, slipping inside and closing the door behind her. "Maude is practically pushing us out the door. She made sandwiches for the train." Her giggle over my mother's antics dies away when she sees my face. "Ellis! What's wrong?"

God, I don't deserve her.

Mutely, I shake my head, a bitter taste filling my mouth. There's only one thing to do here. I don't like it, but there isn't time to explain. I'll have to hope she trusts me, that she understands, and that she gives me the chance to salvage this.

"Something has come up. You need to go to Paris alone."

"Oh." Her shoulders sink, and I've never loathed myself more. "Is everything okay?"

I nod unevenly. "Yes. It will be fine. I'll... I'll explain when you get back. This is unavoidable. There's no reason why you shouldn't enjoy yourself, though."

Josephine stares at me, her warm eyes full of questions. "Should I be worried? I'm trying not to freak out here, but you're not giving me anything and—"

"Please," I blurt out, shaking my head to stop her flow of unbearably compassionate words. "I swear to you, *mon amour*, I'll explain when you get back," I tell her, firmly ending the discussion before moving past her to the door. "Let me drive you into the village. The train is leaving at the top of the hour. I'll email you the hotel reservation."

I'd spent hours booking the place, scouring hotel reviews and imagining how her naked body would look stretched out over the crisp white sheets.

For whatever reason, I kept getting caught on the fantasy of walking into the ornate lobby with her, carrying both of our luggage cases in a silent message that we were arriving together, and we'd be leaving together too. I wanted this so badly. One goddamn weekend with the woman who makes me whole again, the woman who is so perfect that now I understand why some men say they wouldn't change a thing about their wives.

There's so much I want from her, so much I want to give her, moments I want for us... After this, I'll be lucky if she stays here as Zoe's nanny.

Josephine doesn't argue.

Neither of us says a word as we walk side by side down the grand staircase. Our suitcases are already standing beside the door, ready to go, and I feel ill when I pick up only hers. Zoe and my mother must still be out in the grounds, so we don't stop as we head to the car, our feet crunching on the gravel drive.

My heart is still pounding, and after putting her luggage in the back seat, I look up to find her standing stock-still beside the passenger side door. Her expression wooden.

"Josephine?" I question with an edge of trepidation. What will I say if she simply refuses to go? How could I possibly explain this? She's never asked me a single thing about Zoe's mother, and I was thankful for it. A day would come where I had no choice but to give her the gory details of my divorce, but I've been so focused on the more immediate problems that I completely neglected to foresee a massive pitfall lying ahead.

There has to be a quota of how many times any man can reasonably fuck up before a woman like Jo decides she's had enough. How would I feel if Zoe brought home a man who'd treated her as I've treated Josephine? The answer makes me hate myself even more than I did sixty seconds ago. I like to think of myself as decent, yet all I can seem to do is hurt her.

Careful to avoid my eye, she shakes her head and pulls open the car door, dropping into the passenger seat without a word. There's nothing to do but follow.

"Please, *mon amour*," I plead as I turn the keys in the ignition, pulling out into the drive. "I wouldn't stay behind if it wasn't urgent."

Jo stares straight forward, still refusing to look at me. "But you won't let me stay, and you won't tell me why."

I could howl. This is unbearable.

"It's urgent," I repeat, my fists tightening on the steering wheel as we stop at the end of the drive to allow a tractor to trundle past. It's only a few minutes' drive, and while *I know* I need to get back to talk to Zoe, I'm desperate to draw this out just a little longer. "I don't want to lie to you, but I don't have time to tell you the truth."

She doesn't respond and I would do anything to step back in time for a few hours. I woke up so happy, so full of hope, and now it's all crumbling down around me. Hell, I'm pushing it. This is my fault. As much as I would like to vilify my ex-wife until the end of time, I can't blame Miranda for this. Protecting my relationship with Josephine was my responsibility, and I failed. Again.

When we pass the first houses on the outskirts of the village, I can't take it anymore.

"Josephine," I choke, struggling to hold back the rising tide of panic. The train station is around the corner. In a matter of seconds, she's going to walk out of this car and go alone to the romantic weekend I planned for us. She'll have space to think, to step away from the intensity of our feelings for each other, and when she gets back, we'll be finished. I'm sure of it.

"If you want me to go, I'll go," she whispers, sounding so tired, so hurt.

"I don't want you to go anywhere," I protest. "Nothing about this is because I want it, Josephine. Please believe that."

I love you.

The words are on the tip of my tongue, yet I pull them back. This woman turned my whole life upside down in the best possible way, and makes every part of it better just by existing. She deserves the whole world, and it's becoming obvious that I am incapable of giving it to her. I have no business telling her I love her for the first time under such circumstances.

We pull up outside the tiny train depot. Every instinct I have is screaming at me to turn the car around and bring her home with me, to hold on to Josephine Sutton with everything I have, and never let go.

The air in the car seems to grow thin as our last seconds together pass in silence.

"I'll see you in a few days." Her words cut deeper than I knew possible. "You don't need to get out. I'll get my bag from the back."

I pull the train tickets from my pocket and press them into her hand, "Josephine—" But my next words are silenced by the heavy slam of a car door.

Twenty-Three

JOSEPHINE

I WATCH my train leave the station.

The ticket Ellis gave me is a ball of shredded paper bits in my hand. I can still see the manic, fearful look he had in his eyes when I walked into his room earlier. Something is wrong, *really wrong*, and he doesn't trust me enough to tell me what it is.

As I slump into one of the well-worn wood benches at the train station, staring at the chipped tile on the opposite wall, I'm not sure he ever will.

It's agonizing to accept, but I'm learning that trusting someone means offering them a piece of yourself, and Ellis has never done that for me. Even with all his promises of wanting this to be real, he still hasn't offered more of himself than the bare minimum needed to keep me.

In all my worrying over this man breaking my heart, it never occurred to me that *I* might be the one who needed to walk away, or that the prospect of not being in Zoe's life forever would be just as gut-wrenching.

I have to keep my lips pressed together to stop a sob from

escaping. The village gossips about us enough, the last thing I need is to be spotted crying my eyes out in the train station.

Ellis doesn't know I stayed. As far as he's aware, I'm on my way to Paris, and I still could be. Just because I didn't take the last train doesn't mean I can't get on the next one and go by myself. Maybe it would be good to get some space, then go back on Monday with a better idea of what I want.

Another train rattles into the station, and I'm only vaguely aware of travelers getting on and off. I don't notice the brown-haired woman taking the bench across from mine until she speaks.

"*Excusez-moi.*" Having spent the past few months surrounded by native French speakers, and being playfully teased enough for my own accent, I know a foreigner when I hear one. She's older than me—maybe thirty—and has a large leather bag beside her. She's dressed in much more formal, trendy clothing than I've seen so far in the village, and wouldn't look out of place at one of my mother's faculty luncheons.

I smile politely. "Do you speak English per chance? My French is a work in progress."

Her shoulders sag in relief. "Oh, thank god," she exclaims in a clear American accent. "I wasn't prepared to embarrass myself this early in the day."

"You're in luck. I'm from Connecticut."

"Oh wow, small world. I lived there for a while." She sighs. "Well, I'm glad to have found a fellow foreigner, but I'm not sure if you'll be able to help me. I'm looking for this address, and I can't connect to the station Wi-Fi to get my GPS going or make a call."

She holds her phone out and I lean forward, squinting at the address. As soon as I make it out, the room around us seems to go unnaturally still. It's a challenge not to let my shock show as I straighten up, staring at the stranger with new eyes.

She's going to the chateau.

Now that I'm looking at her—*really* looking at her—a ball of suspicion and dread drops into the pit of my stomach. Her face is familiar. Not because I've ever met or seen her before, but because I see parts of her every day.

This is Zoe's mother.

"I know where that is." I tell her, surprised by how even my voice is.

"You're my savior," she says with a grateful smile. "Can you point me in the right direction? I can't imagine this town is huge."

I can barely process what she's saying, because Ellis's ex-wife is going to see them, and he *sent me away*.

"I—" My words falter, and I clear my throat, struggling to speak. "I work there."

The woman across from me, Zoe's mother, the woman Ellis once pledged to spend the rest of his life with, is staring at me too now with a look of dawning realization. "You're Zoe's nanny."

My answering nod is jerky and uneven. "Yes."

Silence falls between us and, with a sudden burst of vicious satisfaction, I know exactly what I'm going to do. "I'll take you." I stand, hitching my overnight bag over my shoulder.

She frowns at me, unsure. "I don't want to trouble you. You're obviously on your way somewhere."

I shake my head. "Nope. My trip was canceled. Let's go."

Without waiting to see if she's following me, I march out of the station, and out onto the hot street. I hadn't realized it, but a while must have passed since Ellis left me here. How long did I sit on that bench, wondering how things went so wrong, so quickly?

"What did you say your name was?" Ellis's ex-wife asks as she falls into step beside me.

"Jo."

I've never disliked anyone this quickly. Ellis might not trust me enough to confide in me about his divorce, but what I've pieced together is plenty.

"It's nice to meet you, Jo. I'm Miranda."

I don't respond, her name settling in at the top of my—admittedly short—shit-list.

A few more minutes pass in silence, and we turn down the long, tree-lined dirt road that leads back to the chateau, passing the clump of bushes I once shoved a basket of groceries into because Zoe was having a meltdown and I couldn't carry them both. Up ahead is the hole in the road that she tripped in two weeks ago and scraped both knees. She screamed all the way back home, and Ellis had to hold her still while I bandaged them up. We can't see it yet, but there's a patch of wildflowers a little way from here that Zoe always plucks for the vase in her bedroom.

So many memories that are hard and happy and everything in between.

Miranda breaks the silence. "How long have you been Zoe's nanny?"

God, just the sound of her voice puts my teeth on edge. "Three months." Long enough to negate any possible excuse for her absence in her daughter's life. Zoe hasn't mentioned her mother or asked for her a single time. Ellis might be a lot of things, but he isn't a liar. I doubt he's been sneaking around, arranging video chats or phone calls between the two of them when I wasn't around.

"You must think I'm horrible." Miranda's tone is mild, as if we were discussing the weather.

Yes. I do.

I don't look at her. "It's none of my business."

She laughs slightly. "I saw your face when you realized who I am. Ellis mentioned he was supposed to go away this weekend, too. Something tells me you're not just the nanny."

That's none of *her* business, but I keep my mouth closed. I have better things to worry about than what this woman thinks of me. Every step we take brings me closer to the chateau, and probably the end of my relationship.

"Do you visit a lot?" I change the subject, endeavoring to keep my voice level. I already know the answer, but I'm curious if she'll lie.

I glance over in time to see Miranda's smile slip. "Not as much as I'd like. I'm a journalist, a foreign correspondent. It keeps me on the road."

"Wow," I reply flatly. "Sounds exciting."

"It is," Miranda answers at last, and there's no way she hasn't picked up on the animosity. "Stressful at times, but I enjoy it."

"Cool."

Though I pretend not to notice, I see her glance at me out of the corner of my eye.

"How long have you been together?" There's no judgement in her voice, or jealousy, only polite curiosity. I ignore her, busying myself by switching my overnight bag to the opposite shoulder. Miranda tries again. "I really don't mean any harm, Jo. I'm thrilled he's found someone. Ellis has probably told you a lot about me, but I swear I'm only about three quarters as evil as he says." Her attempt at humor falls flat.

Probably because Ellis hasn't told me a single thing. Until fifteen minutes ago, her existence was all I knew of Miranda.

Far ahead, I can see the first pillar of the stone columns which flank the chateau's iron gates. If my stomach sinks any more, it'll be dragging behind me on the ground.

"Why don't you tell me why?" I ask wildly, so desperate for any kind of distraction that even listening to Miranda talk seems preferable to wondering what will happen when we turn that corner.

"It's not an unusual story. We met in undergrad and, well, you know what Ellis is like. If you meet a man who is good and kind and reliable, you marry him. It's what anyone would do. I let my dreams get caught up with his, and before I knew it, I was married, living in the suburbs and having his baby."

The weary tone she uses to describe this life makes no sense to me. That sounds like paradise. Spending my days surrounded by people who love me? How could she not want that? How could that not be enough?

I swallow, slowing my pace just a little. "It didn't work out, though."

"No," Miranda confirms, her voice hollow. "It didn't. I had Zoe, and for a while, I thought I could ignore the restlessness. I figured it would pass. My mother told me everyone feels like this from time to time." She lets out a hollow, humorless laugh. "It didn't, though. Ellis didn't understand. He tried, but..." She shakes her head.

"I don't regret my daughter, but I do regret becoming a mother. I wasn't suited to it. I was barely keeping it together, and suddenly she was having all these huge, overwhelming issues. It was a struggle to connect with her, to connect with Ellis, all of it. I felt like an imposter living in someone else's life. How it ended wasn't pretty. I'm not proud of it, or my lack of presence in Zoe's life, but it's better this way."

Better for who? I want to ask. Miranda threw away the two people I want with all my heart. The newfound loathing is a welcome distraction from the heartbreak.

As we round the corner at the gates, we pause, staring up at the beautiful structure before us for very different reasons.

"Wow," Miranda offers, breezy and cheerful, as if twenty seconds ago she wasn't trying to justify why she abandoned her family. "Looks like a tough work assignment."

We've reached the middle of the drive before the heavy wood door bursts open. Ellis is standing there with Zoe in his arms, and his face is chalk white, horror evident even from here.

"Hi Jojo!" sings Zoe, waving at me enthusiastically.

I plaster a smile on my face for her benefit, and wave back. "Hi, honey girl," I call, but there's no disguising the tremor in my voice.

Maude appears at Ellis's shoulder, and when she sees me and Miranda, her expression darkens. I don't look at them, though. My attention is on Zoe, my heart aching when I see the pinched look on her face, a sure sign of trouble approaching.

It's hitting me all over again that she's never mentioned Miranda to me. Not once. The kid talks about the man who sells ice-cream in a shop back in Connecticut, but she's never said a word about the woman who brought her into this world. Without warning, I stop dead in the middle of the drive. Miranda pauses too, looking at me quizzically.

"Are you alright?"

God, I can only imagine how I look right now. "No," I tell her, and my voice is so low, so threatening and unfamiliar, that if I didn't know it was me speaking, I wouldn't have recognized it. "I love your daughter, Miranda. She's curious and funny and amazes me about twenty times a day. You're not here for her, though, you're here for *you*. If you have any awareness at all, you must know that these *whenever you can* visits are going to hurt her. Haven't you done enough damage? When is it enough? Either step up and be her mom, or..." my words falter.

Or let me *be.*

That's what I was going to say. That's what I want. Will Ellis ever let me, though? Or will I forever be striving to be good enough to cancel out this woman's bad?

233

I shake myself. "Never mind. Enjoy your visit." And I turn, continuing on toward the chateau, keeping my gaze trained down. If I meet his eyes, I'm going to cry, and I refuse to do that in front of Zoe. Not now.

As my foot finds the first of the steps into the house, I hear Ellis's voice, quiet and pleading. "Josephine."

I don't stop and look at him. I walk straight into the house, Maude's voice carrying after me, speaking in rapid, clearly furious French. The tears finally break free when I'm halfway up the stairs. It's not until I've reached the long upstairs hall which leads to all our bedrooms that I hear him.

"Josephine! *Merde*—Jo. Please stop!"

Reluctantly, I slow, sniffing and wiping the tears from my eyes with the back of my hand. It takes a lot for me to override the urge to run as far from him as I can, but this is important.

I wait, hating that my heart twists at the broken expression on his face when he stops three feet away from me, his chest heaving. "Go back down, Ellis. You should be with Zoe. I have nothing to say to you."

"Maude has her," he says in a rush. "I need to explain."

I scoff. "No. You don't. You didn't have time, remember?" His hands come out, preparing to touch my face like he must have done a thousand times by now, but I step out of the way. Ellis's expression flickers with panic. "You keep telling me you want this, but I think you're terrified, Ellis. You think I'm going to leave like she did, and I've been trying to prove you wrong for months without even realizing it. Since the very first night, you've been sabotaging our relationship. Better to have it end sooner rather than later, right? Better to never give me the chance to hurt you the way she did?"

Ellis shakes his head, looking paler than ever. "That isn't true."

"It is!" I cry, raising my voice for the first time. "Do you trust me?"

The question hangs in the air between us. Ellis swallows. "I think that in time—"

"No." My voice breaks. "This isn't an *I think*, Ellis. It's not fair. I'm not Miranda! I love Zoe! How do you not see that I would do anything for your little girl? How do you not see that I would do anything for *you*? If that still isn't good enough, there's nothing I can do to change your mind."

Ellis's face transforms from anxious to devastated. "I do trust you."

"No. You don't." I swallow, and when I speak again, my voice is hollow. "I can't do this anymore. No more arrangements, no more back and forth, no more letting you twist me up and think we have a future when we don't. You're not a bad person, you might even be an amazing one, but I deserve better than to spend god knows how long trying to prove I'm not your ex-wife." He makes a noise in protest, but I hold up a hand to stop it. "Don't worry. You don't need to find a new nanny. I'm staying *for Zoe*."

He stares at me, his chest heaving. "Josephine, I—" His words falter as, from downstairs, we hear the echo of Zoe's familiar cry. We look toward the grand staircase in unison, and —unthinking—we both start toward her.

That's not my job, though. I'm not a part of this family and Ellis has made sure I never will be.

"Go." My voice wavers. "Make sure she's okay."

I turn away first, so he doesn't have to.

Twenty-Four

ELLIS

I FIND Josephine's balcony door closed and locked when I finally get Zoe to bed.

As expected, the visit with Miranda rattled her. By mid afternoon, she had retreated into herself, not responding to questions and staring at the wall. To her credit, Miranda made an effort. She came prepared with books, toys, candy... none of it was accepted.

"She's not a baby anymore," I told her at the end of the day, following her out onto the drive. "She knows who you are. She sees other children with their mothers and doesn't understand why it isn't the same for her."

My ex-wife stared at the dirt road beneath her designer shoes for a long moment. "I'll call you in a few days," she finally managed, then, smiling valiantly. "I like the nanny."

My heart lurched, throbbing painfully at the thought of Josephine closeted away upstairs. She hadn't come down all day, though my mother had gone after her and came down nearly an hour later, giving me a withering stare that said plainly just whose side she was on.

"She's very good for Zoe," I manage, and Miranda's eyebrows lift.

"A little young for *you*, though."

I stepped back toward the house. "I'm not having this conversation."

Miranda only laughed, calling after me, "I'm sure I won't be invited to the wedding, but I'll be sure to send a gift!"

There won't be a wedding, and the reminder is like throwing salt on a fresh wound. Only a few hours ago, the woman we're speaking about told me she was finished with me, and I don't blame her for it.

Her words about deserving better were true.

Her words about me not trusting her were too.

When my marriage ended, I felt vindicated in that I at least had the moral high ground. I had tried, I had been faithful, *she* hadn't. I stepped up to raise Zoe full time, while Miranda took a job that would require her to be on the road eleven months out of the year.

Now, I have none of that certainty. I have no one to blame for the end of my relationship with Josephine except myself, and I can't stand it. The need to race upstairs, to try to salvage this, is almost overpowering, but I don't do it. After all I've put her through, the least I can do is respect her decision. I destroyed any possibility of a relationship between us, and now I need to live with it.

The rest of the day passed in a miserable, endless blur. Josephine didn't come down for dinner. My mother snapped at me whenever I looked at her. Zoe had an epic meltdown over her mac and cheese being too watery. The first mercy I receive all day is both of them going to bed early. Being alone with my thoughts is worse. There's nothing to distract myself with, nowhere to hide from my own regret and self-loathing.

My heart forms a new crack whenever I remember Josephine's face when she walked up the drive toward me,

Miranda at her side. She was broken. *I* had broken her, and still she put a smile on her face for my daughter.

I knew long before today that I didn't deserve her, but now... *Jesus.*

In a bid to find something to do other than sit alone with my miserable thoughts, I wander downstairs to the library. My work is all where I left it yesterday—*god, how was it only yesterday*—when I went in search of Josephine and found her in the meadow.

Filled with a hollow, miserable acceptance, I sit down at my work station and hit the power button on my computer, taking the first book from the stack beside me. As I open it, a familiar piece of stationary flutters to the ground at my feet.

Mari,

The doctors tell me it's cancer. It's in my blood, my bones, my brain. They don't say it, too busy waffling on about experimental therapies and treatments, but I know the truth of it. I'm a dying man. Which means I'll leave this earth without ever again seeing your face, hearing your laugh or feeling your skin on mine. Not that it's a surprise. It's been years now since I gave up hope of our Second Edition.

But did I truly give up?

Still, I've collected the books.

Still, I've written the notes.

Still, I've remembered the days, weeks,

months we had together, wishing they had been a lifetime instead.

If you find this—and I pray to god you do—please believe that I have regretted my choice every day since I made it. I was a coward, and I thought turning my back on the money, on my life, was too great a price to pay for one woman.

No one has ever been more wrong about anything.

I loved you when I was twenty-two years old and spotted you across the room at that party, and I love you still. These books, and the other shit, will be left to Weston. It brings me some peace to know that after I'm gone, you'll have your hands on them at long last.

Your Luc

I must read it at least four times before my hand falls back to my side, still clutching the letter. Pieces of the puzzle are falling into place, and I can see clearly now why I'm here. Jean-Luc Perdue was in love with a woman who worked in the library at Weston University, and he made a decision that ended their relationship. He regretted it. The man spent the rest of his life hoping, but never got the second chance—*the Second Edition*—he so desperately wanted. When he saw that he was going to die without ever seeing her again, he left the school with everything in the hopes *she* would be here instead of me.

He wanted her to find the decades of notes shoved between the pages of thousands of books that were collected in dedication to a lost love.

The very room I'm standing in, and the reason I'm here, is because Jean-Luc Perdue's mistaken belief that there is anything in this life more important than the people we share it with.

As the memory of Josephine's tear-streaked face flashes in my mind's eye, and I sink into my chair, heart in my throat. We are not Luc and Mari. Theirs is a different love, played out decades ago, and yet the parallels are too obvious to be ignored. There's a difference, though. Luc never got his second chance.

I did.

It began the day I found myself unexpectedly reunited with the beautiful young woman whom I spent one night with, but was too broken and afraid to call. I'm still that man. Even with all I feel for Josephine, even knowing without a shadow of a doubt that she is nothing like Miranda, it hasn't been enough because *I'm broken*.

She left, and I never spoke about it again. To anyone. For three years, I've focused on Zoe, allowing myself to get lost in the trials of single parenthood, and until Josephine, never realized how deeply the dissolution of my marriage had affected me.

Lifting the stationery, I read his letter again, the sorrow and regret seeping into my veins with each word. This time, my gaze lingers on the top of the paper. *Mari.* It's an unusual way to spell *Mary.* That is, unless it's not her full name. A connection occurs to me, one that must be coincidental... but what if it weren't?

Could it be possible? I can barely bring myself to consider it. The odds seems too high, and yet *it fits.* She would be about the same age as Perdue. They would have gone to Weston around the same time.

My fingers are numb as I pull out my phone, which hasn't been touched since I discovered the text message which put this entire, horrible day in motion. Scrolling through my contacts, I stop at the name of my mentor, the woman who waited to retire until she was confident I could keep Montgomery afloat.

Marian Silver.

It's still early enough in the day for me to call her, so I do, filled with a terrible sort of anticipation. When it stops, replaced by a cheerful, *"Hello?"* it occurs to me I have no idea what I'll do if I'm right.

"Hi Marian."

There's a delighted laugh through the phone. "Ellis! My goodness, it's good to hear your voice. It's been months."

"I'm sorry about that. Life got away from me for a while."

Marian sighs. "Yes, I would imagine it did. Why don't you come for lunch this weekend? We have the grandkids on Sunday afternoon. If you come by then, Zoe can play with them. She and Adeline are the same age!"

I let out an uncomfortable laugh. "Unfortunately, that would be rather difficult. I'm in France at the moment."

"You're kidding! Well, whenever you get back then. Are you there visiting your mother?" In the background, there's a loud mechanical rumble and Marian squawks in protest. "David! David! Oh, never mind." A moment later, a door closes, and the sound lessens. "The man can't hear a thing, and he leaves his hearing aids all over the place." There's an unmistakable fondness in her voice, though, the same one I recognized whenever she spoke about her husband during the four years I worked under her at Montgomery.

"I'm actually here for work." My mouth has gone dry, "Can I ask, did you once know a man named Jean-Luc

Perdue?" Marian is silent for so long that I lift the phone to my ear to check the connection. "Are you there?"

"Sorry. Yes. I'm sorry, Ellis. You just... you took me by surprise. I haven't heard that name in a very long time. Have you seen him?"

"He's dead," I tell her with regret. "He passed away several months ago and left his estate to Weston University. There was a large collection of rare books. I've been here sorting through them."

There's a sniff. "I don't know what to say."

"How did you know each other?"

Marian sighs. "He was my boyfriend. We dated our senior year at Weston."

"What happened?"

"I... well, I don't mind telling you that it was a very passionate relationship. We loved each other. He asked me to marry him, actually. But, as you can see, his family had quite a lot of money, and they didn't approve of him marrying a poor librarian from Queens. The daughter of a garbage collector."

A hollow dread is growing inside me as I listen to her story. "So he ended it?"

"He did." She pauses, and I wait, staring blankly at the books stacked beside me. "It took me a long time to get over it, but then I met David and he's been a wonderful husband. I'm very fortunate. Luc wrote to me years later, after I was engaged, telling me it had all been a mistake and that he still loved me. He had this analogy about our second edition being better than our first."

My heart seems to be beating differently than it was before, the hollow thud resounding through my chest and echoing into my head. "Did you respond?"

Marian's answering laugh is watery. "Yes. Goodness, you have me tearing up. I haven't spoken about this to anyone in decades. It took me weeks to write the letter, and another month to send it. At the time, I still loved him very deeply, and it was difficult to turn him away, knowing he felt the same way I did." Her voice cracks, and I feel a stab of regret at causing distress to the kind faced older woman who saw me through the beginning of my career.

"I'm sorry, Marian," I croak out. "I didn't mean to bring all this up again."

She shushes me. "Don't be sorry, Ellis. I am curious how *you* found out about the connection, though."

Telling her the story takes over an hour. There are a fair amount of tears on Marian's part, and after we've bid our goodbyes—me promising to send the notes to her as I find them—I let the phone fall to my lap. I'm even more exhausted than I was before the call.

I feel confident that my former mentor doesn't regret her choices. Marian loves her husband, just as she loves her children and grandchildren. Still, the pain in her voice was hard to dismiss. After all this time, decades of absence, an entire ocean, and a single terrible choice between them, Mari still loves her Luc.

Luc, who spent his entire adult life wishing he'd fought harder for the woman he loved, *a woman who loved him back.*

Mari, who had to live with the knowledge that by no fault of her own, she was forced to make a choice that closed the door on that love.

Is that what I've doomed Josephine and I to?

Vision blurring with exhaustion, I get to my feet, setting Luc's last note with the others on my way to the door. The chateau, which has become so familiar to me, feels faded and surreal as I move silently through halls toward my bedroom. How is it possible that just last night, I was filled with joy? Christ, I was so sure that I'd done it, that I'd fixed us and we would have a real future. Now, the woman I love is laying behind a locked door, her heart broken because I didn't heal mine.

I barely have the energy to undress and collapse onto the mattress. Even as I lay still, my eyes closed and my body pleading for sleep, my mind is wide awake and spinning. Once, I thought loving Josephine Sutton would be the ruin of me. Now, I know that my end would come from living with the knowledge I could have loved her, but ruined it.

There's one more difference between me and Jean-Luc Perdue—*I still have time.*

And I have no intention of wasting it.

Twenty-Five

JOSEPHINE

"YOU'LL TAKE care of them, won't you?"

Maude's hand on my arm tightens as we stroll after Zoe through the garden behind the chateau, taking one last walk together before she leaves for home. The two of us have gotten close over the last few weeks, but yesterday afternoon, when I retreated to my bedroom with a newly broken heart, it was Maude who came to check on me.

She held me while I cried, murmuring gentle words in French that I could only half understand, and furious ones about Ellis in English, probably for my benefit.

"I'll take care of them," I promise. The anger I felt toward Ellis faded overnight. He hurt me, yes, but it wasn't intentional. I know him well enough to be sure that he wasn't conscious of what he was doing to me.

Now I'm just sad.

It's ironic that all this time I've been worried about him breaking my heart, and instead I broke my own.

"How did it go? With Miranda?" I ask after a minute of silence.

In the corner of my eye, I see Maude's expression tighten.

"Uneventful, thankfully. There was some confusion and tears at first, but after that, Zoe wasn't interested at all. Barely looked her way the entire time I was in the room with them. Ellis was hovering, which didn't lower anyone's blood pressure. You know our Zoe. She likes her space. The woman came and went in three hours. I suppose she'll stop by again at Christmas."

Somehow, it never occurred to me that we would be here for the holidays, but of course we will. Ellis's work assignment has officially been extended until March. Even with all that's happened, I would rather be here than in Connecticut, where there will be pressure to decide the next steps. My mom, obviously sensing I need space, has been giving it to me, and I'm grateful. That will all end when I go home, though, and I've been too focused on Zoe, Ellis, and my newfound sewing hobby to reflect on something as inconsequential as my career path.

Consciously or not, I've been holding my breath, waiting to see if I should be making room for Ellis and Zoe in my future. Maybe it's time to put more thought into it.

Maude and I don't speak as we round the last corner of the chateau and approach the drive, but she hugs me when we stop beside her car. "Does it make me selfish to hope you two will work it out?" she asks, patting my cheek fondly.

"No." I smile sadly, not having the heart to tell her that her hopes are futile. "We'll see you in a few months."

Stepping back, I watch Zoe endure several minutes of goodbyes. At some point, Ellis steps out of the front door and, as if by habit, my eyes move to his for a fraction of a second, before the shooting pains through my heart remind me to look away.

"*Conduis prudemment, maman***," he says, moving to my

---

*   Drive carefully, mom

246

side when Maude has finally released Zoe, and honey girl has crossed back to me. Reaching down to take her hand feels like the most natural thing in the world.

Maude scowls at him but accepts a hug nevertheless. "*Vous allez le réparer, n'est-ce pas?**"

He only smiles vaguely in response, leaning down to kiss each of her cheeks before drawing away to stand on Zoe's other side. The three of us watch as Maude leaves, her car kicking up dust from the drive in its wake.

Zoe sniffs.

"She'll be back in a few months," I assure her gently, giving her hand a little squeeze. "And she only lives a few hours away. Maybe we'll make a day trip one day and go visit?"

I'm careful to keep my tone bright and a smile on my face, but I'm acutely aware of Ellis being so close to me. How do people do this? Break up with someone and pretend everything is fine? Replace intimacy and connection with careful, strained interactions?

It's unbearable.

"Can we sew my dress?" she asks, rocking back and forth on her heels, hands fluttering at her sides. All day she's been a little more on edge, and this is the most she's said to me since I mustered up the courage to go down to breakfast. Considering the day she had yesterday, I'm happy to give her anything she wants.

"Of course." The two of us turn toward the chateau, but we don't get far before Ellis calls after us.

"Jo? Could I have a moment?"

My stomach twists, but I don't look back or stop. "Can we talk later, Ellis?"

"It's about the notes." There's a hopeful, pleading quality to his voice that makes fresh pain rip through me. Isn't this

---

* You're going to fix it, aren't you?

whole situation hard enough without him forcing me to stand here and talk to him? Can't he see that I'm holding on by a thread here?

"Fill me in at dinner!" I call, pulling open the big iron handle of the door, ushering Zoe inside.

It isn't a relief when he doesn't follow.

Still determined to keep a brave face for Zoe, who deserves some stability after Miranda's visit, the two of us head upstairs to my room. The dress we've been working on for her, a pink, tulle monstrosity that she saw the pattern for online and absolutely had to have, is half done and hanging in pieces in my closet. As I go to get them, I hear Zoe's voice.

"What does this say?"

Curious, I poke my head out of the closet. She has a strip of paper in her hand.

Josephine,
    The night we met, I thought so lowly of myself that it didn't seem possible you would want me.
    I still can't believe it.
    Your Ellis

My heart is in my throat as I push the note into my pocket. *What is he doing?*

"Just for the shopping," I lie to Zoe, busying myself with laying all the dress pieces out on the table. Ellis has kept me at arm's length—metaphorically anyway—for so long. The man keeps his feelings behind a thirty-foot wall of barbed wire, rebar enforced cement, that's probably monitored by some kind of alarm system programmed to go off in the event of emotional intimacy.

When I move to the cookie tin where I keep my threads, my heart vaults into my throat. Another note, just like the one Zoe just gave me, is resting on top.

Josephine,

When my father died, I didn't cry. We were close. I loved him, but he had been so sick for so long that when he finally passed, I was relieved. I've always been ashamed of that. So much so, that I think a part of me didn't believe I deserved to cry for him.

He was a good man, a good parent, and I think about him every day. He would have adored you, just as my mother does, and my daughter, and every person whose life you touch.

Mine included.

Your Ellis

My hand trembles as I put the note in my pocket with the other, casting a wary look around my room for evidence of more. My eyes catch on a piece of paper sitting on my bedside table, and I have to press my lips together to stop myself from making a noise of shock.

This one is much longer than the others, and my eyes are burning before I've finished the first paragraph.

Josephine,

It's hard to admit, but I rushed into my marriage. There were issues from the start, but I was sure that if I wanted it badly enough, if I dedicated myself to my wife, it would all be okay. For a while, it was, but things got so much worse after Zoe was born.

I didn't want to accept it, but I knew she was cheating for a long time. She didn't really try to hide it. The scent of a man's aftershave on her shirt, late night disappearances, mysterious phone calls and weekends away at conferences that didn't exist.

For over a year, I turned a blind eye, kept going to marriage counseling, kept trying to keep my family afloat. It all came crumbling down when Zoe was three. She had a fever, and I picked her up early from daycare. We got home, and I had to pull her back out of the house because Miranda was having sex with her boss on the couch.

He left. We fought. She left. I expected her to come back, but then I was getting served with divorce papers at work. She took a job that would take her out of the country, and that was it.

For so long, I just tried to be a good father. I ignored the guilt, the sense of unworthiness, of failure, of rejection, and of loss. All of it stayed buried until I met you.

I'm so sorry, mon amour.
Your Ellis

Wiping tears from my cheeks with the back of my hand, I clear my throat and turn back to Zoe. "Let's finish your dress, honey girl!"

She's looking at me strangely, and I know she must sense the poorly concealed grief, but I thread the machine, pull the fabric into place, and soon she's absorbed in the rise and fall of the needle.

Meanwhile, I'm spiraling.

Why is he doing this? We broke up. I made it *really, really* clear that I'd had enough, and I don't know what he's trying to accomplish here, but I refuse to believe it's some kind of grand gesture. The current, ruined state of my heart is evidence that blind hope is a very dangerous thing, and I refuse to make that mistake again.

The notes keep appearing all morning. I find them in my purse when we go to the village for milk, in the drawer with the silverware and on my favorite bench in the garden, weighed down by a stone. All of them are different, Ellis baring some small piece of his heart.

I'm a wreck.

Twenty-four hours ago, I was sad, but proud of myself for

standing up for what I deserve. Why does he have to make this so much harder than it has to be? I'm determined to not let myself get sucked in, but when I open the refrigerator in search of a snack mid-afternoon and find the note taped to the little box of chocolates I keep hidden behind the lemon juice for emergencies, I can't take it anymore.

Josephine,

I hate that I have no firsts to offer you, but if I can heal what I've broken between us, I swear on my life you'll have all my lasts.

Your Ellis

I'm not sure whether I should cry or scream. Either way, there's only one person I want to direct it toward.

Leaving Zoe hunched over a coloring book at the kitchen table, I stride down the hall and cross the entryway to the library, shoving open the glossy wood door without knocking.

Ellis is standing beside his computer, a book in one hand and his other on the keyboard. He looks up sharply as I stride into the room, my cheeks burning and my chest so tight it might crack.

"Why are you doing this?" I demand, brandishing the note.

Calmly, Ellis sets down the book and straightens up. "I'm trusting you."

"We *broke up*." I half cry, half laugh. Apparently, there's only so long a girl can ride an emotional rollercoaster before she loses her mind. "You hurt me, Ellis. You hurt me over and over again. Can you seriously not respect that I'm done after all that? Do I need to start dating someone else for you to get it?"

His expression goes from patient and benign to

murderous in seconds. "Don't joke about that. You won't be dating anyone else."

My mouth falls open in furious disbelief. "You have no right to tell me what I will or won't do. Not anymore."

"I have every right." Ellis takes a step forward, his gaze burning right through me. "You're in love with me. You don't want anyone else. Which is lucky, because I'm in love with you, and I certainly don't want any other woman."

I make a quiet, wounded noise. He loves me?

"Ellis. *Please*." What am I begging for? Do I want him to keep going? To stop? I have no idea.

Like he senses weakness, Ellis advances, striding over the worn carpet, his pale eyes bright and wild. "Every word you said to me yesterday was true. I've been a coward, and I've been pushing you away rather than confront why. There's a lot I never dealt with after my divorce, but I need to now. I love you, and I want this to work, so I'm fixing the problem. Losing you isn't an option."

His hands lift to my face. *I hate* that he's saying all the right things, and that when he touches me my body goes soft and warmth spreads to the places I assumed were dead.

I hate him. I love him. I'm scared. I'm happy. I want to run. I want to stay.

Ellis must be able to tell I'm beyond words, because his expression softens, and he leans in, kissing the corner of my mouth with a tenderness that makes me want to cry. "You don't trust me right now," he murmurs, still holding me close. "You put your heart in my hands, and I let you down. You've been so brave, *mon amour*. Right from the start. Now, it's my turn."

I'm shaking my head. A sob escapes my lips despite how hard I'm trying to hold back the overwhelming rush of emotions. Never have I wanted anything more than to say yes to him, to throw myself back into his arms and trust that the connection between us doesn't exist to bring me nothing but pain. God, I want it so badly, but I'm scared in a way I wasn't before.

Now, I've learned how terrible it is to lose him.

"I found out why Perdue was writing those notes." His remark about that earlier was driven completely out of my mind when I found *his* notes. Now, my eyes widen, temporarily distracted from my inner turmoil. Ellis's smile is sad. "He fell in love with a young woman in college. Mari, the daughter of a garbage collector from Queens. Perdue asked her to marry him, but ended the engagement when his family disapproved. By the time he realized his mistake, it was too late, and she was marrying someone else."

I wait as he gathers his thoughts, my chest hollow and pulse hammering on too quickly given the circumstances.

Ellis's voice is laced with sorrow when he continues, "He collected these books, second editions as an act of faith that he would have a second chance to love her. He wrote the notes because he was sure she would someday be here to read them herself."

Sorrow blooms inside me for these two strangers. "But she never came?"

"No." He shakes his head, grave faced. "He realized at the end. That's why he left his estate to Weston. Mari is short for Marian. She was my mentor, my predecessor at Montgomery. He thought that she would see them, that she would finally know he never stopped loving her."

Tears are spilling down my face, sorrow for these two strangers clogging my throat. "Is she still alive? Marian?"

He nods. "She is. I spoke to her yesterday to confirm all this. I'll be sending her the letters." His thumbs wipe my tears away. "She still loved him, Josephine. After all this time, they loved each other, but Perdue was a fool and they missed their chance."

A breeze brushes past us from the library's big open windows, a jarring reminder that there is a world outside the moment we're locked together in. I can barely breathe, barely think, barely move.

Ellis's pale eyes are shining, and his voice is rough when he speaks again. "I don't want to wake up decades from now, still loving you, and wish I'd done more. I don't want to lose you because I was too afraid to face myself. You don't have to trust me, I know I haven't earned that privilege, but let me trust you. Let me fight for us, *mon amour*. Let me become the man you deserve."

Fresh tears are spilling over my cheeks, and a sob bubbles from my lips. Will I wake up years from now, filled with regret at not giving him the chance to fix it? Will I wake up months from now, nursing a shattered heart and hating myself for giving him yet another chance he didn't deserve? Both possibilities are gut wrenching, and yet there's one that is so much worse.

I open my mouth, but nothing comes out and I stare up at him, silently pleading for one last push, some way off the horrible, pointed ledge I'm balancing on, too terrified to fall one way or the other.

In the way he always seems to know what I need, Ellis gives it to me. "All you have to say is yes. Say yes, and I'll trust you until you trust me again."

Another breeze sweeps through the library, and I close my eyes, feeling the fear and hope and love. Love that's so big, so overwhelming, that I know won't fade. Even if I walked out this door and never saw him again, I would spend my life wondering.

I open my eyes and say the word. "Yes."

Twenty-Six

ELLIS

6 MONTHS LATER

"**I TOLD** you the shoes were a bad idea."

Josephine's giggle is muffled in my shoulder, and her arms tighten around my neck playfully. "Maybe I wanted to recreate our first date."

People we pass on the road are staring at us. We're making a scene, but—much like the first time we did this—I can't stop smiling. It's saying a lot that even with all the big moments we've shared since arriving in France, this was the biggest.

There's a small church in the village, managed by a cranky old priest. He pursed his lips at the "date of divorce" on my section of the marriage license, but made no other objection to the last minute affair. Likely because my mother was sitting behind us in the pews, glowering at him.

I wouldn't cross her either. The woman wanted Jo to be her daughter-in-law from the beginning, and her opinion on the matter hasn't swayed. When I called her up two days ago and told her we were getting married before going home, the scream that came through the phone nearly blew the speaker.

In an ironic turn of events, it was Weston's rule against student-faculty relationships that got us here. I would have married her months ago, happily, but it seemed important to make sure Zoe had adjusted to Jo being my girlfriend before adding a ring to the mix.

The adjustment period wasn't really necessary. To Zoe at least, our day-to-day life hasn't changed all that much. Jo still spends her time with Zoe, managing to strike a perfect balance between teacher, nanny, stepmother and friend. I work in the library. Our evenings are enjoyed together as a family.

Then, she's mine.

It was always true, but now we've made it official.

When Jo decided to go back and finish her degree so she can teach, I went through the Weston HR handbook again, looking for a loophole that might save us from sneaking around for months on end. I found one. Spouses of faculty and staff are exempt, provided their marriage pre-dates enrollment.

Tomorrow is the last day to register for the fall semester.

While I doubt President Sutton will see it this way, Josephine is confident that her mother won't risk a scandal just to make my life uncomfortable, and I trust my wife.

My wife. It's barely been fifteen minutes since I put the ring on her finger, and I can't get over it. *My wife.* Even six months ago, the idea of getting married again would have made me nauseous. Now... *God*, I'm so happy.

"What are you thinking about?" Jo asks, nipping at my ear.

My hands tighten on the backs of her legs. I can hardly wait to get her alone and fuck *my wife* for the first time. The little tease walked out of the bathroom in pure white lingerie minutes before we had to leave for the church, and I'm not sure how I didn't collapse with the amount of blood rushing to my cock. "What I'm going to do to you when we get home."

Maude, rather conspicuously, whisked Zoe off for an afternoon of bonding, making sure to tell us—twice—that they'd be back at five thirty and not earlier.

Jo laughed. I winced.

My bride sighs happily, laying her cheek on my shoulder. "I should probably call my parents later to break the news."

"Are you nervous?" Her relationship with them seems to be going through a period of adjustment. Jo is different from when they were all together last, and I don't believe the Suttons know what to do with the strong, independent woman who has taken the place of the girl who was once so eager to please them.

"Maybe a little," she admits as we turn the corner onto the chateau's drive. "My mom definitely suspects we're together, but it probably won't go over well when she finds out it's serious."

I chuckle. "Serious? Is that what you call marriage, *mon amour*?"

"The *most* serious?"

"Damn straight," I say in my best American drawl. Whatever I lost of my accent has returned in the time we've lived here. Josephine's French has gotten very good, and Zoe seems to have developed a strange hybrid language. I'm grateful we'll have the summer to get her back on English before school starts.

Josephine bursts into giggles. "Don't do that again. It sounds *wrong*."

"Are you sure you don't want to—*ah*—play football?" It comes out like a question, and my wife's laugher fills the warm spring air. Have I ever felt this light? This wholly and completely overjoyed? Even the happiness of my daughter's birth was colored by the brand new weight of responsibility and fear that comes with fatherhood.

Now I have this woman, *my wife*, and if the struggles at the beginning of our relationship have taught me anything, it's that there is nothing I won't do for her, or her for me. This is forever.

We're approaching the chateau, and I know exactly where we're going. I open the door and she squeaks in surprise when I set her down, then turn to lift her right back into my arms, carrying her across the threshold and directly toward the library.

The room is still full of books marked for donation or sale, but the most valuable of them are gone, and so are Monsieur Perdue's notes. My role is done. Our flight home leaves this time next week. Now, my only responsibility is to pleasure the love of my life until she can't stand.

"So, I've been thinking."

"Oh?" My lips curl into a dangerous smile when I stop beside my work table and finally allow her back on her own two feet. We aren't separated for long. Seconds later, familiar hands are smoothing over the lapels of my suit. "Pray tell, what were you thinking about Mrs. Delvaux?"

"*Sutton*-Delvaux. I'm hyphenating."

I don't care what her last name is, as long as my ring is on her finger. "My apologies." I chuckle, unable to stop looking at her for even a second. *Astonishing is an understatement.*

Her hair is loose and tumbling around her shoulders in loose waves. She made the dress she's wearing, and even with the smear of jam from Zoe's hand when we left this morning, it's perfect.

"You're the most beautiful woman in the world, *mon amour*." I lower my lips to hers and kiss her reverently. "Tell me what you were thinking?" I ask when we break apart, because I'm so aroused it's making my gut ache, and in about sixty seconds, I'll be so lost in her I won't remember to ask.

God, she's my wife.

Her fingers move to my tie, loosening the knot, bright eyes sparkling in the spring sunlight drifting through the high windows. "We should move here."

My eyebrows shoot up. "Here?" I gesture to the magnificent building around us. "You are aware I'm a librarian, yes, *mon amour*? And you are planning to teach high school physics? Neither of our professions is historically well compensated."

Josephine's laughter rings through the quiet room. "Damn, really?" she teases, her smile wide and effortless. "The chateau was very misleading."

"I'll make it up to you." My hands roam over her sides, hunting for the zipper of the dress. The garment comes easily away from her body, falling to the floor around her—admittedly sexy but very painful—shoes. My mouth goes dry. Despite the innocent color, the lingerie is even more wicked than I remember, and now there is an addition. A narrow, lace garter is pulled high up on her thigh.

I do the only sensible thing; drop to my knees.

"Ellis," she breathes, twisting her hands through my hair as I lean forward, burying my face in her mound, breathing in the familiar scent of her body getting ready to take mine. "I meant move to France. After I'm done with school. We're happy here, Zoe is happy here."

As I consider this, I kiss my way down to the band on her thigh. It doesn't take me long. "Okay, let's move here."

"Just like that?" She giggles, squirming as I brush my lips over the delicate skin of her inner thigh.

"Yes."

I'm finished with this conversation.

My teeth graze her skin as I bite the garter, dragging it

down with a level of self-control that ought to get me nominated for sainthood. My little wife is less patient, and she presses into my touch, her breathing ragged.

"You look like a goddess," I murmur, my hands moving to the straps of her shoes, loosening them and helping her step barefoot onto the floor before me. "God, *mon amour*. Look at you. Are you wet for me?"

Josephine moans, hands finding the table behind her as I lift her thigh over my shoulder, offering me a perfect view of her cunt covered only by a narrow strip of white lace. Palming my erection, I lift my eyes to meet her heavily lidded gaze.

"Answer me. Have you made a mess of your new panties?" As if I can't see the damp spot from where she's soaked through them.

She bites her lip, holding back a mischievously smile and shakes her head. "No, Daddy."

At this rate, I'm going to have an imprint of a zipper on my cock, but as much as I'd like to take it out and get some relief, I know full well that if there was only lace separating me from being inside her, there would be no holding myself back.

Today, I want to play with my food before I eat it.

Humming thoughtfully, I inch closer to leave a chaste kiss on her inner thigh. "What happens if I've found you lied to me, *mon amour*? What should your punishment be?"

She shifts against me, trying to get closer. "You can do whatever you want to me."

I pretend to consider this. "That seems acceptable. I'm sure I can think of something. Now, let's check, yes?" Hooking her panties to the side with one hand, I part her flesh with two fingers and spread them in a V, exposing her to my shameless inspection.

Soaked.

Her hands find my hair again. "I'm sorry, Daddy."

"I don't think you're sorry at all, you little tease." Giving her ass a quick squeeze, I roll to my feet. Josephine's lips part and she tilts her head back, obviously expecting me to kiss her. Instead, I bow forward and growl in her ear. "Go over there." I jerk my chin toward the nearest row of books. "Turn around and bend over. Hold on to the shelf."

She hurries to comply, and the moment I see her like this, bent over and offering herself to me, her beautiful form silhouetted by dozens of books... *Merde.* I can't take the goddamn pressure. My cock is going to fall off if I don't get it inside her soon.

My hands are clumsy as I fumble with my belt, losing the battle to take this slow. It's been nearly a year since this beautiful young woman stumbled into the library at her parents' house and the connection we shared then pales to what I feel for her now.

The moment my cock is free, I lean over her, bracing my hand on the shelf beside hers, and guide my tip through her seam, gathering her arousal, before driving forward in a single, ruthless thrust that tears a scream from Josephine's lips and a roar from mine.

Jesus Christ. I will never get used to how good she feels.

"I was going to worship you today. I thought I'd make you feel like the princess you are, but that's not what you need, is it? You don't need to be a princess, you want to be *mine*."

I don't think I've ever been this out of my head. The need to claim her is as vital as the air in my lungs, anticipation and urgency pressing down on us both. This is my wife, the love of my life, and one of the two greatest things to ever happen to me. She also has a body tailor made to drive me mad, and a cunt that threatens to milk the cum right out of me with how hot and tight it is.

There's no way to hold back.

Josephine's fingers tighten on the shelf and she's driven to the tips of her toes each time I plow forward, her cries filling the quiet room in time with my thrusts. "You're so deep," she half cries, half moans, and I lean forward, using my free hand to drag her face around and claim her mouth in a messy, bruising kiss.

"Arch your back a little more," I grunt, dropping my forehead to her back and wrapping an arm around her waist, pulling her ass higher. "There you go. That's better, isn't it? Such a good girl, letting me go at it as hard as I like."

Her cries get louder, but even without that clue, I would know she's close. Pressed together as we are, I can feel every muscle in her body straining, reaching for something just beyond her grasp.

"I'm going to come, Daddy," she warns me, her voice high and needy. In this position, she can't do more than take what I give her. Everything she's experiencing is because of me, and the rush is intoxicating. *God,* do I love it. God, do I love her.

Shoving my hand between her legs, I find her clit and pinch the swollen bundle of nerves between my fingers.

She loses it, coming with a sexy little cry of surprise, wetness flooding over my cock. "Every time," I growl, fucking her through it. "Every time you take me so well. You never complain when I'm rough, do you *mon amour*? Do you like it when I make this tight little cunt ache?"

We're both panting, the wet slap of skin on skin coming faster as I start to chase my own orgasm. This wasn't how I planned tonight going. I wanted to make this last, but it doesn't matter. We have all the time in the world.

I come with a roar, hunched over my wife and wedged as deep as I can inside her.

"*Oh god,*" Josephine moans, her knuckles white on the bookshelf with how hard she's holding on, my cum coating her inner walls. "I loved that."

Yeah, I loved it too.

We both sag at the same time, falling in an undignified,

boneless heap onto the ancient wood floors. Josephine is still wearing her bridal lingerie and I'm somehow fully dressed, my pants and briefs caught comically around my knees.

"Wow," she says softly as our breathing slows. "I think I like being married."

I lift my head to look at her, and Josephine squeals, having realized her mistake a moment too late as I flip her over, tickling her sides. "*Think*!" I exclaim in playful disbelief. "You *think* you like being married?"

"I know!" she gasps through peels of laughter, trying to push me away without success. "I know! I know!"

When my hands slow, my cheeks are aching from how big my smile is. Josephine is beaming right back, as if it's every woman's dream to be bent over in a library and fucked senseless on her wedding day. "I love you so much." I run my hand down her side to settle on the curve of her waist. "It's such a gift you've given me, *mon amour*."

Her smile softens. "Our second edition?"

By now, we've talked a lot about Jean-Luc Perdue and his lost love, Mari. Up until the last shelf of books cleared, I was still finding his notes here and there. This entire room was a testament to the power of love and regret. It seems strangely poetic that it was here, where I decided, once and for all, that I was going to confront my fiercest inner demons so I could keep Josephine Sutton.

It was worth it.

Epilogue

JOSEPHINE

5 YEARS LATER

"I WANT A SISTER."

The car door slams heavily as my step-daughter pulls it closed, dumping her backpack on the floor at her feet.

I blink. "What—"

The orange vested school pick-up attendant waves at me impatiently and I put the car in drive, staring straight forward as we inch toward the exit of the parking lot. The local high school where I work is located adjacent to the middle school Zoe attends, and lets out thirty minutes before her last class ends for the day. Ellis is at work until five, so this is our typical family routine.

Minus the sibling request.

"So, what brought this up?" I ask conversationally, glancing at Zoe, who is staring at the screen of her brand new cell phone, completely expressionless.

She shrugs. "Callie has a sister, and she likes her. Margo's brother is disgusting, so I don't want one of those."

My heart seems to be beating faster than usual as I fight to keep my expression impassive. "Even if Papa and I *were* to have a baby, we couldn't control if it were a boy or a girl, honey girl."

Zoe wrinkles her nose. "Whatever."

Whatever is a recent addition to her vocabulary and seems to be getting used with increasing regularity as we enter her pre-teen years. It's not my favorite.

I blow out a long breath, still reeling. In truth, Ellis and I have never put that much consideration into having a baby. We were both only children, and with Miranda's still inconsistent presence in her daughter's life, I didn't want Zoe to feel displaced or worried that I would love my biological child more than her. We concluded that when we move to France and our lives settle down a little, we would revisit the discussion.

It's been five years, though, and while we visit Maude often, we haven't discussed moving in a while. Things have been chaotic. Ellis was promoted to director of Weston's entire system of libraries, I finished my masters in education and started teaching, Zoe made friends and an international move was put on the back burner.

As we pull out of the school parking lot, heading toward home, I try again. "Babies are loud. And messy."

"I know that," comes the clipped reply from beside me. "You're being super annoying about this. Papa wants one."

That has my attention. "*One*, what? A baby? What makes you say that?"

"He told me. When I asked *him* for a sister."

"When was this?" I demand, my eyes wide.

"Three days ago. He said," she adopts a deep, French accented voice, "*I would like that very much, but Jo is still young and I don't want to pressure her. Maybe someday.*" She huffs. "He got emotional after that and told me I was more than enough for the both of you and that you loved me and all this sappy stuff."

I can't help but laugh. "We *do* love you. And you *are* more than enough for us."

"Gross. Can you drop me at Gram and Pops?"

My fingers tap restlessly on the steering wheel, struggling to think past the bomb Zoe dropped in my lap. "Nope. You have a history test tomorrow. We have flash cards to make."

My parents didn't attempt to conceal their disapproval that I went to France as Ellis's nanny and came home as his wife. However, the frosty reception he received was *not* extended to his daughter. Within a few months, Zoe was calling them Gram and Pops, and had become the—very spoiled—apple of their eye.

When we get home, it's a surprise to see Ellis's car in the drive, and the garage door open. Zoe makes her escape quickly, undoubtedly hoping to avoid history flashcards as long as possible, but I go in search of my husband.

I find Ellis, still wearing his Weston ID lanyard and—as I've dubbed it—naughty librarian sweater, pulling down the big storage totes we keep summer stuff in.

"Hey, you," I say, picking my way around bicycles and the snow blower to get to him. "You're home early."

His expression softens at the sight of me, and he abandons the storage bins to pull me into his arms the moment I'm close enough, kissing me sweetly. "Hello, *mon amour.*" Another kiss, and he releases me to return to his digging. "I'm just stopping by to pick something up. There's a retirement party for one of the archivists in an hour and I signed up to bring lawn games. Have you seen those?"

I lean my hip against the wall, fighting a smile. "We got rid of them at the garage sale last year because we don't like lawn games."

He curses under his breath, letting the plastic cover in his hands fall to the floor with a clatter. "You're right. I remember now. Well, we'll have to learn to like them, because I'm buying more on the way back to work."

"Sounds good." I watch him start to put boxes back, my heart in my throat. "Do you want to have a baby?"

Ellis looks up sharply, expression going from shocked to annoyed in the blink of an eye. "Damn it, Zoe." He offers an apologetic grimace. "I'm sorry. I told her to drop it."

"Zoe has never in her life dropped anything because someone told her to."

"Fair point." He heaves a sigh, looking worried. "Truly, it isn't a rush to me, *mon amour*. I consider myself an exceptionally lucky man as it is. Wishing for any more would be greedy."

My heart squeezes with affection for my husband and I draw forward, wrapping my arms around his neck and lifting my chin in a silent kiss request. He doesn't hesitate to grant it. "I love you," I murmur when we break apart, gazing up into his pale eyes. "It's kind of funny Zoe picked now to say something. I might have been thinking about it recently."

The confession makes Ellis brighten. "*Have you?*" He beams down at me and leans in for another kiss, this time with considerably more heat than the first. I giggle when his hands wander lower to grab my ass, dragging me closer.

"Not right this second." I swat his arm playfully, but I'm having a hard time keeping my smile at bay. *Are we really talking about this?* "We should probably decide on the whole international move thing before throwing my birth control out the window."

Ellis nips at my bottom lip. "Your parents will kill us if we go anywhere."

"Mom is retiring soon." I shrug. "They want to travel. I don't think it's the end of the world. Besides, Maude has been having all those issues with her insulin levels. It would be great to be close to her. Plus, Zoe has always been happier there. She never wants to leave at the end of summer break."

My shoes shuffle loudly over the cement floor as Ellis backs me over to the long workbench and lifts me up so he can stand between my parted thighs. His lips curve in amusement. "It sounds like you have it all figured out."

"Not all of it," I admit. "You love your job. If you wanted to stay at Weston, I would understand."

"I do love my job." Ellis drags his hands down the outside of my thighs, his eyes on my face. "But I love my family more. Why don't we discuss it with the young, stubborn one, and go from there?"

He poses it like a question but we're both smiling, because *we know* what she'll say. This move has always been the plan. France is where we fell in love, where I fell in love with *both of them,* and it feels like home. There's still a lot to consider, jobs and houses and schools, but excitement is kindling to life inside me.

"We're coming full circle, huh?" I muse, playing with the ends of his hair, which has gone almost completely gray in the past five years. I'll never get over how handsome he is.

"We are," Ellis agrees. His smile slips slightly, turning to something soft and hopeful. "You've really been thinking about a baby?"

God, with the way he's looking at me, if I wasn't thinking about it before, I would be now.

I nod, my heart so full. "I have the world's hottest husband who also happens to be the best dad ever. Of course I've been thinking about it. Though, maybe we shouldn't risk it. Zoe has requested a sister, and I think we'll be in trouble if we mess up."

He trails his fingertips over my collarbone, making the muscles below my bellybutton flutter. "I'll confess I may be out of my depth with the surly teenage attitude."

I squirm closer. "We'll figure it out. Will you still want me when I'm giving you surly pregnant lady attitude?"

Ellis scoffs. "I'll always want you."

"You can't know that!" I object playfully.

My husband lifts his eyebrows, lips curving into an amused smile as he pulls my body more securely against his own. "I think you'll remember I tried very, very hard not to want you at the beginning. How did that work out for me?"

* * *

Thank you for reading Second Edition! If you have a moment, please consider leaving a rating or review for the book. It is an enormous help to indie authors such as myself, and I genuinely love hearing people's thoughts on my work!
—Cleo

Bonus Epilogue

Want more of Second Edition?
Catch up with Ellis, Jo and Zoe, six months after they leave
France in this bonus epilogue!

About the Author

Cleo White's affinity for all things dramatic, and hopelessly romantic began the day she was born, which happened to be in the middle of a record-breaking snowstorm on Valentine's Day. Her love of literature came soon after, and she spent the better part of her childhood with both a book and a notebook full of unfinished stories in hand. Later in life, she found a love of writing spicy books with complicated characters and dysfunctional family drama. Cleo currently lives in Vermont with her husband and two daughters. When not writing, she can be found hiking, gardening, painting, and consuming excessive quantities of caffeine.

To stay up to date with upcoming releases and receive exclusive bonus content, subscribe to my newsletter at www.authorcle-owhite.com

Also by Cleo White

In the mood for more forbidden insta-love, age-gap, spicy goodness?
Check out Cleo's other books!

<u>Out of Sight</u>

In Pieces

Age of Shade

<u>You're It</u>

Second Edition

9 798330 292301